KEEP ME SAFE

ALLISON MELDRUM

The Book Guild

First published in Great Britain in 2025 by
The Book Guild Ltd
Unit E2 Airfield Business Park,
Harrison Road, Market Harborough,
Leicestershire. LE16 7UL
Tel: 0116 2792299
www.bookguild.co.uk
Email: info@bookguild.co.uk

The manufacturer's authorised representative in the EU
for product safety is Authorised Rep Compliance Ltd,
71 Lower Baggot Street, Dublin D02 P593 Ireland (www.arccompliance.com)

Typeset in 11pt Minion Pro

Printed and bound in Great Britain by CMP UK

ISBN 978 1835742 839

British Library Cataloguing in Publication Data.
A catalogue record for this book is available from the British Library.

To my Mum and Dad, Mo and Doug Brodie, who collectively nurtured my love of books.

1

Good and evil are so close as to be
chained together in the soul.
—Robert Louis Stevenson

KIRKALDY, SCOTLAND, 2023
MONDAY

"I understand you're here today to talk about a murder you witnessed ten years ago?"

The psychologist made it sound so matter of fact. Maggie should have seen it coming and practised a response, but it was easier not to think about this moment. She knew psychologists did this. They probed gently but with a sharp point. Her world comprised interviews where *she* was in control, asking the questions. Maggie was out of her comfort zone. The tables had turned. A heat rose through her torso, quickening her breathing and hinting at a growing nausea.

"I promised my boss, Lexi, that I'd come. She found me one day… I couldn't stop… Well, anyway, she – my editor,

Lexi – reckons past trauma is interfering with my work."

It was a stitched-together sentence, but all she could manage for now. How could she tell a total stranger about being trapped in the loos at work because she couldn't stop washing her hands?

"Can you tell me more about what may have caused this trauma?"

Maggie refused to make eye contact with the woman asking the questions. That was a stretch too far. It was bad enough feeling the heat of her stare sear through her skin. She just kept waiting and listening and looking. She gripped her pen, expectantly, above a notepad – ready to capture the ins and outs of Maggie's story. The tears in the plastic of the standard-issue National Health Service chair she was sitting on rubbed against exposed thigh and made her itch. Maggie's bones were protected by very little flesh and the fabric scratched through the Lycra of her cycling shorts to the small of her back.

"I saw a man murdered ten years ago in the woods – just out there – and I never told a soul. Except Lochie. I told him."

Maggie pointed into the middle distance somewhere, and the therapist cleared her throat. Psychologists are probably used to working harder to tease out the big stuff. Maggie didn't see the point. She needed to get this done. Rip off the plaster. Fast. And get the hell out of here. It was a windowless room, and the air felt stagnant.

"Who is Lochie?"

"My brother. He's my brother and pretty much my only real…"

"Only real what?"

"Never mind. He's just, he's my brother – like I said."

She stopped herself saying *only real friend*. It would sound too pathetic. But the therapist saved her. After clearing her throat and leaning forwards in Maggie's direction, she spoke slowly again. A little too patronisingly.

"Before we go on, please remember I am duty-bound to disclose anything to the authorities that presents a significant risk to you or the public. Do you want to continue?"

Maggie glanced up long enough to catch the end of a sharp eyebrow being raised in her direction. Saying the word 'murdered' was one thing. It was just a word. But it was all the messy detail behind it that was festering under her skin. There was no choice, though. Lexi was serious. It was no empty threat. She'd have HR convinced Maggie wasn't fit to work. Tell them about the day she found her in the toilets. She couldn't let her do that. If Lexi took her job away, she'd have nothing that really mattered to cling to. Copping out now was not an option.

Maggie nodded as the stiff woman sitting opposite her navigated the silence that hung between them.

"Do you know much about EMDR therapy, Maggie?"

"Mmm… a fair bit. Eye movement desensitisation and reprocessing. Something to do with using my eye movements to move from the crap memories to *a place of safety*."

She laboured over the last four words, feeling like they didn't suit her voice. Like trying to put on a trendy outfit that she'd hired for an event with a dress code.

"That's correct, Maggie. Yes. But not yet. First, we need to isolate that trauma. We need to take you back there. Do you think we can do that today?"

Her rational brain screamed *No*. She'd rather be anywhere else but here. But she had made it this far. *Get on with it. Treat it like a vaccination before travel. Just tick the box and get back to work.*

Maggie nodded for the second time.

"Please try to relax and close your eyes whilst you take yourself back to that day. Can you remember where you were? Anything about it at all?"

Her brother had warned her it was blowin' a hoolie that day. It was late May, and she'd dressed for everything the North Sea coast could throw at her. Feeling the late afternoon sun hit her cheeks, she pulled the leather strap over her neck, unzipped her rucksack, and stared at the hazy coastal sky. A dark shape in her peripheral view broke her upwards gaze. The workings of her mind didn't feel normal from a young age. She was used to being harassed at every turn with heavy, sludgy thoughts. Torturous *what ifs*, mostly. It was almost always Lochie who would reassure her they were ludicrous and eventually she would move on. Before the next one came, hot on its trail. But this time, the threat was real. Something in her stomach twisted and told her to back the hell off.

Her senses were pleading with her for attention. Tugging on her brain like a stroppy toddler.

She sank deeper into her memory of the sights, smells and sounds of that day, but was still aware of the therapist listening. Her presence had faded into the background more.

Maggie remembered a large oak tree just off the side of the path, nestled feet away from a fast-flowing burn. It lured her to hide behind its embrace, and she shifted her body out of view of the approaching figures. Being small in stature was a gift in such moments. The Kirk Woods sat between two neighbourhoods in Kirkcaldy, dividing a neighbourhood of large, orderly, stone-built Victorian homes from one of a different, harder place. Despite growing up in Kirkcaldy's more chaotic world, she found solace in organising things that fit neatly into boxes, with clear borders she could control. It helped her fight off the dark, haunting thoughts and physical urges to correct, straighten, and order everything around her.

Inside her rucksack was the compact digital camera she'd stashed in there when Lochie wasn't looking. It was one of the few things he owned that cost a fair penny, and the nudge of guilt prodded her skull each time she grabbed it from his wardrobe. She remembered checking the ground beneath her. Discarded needles, dirty wipes, or abandoned food could be anywhere. Carriers of invisible disease that might seep into her body covertly.

Maggie rubbed her hands together in her lap. An involuntary movement that brought her back into the room for a moment.

She heard the light scratching of notes being scribbled on paper at speed.

"Keep going, Maggie. Tell me what happened next."

She remembered looking for a way out before it was too late, but a relentless nosiness was forever getting Maggie in trouble.

Lochie had told her to avoid this route on her own. It was a hangout for all the town nutters, junkies and some interlopers. Most locals were born and bred in Kirkcaldy, but it was easy to spot the outsiders. Lochie treated them sometimes at the hospital where he worked.

Maggie ignored his warnings that day because she was so close to being late for work at the carvery restaurant. Being late meant plate-washing duty. She'd refuse to do it and lose her income. Maggie was saving up for her future. She wanted to study journalism and write about things that would make a difference. Just this once, she told herself, it would be fine to take the shortcut through the woods. The odds were stacked in her favour.

Maggie felt her voice echo around the walls and floor of the consulting room as she battled on, letting her memories seep out of her pores. As she spoke, her eyes remained fixed on her hands, rubbing at the raised veins and dry, peeling skin.

She remembered it was late spring on the day it all happened. That haunting time of day when towns on Scotland's east coast spewed out a quick burst of dazzling low sun. Her hands rested against the deep crevices of tree bark – dampness rising from beneath her feet. Nature's smells often comforted her. But something cut through the air that day, jarring against the natural pungency of the woods. The scent of approaching company.

"That's when I saw them."

"Who did you see, Maggie? Can you describe who you saw?"

"Two men appeared from the direction I'd been

walking, too far away to have noticed me. They arrived separately and were only interested in each other."

Maggie noticed her fists clench together on the armrests as danger resurfaced in her head. She remembered her idea to escape through the overgrown shrubs lining the path ahead, but the burn blocked her route onwards, and there was no way back without being seen.

"Can you describe who or what you saw, Maggie?"

"One man was small. The kind of bloke my brother would call a bit of a runt. A snood and beanie hat covered almost his entire face, leaving just a strip of flesh and his eyes visible. The other one was further away and harder to make out. He had more heft about him. He owned the scene. The other lad looked out of his depth – nervous but trying to hide it."

She recalled a sharp gust of wind which carried the odour of smoke and stale clothes in her direction, making her recoil further into the smell of wet pine. Then she sat motionless, watching the two face up to each other at the path's edge. Raising the viewfinder of her brother's camera to her eye, she clicked away, taking time to zoom in on the faces of the two men. No words were audible, but there was an exchange of an item too small to identify. Something transferred from the big man to the wee man, who grasped at it with his fingerless gloves. His fingernails, she sensed, would be black as soot.

Maggie rested her chest against a tree trunk and felt her heart work double time. There was no escape for her now in either direction without being seen or heard.

Shit.

Don't move.

Don't even think loudly, Maggie.

Close your eyes, make everything disappear. Count to three… very, very slowly.

A series of pictures were snowballing in her head as if she was right there, again. Ten years ago. Staccato images formed – a blade, piercing blue eyes that shone with light seconds before a darkness washed over them.

Maggie was lost to her memories of that day, encouraged by a voice coming from somewhere and asking her to keep talking.

"What happened then? What did you see?"

Before she could answer, a sharp knocking sound punctured her thoughts.

A repetitive *rat-a-tat-tat* sound pierced Maggie's subconscious in the place that images were forming. This wasn't part of her memory. Her body spasmed briefly at the sound and her mind drifted back into the consulting room. The staring woman stopped writing and looked over Maggie's head to a space behind her.

"I'm so sorry. I thought this room was vacant."

Maggie turned around, following the sound. A man she'd not seen before was standing in the doorway. He mumbled something and retreated, lobbing a string of apologies into the air. Then he closed the door again, leaving Maggie alone with the woman, her notepad and the memories of her own words hanging in the fetid air.

The interruption killed the momentum. She sprang up from the scratching chair so fast that a wall of dizziness hit her like a drug but was out of the room in seconds.

She must bury the memory of that day again – in her own head. Just as Lochie first told her to ten years ago. To speak to no one, especially not the police. *Don't mess with these kinds of people*, he said. *It'll only come back to haunt you.* And for so long, Maggie had done as she was told. And it worked – for about a year. Until the need to speak up fought back with such a force that she almost gave in to her own instincts. Until a new reason arrived to keep her quiet. It was more compelling than ever. It sat like a heavy cloud above the embers of her conscience until the temptation to speak was extinguished again. Maggie hid her memories where no one could find them. They got comfortable in that dark place, alongside the memory of her mother's lifeless body.

2

TUESDAY

Making her way into the editorial office of the *Fife Standard* for her early shift the next day, Maggie couldn't shake the feeling of being rinsed out by yesterday's therapist. Flashbacks peppered her sleep and a sense of vulnerability lingered in her head like the after-effects of cheap wine. She tried to reassure herself that she'd not shared enough to be 'reported to the authorities'. There was always the option to deny everything if trouble came knocking.

Maggie's boss and editor-in-chief, Lexi Brodick, sat in an office surrounded by glass walls, with cheap, yellowing blinds. Lexi earned her newsroom stripes when smoking on shift was as common as dropping the F bomb in every other sentence. Maggie didn't understand the need for blinds in the boss's office, anyway. There was precious little sunlight around for ten months of the year anywhere in Fife. They offered no extra soundproofing, evidenced by the spectrum of swear words which carried from her office to the surrounding newsroom. Maggie estimated Lexi spent an hour applying her make-up every day, but the profanity escaping from her scarlet-rimmed lips remained unconcealed.

Lexi's forehead wrinkled as she studied the top-line news streaming in through reams of digital sources on her wide monitor. Watching her in action was an unnerving time, prompting Maggie to pummel a stress ball before returning it to the middle drawer, where it sat on a neatly folded piece of kitchen roll – next to a four pack of miniature hand gels. She rearranged the notebooks on her desk in height order and ran a wet wipe across every inch of the laminate wood.

Lexi would soon start to pace around the room, jabbing her designer heels into the stained carpet tiles. This always climaxed with her door being opened, a name being called, and a chosen victim lured inside.

"Maggie Shields. In here, now."

Shit.

Maggie's number was up today.

Today, of all days, she wanted to be left alone. Not just because it was the anniversary of her mum's death. Reliving memories that should have stayed buried exhausted her, and she had no appetite for Lexi's grilling. Rumours of Tom Aitken, a local councillor for Kirkcaldy West, channelling exploited refugee labour to businesses who could afford to pay a living wage had kept her busy that week. It wouldn't win her the Pulitzer, but it was enough to get her teeth into. But she knew better than to resist the summons. After grabbing one notebook and readjusting the others, she rushed to the glass-walled cube.

"What are you working on at the moment?"

Lexi asked this a lot. Even if she wasn't especially interested in the answer. It was shorthand for *I'm watching you. There's no place for drifters in this business.*

"I'm… eh… chasing a strong lead into Tom—"

"I need a showstopper from you, Shields. We're getting battered by vloggers and TikTokkers and Christ knows who else, and my pension pot isn't big enough to fund a one-way ticket to the Caribbean yet."

Her boss threw down a pile of tabloid front pages on the desk between them. They were awash with celebrities behaving badly and headlines like 'Bankers in Brothel Brawl' or 'Royal Rumble in Celebrity Jungle'.

A wave of depression crashed into her soul.

"This is what that lot out there wants to read," said Lexi, gesticulating to the outside world.

"Forget your moral high ground, lass. Fife readers don't have the appetite for it. They're too busy trying to keep their heads above water. The country's knee-deep in a cost-of-living crisis. We have two ways to keep their hard-won attention on our wee rag."

She paused, but not for a response.

"Either we show them how to survive – who to complain to, where the new jobs are coming from, how to save money, that kind of thing – or we give them a generous helping of utter nonsense escapism. Ideally, a bit of both. Got it?"

This time it sounded more like a question, but Maggie knew better than to respond. This was a speech. Most definitely a one-way thing.

"You want to be an investigator, aye? Well, pick a topic folk give an actual arse about. And I mean real folk. People who watch soaps on the telly every night and go to work every day in jobs they bloody hate just to make it to the weekend again without falling further into debt."

Maggie couldn't help wondering what the mighty Lexi Brodick would make of some compulsory EMDR therapy, but there was no time to dwell. The boss was opening her door – a clear sign the rant was done for today. It would be someone else's turn tomorrow.

"And, Maggie..."

"Boss?"

"Stop looking like a miserable, nippy wee bairn, eh? Did you show face at that appointment yesterday?"

"Sure did."

It wasn't a lie. She turned up. What Lexi doesn't have to know is that she bolted after the first fifteen minutes.

"No overnight benefits then, I see? Can you tell that face of yours to smile occasionally?"

Not that Maggie never smiled. She knew very well how to look happy. But she could not fake it. Her face had always been a clear a window into her mood. But she was fine with that. Proud of it, in fact.

"Sorry, boss. Tough day."

Lexi raised one heavily pencilled eyebrow over the rim of her glasses.

"Is there something I need to know about?"

Maggie responded with her coldest stare – a definite decline.

"Well, how about you jog on out of here and distract

yourself by finding tomorrow's front-page splash, yeh?"

Maggie was on her feet and heading for the door whilst she had the chance. She fought hard to swallow the lump of anger building in her throat as she trudged back to her desk, pulled out her seat, and thrust her body down like a petulant child. The words 'nonsense escapism' were nipping at her head.

The screen attached to the wall behind the reporters' desks was halfway through the late morning news. She spun round and craned her neck upwards to hear them discussing the aftermath of Storm Ivor. The VT package ran images of frail-looking elderly folk being shipped to safety in dinghies down the high street. Maggie's mood nosedived further. The thought of doorstepping a family knee-deep in stagnant flood water or pitching up to a church hall filled with displaced locals, rammed together like homeless, angry sardines, was too much. She had to get out of here before Lexi sent her to get a vox pop. She often gave Maggie this task on account of folk being less intimidated by a petite female sticking a microphone in their face.

"And finally, turning to a developing story in the Kingdom of Fife."

The newsreader was back on the screen, complete with airbrushed face and a painted-on expression of concern.

"Police Scotland are expected to make a statement shortly to confirm the apparent disappearance of international rugby star and Fife resident Mark Anderson, who's been reported missing by his wife Valerie Anderson today. It's understood that Anderson – who has over one hundred fifty rugby caps for Scotland and The British

Lions and a formidable reputation on the international sporting stage – was last seen by his teenage children over three days ago at the family home near St Andrews."

It had all the elements of a newspaper shifter. A page three lead at the very least. Might even make a lively double-page picture spread, too, if it rumbled on. Well-known, home-grown, easy-on-the-eye sportsman vanishes overnight. Glamorous, grieving wife left reeling. Might sell more copies if he had been a footballer, but it still had potential.

If she could get some decent background on this rugby boy and turn it around for tomorrow's paper, she'd get Lexi off her back and get back to Aitken faster.

The problem was, Maggie could write everything she knew about rugby on the back of a stamp. The sports desk might already be across it, so she'd have to make it her own. Go for the human-interest angle. Hardly the issue-led investigating she was aspiring to, but it might keep her out of Lexi's glass cube for a few days.

Reunited with her stress ball, her hands got to work on its malleable rubber, pounding it like hell.

The story might be self-limiting. Anderson had to be off shagging someone other than his wife, and he'd be quick to crawl back home when he missed her Sunday roast, so she needed to move fast. The sports fans Maggie knew in life understood the world of football, not rugby. They spent their weekends supporting Raith Rovers at Stark's Park, chanting songs that would make your eyes water. Posh boys played rugby at the private schools or down in the Borders.

Maggie spun in her chair, surprised to find the *Standard*'s sports hack Harris Roberts at his desk. He often spent his days in the stands or in nearby boozers and was more used to press conferences about transfer windows and injuries than Maggie ever wanted to be.

"Oi, Roberts. You across that missing rugby boy story?"

He leant back in his chair, taking the opportunity of an interruption to flex the muscles inside his tight-fitting shirt.

"Nah. The boss said not to bother. Told me to stick to the players that turn up to the games. Tell the punters who's got form, who's injured and who's going to be sent to the bench. Helps us sell more advertising space to the big online gambling sites with deep pockets."

An unexpected flutter of relief flew through Maggie.

"Why? Can't imagine it's your thing, Shields."

"It's not. But I need to get out of here before she sends me down to doorstep flood victims. These poor folk are dealing with enough, and then we pitch up with our recording devices and predictable questions – that's not what I signed up for."

Harris shook his head and belched into his own hand, briefly offending himself.

"Oops, 'scuse me. Coffee on an empty stomach. Well, good luck to you with that lot. I'm off for a bacon roll. You want anything?"

She ignored the offer. If the police were releasing a statement about Anderson, it was an excuse to put in some face time at the station. There might be something else brewing that she could squeeze out of them whilst she was there. She just had to ask the right person.

Releasing her stress ball for a moment, she let her fingers run across the edges of her notebooks, feeling the joy of their aligned spines run through her senses, straightening things out in her own mind.

*

By the time Maggie reached the St Brycedale Road branch of Police Scotland, the press conference was in full swing. An OB van belonging to the TV crowd took up three spaces in the car park and the usual faces were all there. Cameras and mics lined up in the front row, hungry for action. A mix of hyper-local bloggers and the odd stringer from the Scottish nationals took up a few other seats. As press gatherings went, it was a sizeable turnout. She found a spot near the back and rummaged around noisily for her Dictaphone and notebook. The police media relations officer paused, took an exaggerated inward breath, and continued.

"As I was saying, we've got some CCTV footage of what we believe to be the last known sighting of Mr Anderson. This indicates he was in the local area shortly before his wife, Mrs Valerie Anderson, reported him missing yesterday evening."

Maggie's phone sprang back to life in her pocket.

"Shit, sorry."

She scrambled to open her zip and silence it as a few grunts reverberated around the room.

"We have a couple of frozen images to share with you today taken from different angles in the Harbour Tavern, which – as you may know – is located on the corner of Whytehouse Avenue. Each image shows our missing person, Mr Anderson, in what could be described as 'heated conversation' with another currently unidentified male."

The interior of the Harbour Tavern was familiar to Maggie, even though she could only remember being inside it once in her life. It was a rowdy funeral wake for one of her dad's friends. But Maggie had etched every detail of the bar into her memory, including the shape of the high stools, the smell of stale beer and the chaotic arrangement of bottles stacked up against a mirrored wall. Her mind worked like a camera. Instant, accurate, and unforgiving.

"The CCTV footage you are looking at now was from eighteen-O-eight hours on Saturday fifth June, but we are appealing for the public's help to determine the ID of the male seen in conversation with Mr Anderson."

Maggie strained to focus on the grainy image from her seat at the back of the room and was about to ask if they'd enlarge it on-screen when a voice she recognised cut through the air.

"Is he a danger to the public? There's always some trouble there after a certain time of night – more CCTV than Buck House around that dive."

The question came from the *Scottish Daily Sport*'s very own Den Appleton, commonly referred to as 'Dennis the Menace' on account of his reputation for never letting the truth impede a good story. Rumour had it that the paper's legal advisors were campaigning to get Den ousted before they found themselves on the wrong side of one more messy libel case. He was based at the national tabloid's Glasgow HQ but ventured further north if he got a whiff of something juicy enough. His presence today made Maggie glad she'd bothered.

"Yes, thanks Den. We are simply encouraging anyone who was in or near the Harbour Tavern or may help us identify this male to contact the team here at Police Scotland."

The media officer clicked on something which highlighted contact details at the bottom of the smart board. Fife police had recently gone to town with an audiovisual upgrade and Maggie wondered how many new cops they could've put through training college instead.

Returning her attention to the black-and-white image from the bar, Maggie tried to focus on the two men. One was in control of the situation. He gripped his victim by the collar, pinning him up against the wood panelling of the pub walls. Something stirred in Maggie's brain. The part that stored memories of faces or names she'd encountered before. But the scene itself made no sense. What the hell was a man mountain of a rugby player with no shortage of cash doing in this grotty wee den, pressed up against a wall, taking a bollocking from another lad two weight divisions beneath him?

"Are you treating Mark's disappearance as high risk?"

Julie from *The Scottish Express* was next to speak up.

The tabloids were hungry for an angle that would generate panic.

"Do you have reason to believe he's come to any harm?"

The questions were firing thick and fast at 'Nina', the media rep. It must have been her first press pack. She looked like a rabbit caught in car headlights. Maggie tried to block out the surrounding drone and incessant camera clicks, standing up to take in every pixel of the photo more clearly. She scanned it for the stuff that others wouldn't see. Something at first glance meaningless but out of place. She kept looping back to the same two questions. Why was Mark Anderson there, and why was he not fighting back?

The face of the man confronting Anderson stole Maggie's attention. It wasn't the weight of his body that held Mark still. The image was out of focus, but raw human pain was unmistakable. She'd seen it in the eyes of her own family and in the face of the dying – strangers and loved ones alike. Lochie's words of reassurance that day ten years ago still echoed in her ears.

Keep out of it, Maggie. These people didn't know you were there, so don't get involved.

But today, the raw pain in the eyes of the man confronting Mark triggered something inside her again. What was giving this man the strength to intimidate a wall of athletic muscle and make him listen?

Maggie locked her stare on their faces, desperate to find some clue. And then it came at her in a wave of reality. She knew this face from her past, and it was from a part of her life she would rather had not been found here.

3

TUESDAY EVENING

Maggie returned to her flat just before nine o'clock. Nudging the communal front door open with the side of her body, she tried to march past the mess of bikes scattered in the stairwell. They all faced in different directions. Filthy tyres rubbing against the wall. Her pulse quickened, but she focused on the stone steps ahead.

One step, no – two steps. Two steps at a time. Start again from the bottom – keep it right. Two steps. And another two. Focus.

Her own front door approached at the first landing, reaching for her like a welcoming hug. The familiar smell of her lavender diffuser seeping under the doorway into the landing comforted Maggie. She unlocked her door, kicked off her slip-on Skechers and stepped from dark stone to fresh laminate wood, desperate to shed the rest of her outside clothes. But something else cut across the lavender. A pungent, heavy aroma. Unmistakably male. Her heart quickened. People told her she imagined smells that didn't exist. The smell of vomit on a bus where there was none, the smell of blood on a café mug, fresh out of the dishwasher. But this time it was real. She pulled her mobile phone out from her pocket, unlocked the screen and hovered her thumb over the number 9, using her other hand to arrange her keys into a weapon. Her hallway was dark and the doors leading off it closed. Maggie never closed her internal doors – she preferred to let the air circulate. Resisting the urge to switch the light on, she noticed a shaft of white escaping from under the kitchen door. A few sharp banging sounds came from within. Cupboards being opened and closed rapidly and the heavy clomp of feet moving across her wood-panelled floor.

Maggie left her front door ajar behind her before taking two more steps towards the kitchen door. She fumbled around in the darkness to find the door handle before a voice cut through the silence.

"Maggie? That you?!"

"Shit, Lochie."

She whispered the curse under her breath and took a long overdue inhale of air, trying to steady her pulse.

"Ah, the wanderer returns at last. How's it going, Scoop?"

Relief engulfed her like a sedative through her veins.

Scoop was Lochie's favourite nickname for Maggie. She pretended to be irritated by it but secretly loved it for the undertone of fondness and pride. But Maggie's pride in her brother mirrored his for her. Lochie's promotion to charge nurse made his job even tougher. But hard graft didn't scare him. She knew he would do anything for his patients and even more for his only sister.

"You forgot I was coming over, didn't you?"

Even when life irritated him, his face remained soft. Lochie inherited their dad's more rounded features and Maggie got her mum's angular cheek bones. His light blond eyebrows raised slightly, emphasising the faint collection of lines gathering on his pale thirty-five-year-old skin.

"Eh… no, Loch. It's just…"

"I knew you would. I tried to call earlier. To remind you."

"Sorry. I was at a press conference."

"Anything interesting?"

Scanning her lounge, the sight of items out of place unnerved Maggie.

"Lochie, could you please take those hospital Crocs off at the door?"

She searched for something to settle her, casting her gaze over the neat row of potted cacti sitting five centimetres apart on her windowsill. Maggie never bothered with regular house plants. They were too needy. An occasional drench of water kept cacti content, allowing them to get on with life on their own terms. She admired their ever-increasing strength and prickly defence – a clear warning to those who got too close.

"What's that smell?"

"That smell, young Margaret, is my slow-cooked lamb casserole. Hope you're hungry."

Maggie considered going vegetarian many times, but Lochie always pushed back, ranting about iron deficiency.

He'd tell her she needed more 'meat on her bones' and that she'd be stuffed if she got ill with so few physical reserves.

"So, what are the good people of Fife girnin' about today, then?"

"Lochie, I'm knackered. Can we talk about something else?"

He accepted the rebuttal without question, silently shrugging his shoulders in response.

Taking in the devastation in her small galley kitchen, she imagined getting it all back the way it needed to be after he'd gone. But he was reading her mind.

"Christ's sake, sit down, Mags. You know I'll wash up later. It's good for you to just let it be for a bit, eh?"

"How do you do that?"

"Do what?"

"Read my mind like that. Do they teach you that at nursing school?"

"I wish! Actually, no. I don't. Ignorance is bliss sometimes."

Pulling out a chair, she sank her tired body into it, exhaustion taking over. Lochie handed her a glass of water, cooled with ice, and placed a cushion under her feet. He had a way of making her feel secure and at ease. Once again, her memories from yesterday's therapy session jumped back into her head.

"I tried to do some therapy yesterday, Lochie."

He stopped in his tracks on his way back to the kitchen, turning his head to one side as if he had misheard.

"You what?"

"I went to a therapist – or rather, a clinical psychologist.

The real deal apparently. Remember I told you Lexi forced me to do it?"

Lochie had returned to the kitchen table, pulling out a chair next to Maggie. His interest in what she had to say felt intense.

"Wow. Maggie. I'm… impressed."

Maggie couldn't avoid the feeling that Lochie looked more unsettled than impressed.

"I had no choice. No one is going to take my job from me. I had to show up."

He shifted a little on the chair and leant towards her, resting his arms on the table.

"And? Well… what did you discuss?"

She could gloss over her great escape from the woman and her scratchy pencil with Lexi. But there was no lying to Lochie.

"I couldn't."

"What? Couldn't *what*?"

"It was too much. The questions. The place. I tried, but just when I relaxed a bit some eejit gatecrashed into the room. It felt like… someone was raking around in my brain. Shit, Loch, I couldn't do it."

She turned her face away from him, shame building inside her like a pressure cooker. When she looked up, her brother's body language had changed. He'd relaxed back into the chair and was stretching his legs out in front of himself. If she didn't know better, it almost looked like relief. Lochie placed a strong importance on privacy. He'd been like that ever since Mum died and the town crowded around us all at once.

"It's a therapy session, Mags. What did you expect? These folk will chip away into your head – into your life – and pull it apart bit by bit."

"Well, anyway. I couldn't do it, Loch. I'll find something else – a self-help book or a podcast or something."

"I get it, Mags. Can't imagine I'd love some stranger fishing around in my memories, drudging up crap from the past."

It was Lochie who got the call from Lexi when she found Maggie in the women's toilets, curled up on the floor with her arms around her knees. It was supposed to be a routine toilet trip and hand clean when she came back from a job. Just once. Maybe twice to get the bits under her nails. But she couldn't escape. She was stuck in a loop: clean, dry hands, touch door to leave, restart. Clean, dry hands… until she found herself on the floor with Lexi staring over her.

"I understand why Lexi wants you to get help. But talking to strangers? They wouldn't understand."

"What, Lochie? What wouldn't they understand?"

He looked agitated. Pointing his eyes upwards and breathing through a gap in his teeth.

"All the stuff that we've – you've – had to deal with."

Maggie listened to the words coming from her brother. They sounded misplaced from someone who spent his days talking to strangers – trying to make them feel better. But maybe this was different somehow. It was their past and their lives being examined.

"Maybe she'll let you try something else? Less… in your face, you know? I can help you research that if you like?"

"Aye, thanks Loch. But research is kind of my thing, yeh? That's kind of what journalists do... like... every day. Anyway, are you making my dinner or what?"

Maggie enjoyed watching Lochie cook. It reminded her of their mum in the kitchen. She made it up as she went along, but it would always come together at the end. He'd make a decent boyfriend to someone. If he ever stopped hanging around with his wee sister.

Lochie talked a lot about family loyalty. The importance of knowing who to trust and who to avoid. How to know who's got your back no matter what. So, when he told her to keep quiet about what she witnessed that dark day in the woods ten years ago, she couldn't – and wouldn't – ignore him. At least, not at first.

Don't talk to a soul about what you saw, he'd said, when he got home and found her shaking with fear, telling him about the photos she took on his camera. She wanted to be brave and speak up to the police – right there and then. But Lochie made her see the truly brave thing to do was to walk away. To get on with your life, far removed from witness statements and courtrooms. Eventually she listened, and it reassured her. Settled her fevered mind. Until a year later, when the urge to speak up almost overwhelmed her.

Tonight was not the time for those memories though. Looking at him sitting opposite her at the table, Maggie wondered what it must be like to be an only child. She craved her own space sometimes – but knew they had to be together tonight.

"I'm going to get changed."

She changed her clothes, sat on her bed for long

enough to feel her breathing settle, and then returned to the kitchen. The nine o'clock news played on the TV, and Lochie put an intimidating dome-shaped pile of meat and rice on the table in front of her.

"Thanks, Lochie. Sorry – it's just late, that's all. I appreciate your offer of help, but I need to find my way through all this, you know, stuff that's going on with me – whatever it is."

Lochie said nothing but nodded at her with a silent reassurance. Reaching for her first mouthful, Maggie heard Mark Anderson's name on the news.

Mark Anderson. Scotland's sporting giant… reported missing by his devoted family.

It pulled Maggie's mind back into work, but Lochie's arm sprang across the kitchen table for the remote control and switched off the TV abruptly. He didn't do much quickly outside of his work. It was a shift in pace that felt uncomfortable.

"Guessing you'll want a break from the news?" he said, in a half-question, half-statement kind of way. It was a sweet gesture. He liked to block curveballs coming her way because he saw them first. Maggie had to keep busy today, and being together at the end of it helped. The gaping hole in both their lives was never far away, but it felt wider and deeper than ever on this day.

"You know what date this is, don't you, Loch?"

He stopped shovelling food into his mouth briefly and looked at her, a little startled.

"Of course. But I thought you didn't *do* anniversaries?"

"Doesn't mean they don't exist, does it?"

Maggie dropped the fork on her plate and stood up, too restless to eat.

Her brother's expression softened as he refilled her wine glass before topping up his own.

"You're getting more like her, you know?"

"What, looking older, you mean? Don't go telling me to wear more make-up and all that nonsense again, mind."

She was pacing now, but he stayed still. Like a stake in the ground to exercise around.

"Nah, just… in little, weird things. Stuff I've noticed sometimes. Like the way you keep your bread in the fridge, instead of a bread bin like normal folk. Or how you send salesmen to the neighbours you don't like. That's *all* her."

Maggie wondered if she could ever fill her mum's shoes in Lochie's eyes. She felt so far from the mark most of the time.

"I don't want you to lose your job, Mags. I know how much it means to you. But I don't think it's right that you're forced to talk to a stranger about all that personal stuff. There must be another way to get to grips with everything going on up here."

Lochie jabbed a finger into his own forehead as he spoke.

"Blimey, promise me you won't ever apply for a job in a psychiatric ward, will you? You are spectacularly insensitive."

The intensity with which Lochie seemed to steer her away from seeing this psychologist again unnerved Maggie.

"I'm on an early shift tomorrow, Loch."

"Alright, I get the hint."

He reached for his jacket, pulling it on whilst he slipped his feet back into the NHS-issued navy-blue Crocs.

"I'll call you tomorrow."

She let him give her a quick hug before playfully pushing him away.

"Save it for your girlfriend. Oh, wait…"

"You're too funny. Take care of yourself, Scoop."

She watched him leave and her gut flipped a little at the sadness on his face as he said goodbye. He would have stayed with her if she'd asked. But she didn't. She couldn't. There were things to do before she could rest.

"Bye, Lochie."

Seconds after closing the door, she began a deep clean of the fridge and every surface of the kitchen until the smell of bleach annihilated everything and made her nostrils and throat sting. Then she slipped on her outdoor shoes, jacket and Marigold gloves and wandered down into the stairwell where she could sort the bikes. She aligned all the handlebars, making sure each one stood upright, and swept away the fallen mud from around them. Returning to her own flat, she scrubbed her hands clean for three minutes. The egg timer sitting on the shelf behind the sink bore witness. Collapsing on her sofa to breathe in the visceral moment of calm and equilibrium in private, her thoughts drifted back to the past.

Fifteen years, Mum. You'd be so proud of Lochie. Healing the sick and all that.

Wiping a rogue tear from below her eye, she reached into the drawer below her coffee table and pulled out an old red padded photo album. It was a comfort blanket. She knew its imperfections and the slightly stale smell instantly transported her to another, happier time. Leafing through the pages, she rested her gaze on photos where Lochie was the star of the show. The centre of attention, laughing, winking, or throwing his arms around his wee sister. Maggie ran her hand over the shining plastic covers on each page as if she could somehow feel her mother's soft skin. Her own eyes felt tired, desperate to close on the day, but they didn't. Something stopped them. One photo near the end of the book drew her attention. She sat up and focused her gaze on the faces staring back at her. Her brother, as relaxed as ever, was standing on a sports pitch alongside four others. They were all pals of Lochie from high school. Seeing them like this took her back to her earliest memories of having a brother who was so much older than her. This must have been taken when she was in primary school. Her brother and his friends seemed so very old and grown up.

Her pulse quickened again as she noticed one face staring back at her from the album. There was no mistaking where she'd seen it earlier that day.

It was the same face she remembered from the police CCTV footage at the press conference. The face that was being publicly tipped as the tidy link between a pub brawl and a high-profile missing person. The same eyes that showed pain and the same arms that held Mark Anderson against the wall in the Harbour Tavern.

4

WEDNESDAY A.M.

Maggie knew her brother would be at work at the crack of dawn. The photo of Lochie with someone who was now linked to a missing person's case caused another disturbed night's sleep. It was taken more than a decade ago, but it meant there was a connection between her brother and the last person to see Mark Anderson before he disappeared. He was a top priority for the police and Lochie might still be in touch with him. She was never one to wait long for answers, so she reached for her phone and started typing.

Call me on your break. Please. Mx

He'd already be at the hospital, in his scrubs, with his mobile phone silenced in a locker, so she'd just have to wait. Work would distract her for a couple of hours, at least. A juicy nugget about Mark Anderson's past or present from Lochie might give her a way into what was going on behind the scenes. There was always something. This job had taught her that fast.

She clicked on the first search result that grabbed her

attention. It was a photo taken before the 2011 Rugby World Cup.

Anderson Captains A Defiant Scotland Squad As They Face Up To Bullish Argentina.

He looked like a man who wouldn't entertain the thought of defeat. There were other images further down. Some with his then-fiancée, Ms Valerie Rollo, but many with his father – Ranald Anderson. This man popped up a lot – like some sort of half-father, half-manager hybrid.

She followed the research rabbit warren where it led, opening a fresh search bar and typing 'Ranald Anderson, Kirkcaldy, Fife.'

The search results filled with pictures of a tall man – thickset and possibly mid to late seventies – wearing a selection of suits with brightly coloured ties. There were blotches of red skin on his face. Most of the photos were of awards events or presenting oversized cheques to grateful-looking recipients. There were several news stories with headlines about 'groundbreaking medical software' and 'patient centric data management solutions'. A jumble of words that Maggie suspected would impress the right folk.

She hovered her mouse over a picture caption that read, Ranald Anderson gifts groundbreaking patient software to Fife Victims of Domestic Violence Shelter.

Next to a lineup of grateful-looking women stood a man clearly experienced in pulling off a photo opportunity. Maggie's scepticism for corporate altruism was surfacing again, interrupted by the sound of her mobile phone ringing.

"Lochie, hi. Listen, you know him."

She heard him clear his throat. His voice sounded hoarse. Even more tired than usual.

"What? Who? Who do I know, Maggie?"

"Or knew him anyway, I mean. The guy on the CCTV."

"I've got patients to discharge, for Christ's sake."

"It's one of your old school pals – think he was the really bright one – no offence, like. McSomething, I think..."

"I'm going. This is not urgent. I thought something serious had happened to you."

"No, wait. Listen. He's the bloke the cops are trying to ID – you know, the one who was last seen with that missing rugby lad Mark Anderson before he did a runner... or vanished, or, well, whatever happened to him."

An eery silence hung in the air between them. Maggie wasn't used to silences between her and Lochie, and it was unnerving her more. Why had he stopped protesting? In her line of work that was usually an indicator that she'd hit a raw nerve.

"Loch?"

As the awkward gap lingered, Maggie saw the top line of a news item ping into her social media feed.

Police name associate seen on CCTV with missing Anderson as thirty-two-year-old Kirkcaldy man, Peter McGill.

It was some hyper-local blogger's site, but it looked genuine.

"McGill. That was it. Your school pal's name."

Nothing came back from him. He hadn't spoken for so long that she wondered if they'd been cut off.

"Lochie? Are you still there?"

"Maggie, I'm going back to work now. I know a lot of Peters… I'd need to look at the photo again to be sure which one it is. Is there no one else you can ask about this? You're the one knee-deep in everyone's business around here."

Maggie squeezed on her stress ball with a purpose. The muscles in her neck tightened.

"I'm asking *you*, Lochie, because there's a picture in our family album of you with this man. It may have been taken bloody years ago, but you looked pretty good pals to me. I just want to speak to you about him. I don't get why there's an issue?"

Maggie heard her brother swear quietly under his breath, but she waited, biting her tongue to stop herself from snapping again.

"I'll talk to you about this after work."

Maggie threw her phone down on the desk and reached over to her keyboard. At least she had a name. Peter McGill. The same name the police would have already run through their systems. She double checked the national feeds and, sure enough, they were running the same headline. The same name. Peter McGill would probably already be in the station answering questions. The police trying to tease out information from someone who chose not to come forward himself. Maggie sensed the familiar desire to burrow herself into this tale, somewhere the police would probably not want her to be. She just needed to find her own way into Mark Anderson's wider family.

*

"He's built like a brick shithouse that one, eh?"

Harris was lurking around her desk, way too close for Maggie's liking.

"Feck, Harris, don't creep up on folk like that! What are you on about?"

"Anderson. He's built for the front row."

Maggie didn't know what the 'front row' was and far less cared, but showing her ignorance was not an option.

"Aye, you could say. Know much about him though, like, off the pitch?"

"How come you're still fishing around this? Didn't I tell you the boss isn't interested? Oh, look lively, speak of the devil."

Lexi was circling the office, leaving a trail of sickly perfume as she went. She leant in over Lexi's screen.

"Where's your head at, Maggie? You got me that front-page splash yet?"

She couldn't decide whether it was best to keep her work on Anderson close to her chest until she had something solid to offer.

Lexi held up her wrist, pointing to her gold-and-jewel-encrusted watch.

"Keep up, Maggie. The job cuts they are a' coming."

She'd heard this line so often before, but it still served its purpose as a reminder of the thread by which she was clinging to employment.

Sod it. Nothing to lose.

"I was just having a nosey around that miss per, boss –

the rugby *celebrity*, Mark Anderson."

"Thought you reckoned he'd just rode off into the sunset with his bit on the side?" Lexi countered, quicker than Maggie was expecting.

"Don't know. Something about the press pack at the police station yesterday. Heck of a fuss being made about tracking down the bloke in the CCTV. Pretty odd that he's just up and vanished, don't you think? Might make a juicy local intrigue piece if it rumbles on?"

Lexi's face contorted as if she'd been hit with a bad smell. A regular event in the newsroom.

"Don't think I'm all that interested in 'rugby land', young Maggie. And there's not much to say from what I've heard. Doubt you'll get anything from the cops to bring it on much."

Maggie nodded out of habit.

"Ah, right enough. But the thing is, I might have a way in to the bloke the cops are trying to ID. You know – the guy pinning Anderson up against a wall in the Harbour Tavern? Police have named him now. Local lad, Peter McGill."

Lexi looked keen to move on, but Lochie's past link to McGill was the best lead on a potential new story Maggie had, and she would not let it go lightly.

"I recognised his face when I saw it in my bro… I mean, on the screen down at the station."

Harris and Lexi turned to face Maggie in unison.

"You know him?"

Harris was trying to catch up.

"Well, I don't know him exactly, but I think I can find out more about him."

"Well, isn't that cracking? Case solved, eh?" said Lexi. Bursting with sarcasm.

Maggie was impervious to the putdown, so she stepped it up a notch.

"I think he was a friend of my brother's."

"Oh, aye? Thought your brother was the squeaky clean one in scrubs – nurse at the hospital, is he not?"

Maggie cleared her throat, waiting for the dryness to soften before she spoke. The sound of her brother's name being bandied about at work felt odd.

"I'll speak to Lochie when he finishes his shift, but in the meantime, I've dug up some background on Mark Anderson already. Fancy taking a…"

"Great. Let's fill the paper with a tribute to the man 'cause he's been a low-risk miss per for a few days then, shall we?"

Lexi's resistance grated on her now. *Why was she not going for this? Or at least keen for me to dig around the Anderson family a bit more?*

"Can you let me take a run at it, boss? There's a fair bit to his wider family, mind. He's your classic posh boy. Went to that fancy-pants boarding school in Perthshire – something Towers. His old man – a Mr Ranald Anderson – dabbled in amateur rugby too, before building up the family fortune in med tech." Harris looked at Lexi, mouthing the words, *What's med tech?* but she ignored him. "Mark joined the East of Scotland team when he was only twelve years old and was quickly promoted to the national A team when the sport became professional."

"Rugby went pro in ninety-five, Maggie. That's a fair few years before Mark hit the scene."

She looked up from her notepad and ploughed on, avoiding eye contact with Harris.

"As I was saying. As soon as he was on the squad, he was rarely on the bench. Injury record was low, apparently. Almost inhumanly low. He started picking up endorsement deals and the like. Young kids coming up through the leagues had a new hero to worship."

Maggie clocked she was losing the room.

"Wait until you hear the picture behind the curtain, though. All very different."

Lexi raised her right eyebrow sharply. There were a few rumblings around the table as her words seemed to stir bodies and minds back to life.

"Apparently Anderson senior was the worst kind of father from hell. Rumours out there that his agenda for Mark's life took its toll."

"How's that then?"

Lexi was at least asking questions – encouragement enough for Maggie to carry on.

"Turns out young Mark tried to rebel. Went a wee bit, you know, off the rails."

Lexi rolled her eyes. Her look of weariness was all-encompassing.

"So, let me get this right. We have 'young, talented sports person has a naughty side'. Hardly the scoop of the year, Shields. You know rugby players puke in their own boots and then drink beer out of them in clubhouses?"

"I get that, boss. But listen, we're not just talking about

the odd lager shandy here. There were reports of drug use. Sustained steroid use for a start and some other pretty strong recreational stuff."

"Why was this not *everywhere* at the time?"

Maggie was ready for the question. Encouraged by it.

"My thoughts exactly. But no one ever substantiated any of it. And turns out the big man Daddy Anderson lawyered up and came down so hard on local hacks sniffing around his son that the rumours disappeared in a puff of smoke. No hard and fast proof, you see. He had them over a barrel every time. And initial enquiries would suggest he's got as many enemies as millions in the bank, too."

"Oh? Why's that then?"

Mike – the fresh-faced business reporter and only bloke in the room wearing a suit – seemed to have woken up for this part.

"Not sure yet. It doesn't feel like tax dodging or anything like that. But there's something there. I'm doing some digging. Might try his nearest and dearest next."

"So, what happened to the rugby boy wonder after his dad shut down all those drug-taking headlines?"

"Mark just kept playing great rugby – for his team and his country. Scottish rugby fans don't have an easy run of it, so when a star player comes along, folk are keen to let the rumours fade – especially if they're not proven."

"Until he lost form spectacularly."

"Yes, thanks, Harris. He retired from the game four years ago, not long after one of Scotland's worst World Cup performances ever. His professional playing days just kind of disintegrated. Apparently, he was 'invited to retire' after that steroid stuff flared up again."

"After pissing hot, is what Maggie's trying to tell us."

Harris Roberts never missed a chance to remind the world just how much time he'd spent in sports locker rooms.

"And then what? He's hardly let himself go to seed physically, has he?"

"Well, I found out he's been thrashing out a living as a high-end personal trainer ever since. Feeding off his dad's links to the private healthcare providers. It's amazing what strategically placed flyers in private physiotherapy and rehab wards can do for business."

"Aye, I've seen the tidy pile he shacks up in along near St Andrews West Sands. Life can't be too rough for him," said Harris.

"Rubbish. It's Kirkcaldy the Andersons live in, not St Andrews."

Lexi's interjection was brimming with confidence. She prided herself on knowing where every well-known face in Fife lived.

"That's the family home," Maggie corrected her, with a bravery that felt good. "It's where his two daughters and wife, Mrs Valerie Anderson, live. But the pair separated a few years back. Around the time of his biggest steroid stooshie. All a bit much for her, it would appear. So, he treated himself to a shiny new bachelor pad in St Andrews – no doubt helped along by Daddy Anderson's deep pockets."

Maggie caught a fleeting glimpse of something that

bordered on resentment in Lexi's eyes. She wondered if it was just because she'd got one over on her.

"Decent work, Shields. But are the cops telling you anything interesting about their missing person investigation?"

"We're very much stuck at the cloak and dagger stage for now. We had the CCTV footage appeal, the last known sighting with the now ID'ed Peter McGill, but not much after that. It's a bit like the shutters have come down with a silent bang. Nothing but a standard line about pursuing any potential leads and remaining in direct contact with Mark's family."

"What about McGill, then? What is it you know about his family?"

Maggie felt something disconnect. She'd only told Lexi her brother used to know *him*. She mentioned nothing about knowing the wider McGill family. It was a subtle difference, but the jump unsettled her. People didn't expect Lexi to make logical errors. She was, however, known for having a deeper and broader knowledge of local gossip and history than anyone in Fife. Maybe she'd had a bad night. Lexi's black-lined eyes were bearing down on her now and her sharp eyebrows stooped towards the centre of her nose, like stamps on her face.

Maggie remembered the McGill family. At least by reputation, that was. But she wanted to keep that to herself for now.

"Yep. Looks like McGill was an old school pal of my brother. Digging into that now, boss."

Maggie sensed Lexi on the verge of another rant about

clocks ticking, but she held back, leaving a rare gap in the exchange.

"I reckon it might be time to pay Val a visit at home," said Maggie. "See if she wants to give the police a gentle nudge through the media."

"Fine. But I'm not having you waste any more time on this unless the cops give you a fresh line on Mark soon."

Maggie was determined to get ahead of the police. The tenuous link to her brother via Peter McGill presented a definite opportunity for inside information, so why was it feeling a little more unsettling than helpful?

Picking up her coat and pushing her chair neatly under the desk, she escaped into the clean, open air. Her usual route from the office took her along the coastal path towards Ravenscraig Park. Sitting proudly on the seafront pointing towards Kirkcaldy Bay, this park was where her mum brought her when she was a child. The place she learnt to ride her bike without stabilisers and fed chips to seagulls the size of golden eagles. Her gaze dropped towards the path at her feet, careful to avoid standing on cracks in the pavement. That was a habit that started very young. Probably soon after her mum died, but now she couldn't remember a time she didn't do it.

Walk on a line and you'll break your spine. She used to chant the words to herself, on loop, until she was sure she wouldn't forget it. Soon after, she graduated to chasing lamp posts.

Get to that lamp post before the next car or someone you love will be hurt.

The mantra introduced her to a game of chance against

the world, like one of those shitty little evil chain letters or social media posts that stalked folk online.

Share this post with ALL your friends or something awful will happen to one of them and they'll ALL know it was YOUR fault.

For Maggie, these mind games were personal. She was up against fate and the stakes were as high as she could imagine. There was no margin for error, just in case something painful and life-changing happened to someone – and it *would* be *her* fault, because she didn't listen to the warning from the bully in her head.

Lochie was her only safety net. Her port in a storm. He used to have friends his own age that he hung out with, too. She remembered a few of them. Faces more than names. Fleeting images of a young Peter McGill darted into her mind. What rose to the surface was talk of a reputation – and not a good one at that. A family to be avoided. Why, then, was her brother's arm draped around Peter McGill in that photograph? Strange way to avoid someone. It was certainly not the first time they had spent time together. Maggie could read photos as if they were moving images.

Her mother's words were coming back to her, ringing in her head as she swirled the memory and photo of Peter McGill around in her mind. She was talking to Lochie downstairs in the kitchen and Maggie was sitting on the floor at the top of stairs, ears resting against the banister.

Don't be dragged into their world now, Lochie. Even that Peter. He might be a smart lad but that family is best avoided. You hearing me? Those McGills are bad news, trust me.

What was her mum's voice trying to tell her from the grave about the last man to see Mark Anderson before he disappeared? Maggie's instincts that something darker had happened to Mark were growing by the minute. She had to dig deeper into this story. Approaching the distressed wife of a missing man had to be tackled with care, though. For all her hunger to chase a story, Maggie's human instincts reminded her she was visiting a woman who was in distress. Val Anderson was a mum too, with daughters whose dad had, apparently, vanished without a trace. But it was time to swap her thoughts for action. Maggie picked up her pace. The coastal wind had turned bitter now, and her skin was stinging from the particles of sand being whipped up in the air. She couldn't face walking back along the sea wall to the office to collect her bike. Pulling her phone out, she dialled for a cab. The call waiting jingle made her move the phone away and look at her emails instead. The usual assault of press releases, news wire feeds and Google alerts swamped her screen in one amorphous mass – except one. It jumped out at her immediately.

Sender: NHS Fife
Subject: Adult Mental Health Services

Shit. The psychologists are chasing me.

Remembering sitting in that room, she felt briefly ashamed about spilling her guts out to a stranger. Someone who couldn't possibly understand what she'd been through – just like Lochie had said. But she forced herself to read on, dreading the inevitable.

Dear Ms Shields,

We are aware that your recent session with our clinical psychologist, Dr Julie-Anne McCarthy, ended prematurely. We understand from Dr McCarthy that your session was interrupted due to an error on the part of our colleagues, so we have recorded this as a 'did not attend appointment'. This gives you the chance to recommence your full six-week block of sessions again.

We have therefore rescheduled your first appointment for the below time:

Thursday June 24th, 2023, 3 p.m.

Unless we hear from you ASAP, we look forward to seeing you at this time. Please accept our apologies for the interruption to your session.

Shit. Not again. Six more sessions with the note scribbling, head-tilting Dr McCarthy and her itchy chairs and stale air? No way.

Maggie stopped reading as the voice on her mobile phone cut through her thoughts.

"Kingdom Taxis. Are you looking to book a car on account or private hire? Hello? Is there anyone there?"

"Shit, sorry. Account please – *Fife Standard* account, passcode STANDARD23 – picking up from Ravenscraig Park – main gate. Name's Shields."

EMDR therapy round two could wait. She was off to visit the home of Mark Anderson's wife and children. Maggie was no stranger to the feeling of a parent walking out on his children without warning. It's what her own dad did less than six months after their mum died. He couldn't provide them with what they needed, so he said. He was a broken man. Lochie would take care of her better than he could, he reckoned. And that was the last they saw of him.

Maggie knew fathers had the potential to let their children down spectacularly, but she needed to find out if Mark Anderson had done this out of choice. She only had a ten-minute taxi ride to figure out how to gain his wife's trust enough to even speak to her. It was going to take all her skills of persuasion and compassion.

5

WEDNESDAY LATE A.M.

Maggie's cab driver wanted to chat, but she wasn't in the mood. She focused on the fare ticking up on the screen above his head, willing the red numbers to stop in a comfortable, tidy place. That would be helpful. No, that would be essential. A three would be great, but a solid ten would be better. No messy numbers. That's never a good sign.

Her mobile vibrated in her pocket, and she welcomed the intrusion.

"Right, I have five minutes before I go back to the shift from hell. What do you need to know about Peter McGill so urgently?"

"Hi, Lochie. Yeh, so – anything really. Is he still local? Is he currently employed? Anything like that, really."

"Maggie, I'm not sure of the answers to all of this, and to be honest, I'm worried about you digging..."

"I'm just asking for a bit more background on who he is, Loch. I know it's awkward for you, but he is a person of interest in this missing rugby player story I'm reporting on."

He inhaled briefly before taking one long, laboured sigh.

"Yes, I know. You're never off duty, are you? Well, for a start, I remember him as Pete. And he was a bit of an oddball at school, to be honest. Really bright kid like you said, but just a bit – I don't know – closed. But don't quote me on that, OK?"

"He was part of a family that Mum told you to stay away from, wasn't he?"

Maggie heard a long intake of breath at the end of the line and waited as patiently as she could.

"Well remembered. But she said that about plenty of folk around here. I've survived OK after getting close enough to have my photo taken with him, as you saw."

"Would you describe him as harmless, then?"

She heard a humourless huffing sound down the phone.

"That depends on who you ask. Some locals were on the receiving end of his capers. But it was all low-level stuff. Joyriding, making a nuisance of himself drinking in the park and the like. Doubt he's capable of dispatching a large rugby player, if that's where you're going with this?"

"I'm not going that far yet. It just feels odd that Mark got mixed up with any of the McGills when they came from such different worlds?"

Despite it being framed like a question, Lochie chose not to answer. Maggie made a mental note to do some digging around Pete's criminal record. This kind of stuff was surprisingly easy to find after it became public knowledge, if you knew where to look. Lochie was opening up now, and she needed to let him speak.

"He turned into a bit of an oddball in the end…"

"In what way, exactly?"

"Just a bit… you know… awkward. Think he sells houses now. We all thought he'd go into something more, you know, techy. He always seemed to hide in his room or play around with computers at school."

Lochie's voice seemed to trail away, so Maggie moved fast to keep him talking.

"Any idea why he would mix with a posh lad like Mark Anderson?"

He let out a theatrical laugh, which felt a bit forced.

"Pete McGill and Mark Anderson? Nah… never would two lads be less likely to cross paths in life, Maggie. My guess is that it was a total coincidence they bumped into each other that day in the tavern."

Maggie didn't believe in coincidences.

"What – and total chance Mark ended up pinned against a wall and then disappeared days later? Come on, Lochie."

Lochie was stalling, holding himself back. She'd seen the footage. She was certain one of those men knew the other would be there that day.

"If there's something you're not telling me, please just spit it out. Or do I need to guess, Loch?"

"Look. You've said it yourself. McGill's family didn't have their troubles to seek. His old man was dead by fifty – chain smoker since fifteen, in and out of jail himself for keeping the wrong company. Life just seemed to push him down the whole way."

"And his mum?"

"Dunno. She used to work on reception at the job centre, but she packed that in a while ago. Think she's in a bad way, health-wise. Rarely seen out of her house as locals would have it."

"Any siblings or other family around?"

"Nope."

She noticed his answers were getting more clipped. His patience was running dry.

"Thought you didn't know much about him, Lochie?"

"Just local gossip, that's all. I work in a hospital, remember. Always plenty to be heard in the wards. I can't avoid drama but you, Maggie, you seem to run towards it sometimes. It worries me, that's all."

"I don't need you to protect me from the darker side of life anymore, you know?"

Maggie couldn't help feeling that he was holding something back. She wished she could see his face. She'd know if he was hiding something.

"Does Pete still live locally?"

"What, so that you can knock on his door and have a friendly chat?"

"I don't know. I just need a way into this. I'm getting a bad feeling about it all, but Lexi isn't exactly sold on me chasing it until the police have more to say. It would keep me away from having to ask flood victims questions that they can't answer. Mark Anderson may be an entitled posh boy, but he's still got two daughters that need him and a wife who… well, who knows what she thinks right now."

It was her best and final attempt for now. If Lochie

wasn't forthcoming, she would have to leave him to get on with his job.

"I don't know. Reckon his mum still lives here, but I'm not sure about Pete himself. Maggie, promise me you won't pitch up to that lad's old estate on your own? There could be all kinds of trouble going on around there. Could Lexi not send someone else?"

"Why? This is my job – and I'm not sharing this story with someone else."

"I've no idea where he lives now. Or where he works. I think he's done a short stretch inside, but he'll be back at large by now. That's if he's not still helping the police with their inquiries, of course. I don't really keep in touch with everyone I once knew as a schoolkid. Do you?"

Maggie didn't have many friends at school. She was wary of other people. Especially after their mum died. Knowing that someone killed their mum and got away with it made her deeply mistrustful of others.

Well, they almost got away with it. At least Maggie and Lochie had that comfort. Eventually, justice was served, even if not in the conventional sense.

"OK, thanks, Lochie."

"Sure. Listen. I've got to go. But please don't do anything stupid on your own. I'm not kidding, OK? And, Mags…"

"Uh-huh?"

"Have you decided to ditch that nosey psychologist yet?"

"Ach, I don't know. Trying to figure out the best way to play it to keep Lexi onside. I'll let you know. You better get back to healing the sick, eh? Bye for now."

She pressed her finger on the call end button, silencing him. Maggie knew when he wasn't telling her the full truth. She would hear something in his voice. The way he clipped the ends of his sentences or tripped over his words. Her senses were onto the warning signs of a lie. And it made the ground under her feet shake.

"Nearly here, hen."

Her taxi driver wasted no time, catching her eye in the rear-view mirror as soon as she'd hung up.

"Blimey, some hoose yer heading to today, luv. That would do me just fine as a fancy holiday home, that one."

Maggie's heart sank as she saw the meter was hovering around the awkward £9 mark.

"Just drop me here, and round that up to a tenner, please."

"Awful good of you, luv. Just sign here for yer receipt – to prove to the high heid yins that you were on a job and not just needing a lift back from the pub, eh?"

Maggie saw the thin film of greasy fingerprints smeared on his digital receipt printer, took a deep breath, and scrawled the shape of an M as lightly as she could with the stylus.

Val Anderson's house nestled in a quiet cul-de-sac off Kirkcaldy's Victoria Road – a wide, imposing avenue with a handful of enormous period houses and walled gardens, each of which was the size of her entire street. She wondered what could have gone so wrong in a man's life to make him walk away from this fairytale out of choice. It made no sense.

Reaching for a wet wipe from her pocket, she scrubbed at her hands before approaching the front door. Two police panda cars sat around the back of the property. She wasn't

Val Anderson's first visitor today. As soon as she climbed the age-worn steps to the grand front door, it clicked open, releasing two uniformed officers from the house. They weren't cops she'd seen before. After just a few years of reporting on a small community like Fife, Maggie had encountered most of the response officers at some stage. She kept her head down as they passed, pretending to be on another call. Any approaching press intrusion was likely to be challenged. If reporters had to wear a uniform, they'd get nowhere fast.

The old iron door knocker was irritatingly high for Maggie, who was only five foot two and, according to her brother, likely to blow away in a mild north-easterly breeze. But what she lacked in height and heft she was determined to make up for in grit.

After giving it a couple of sharp knocks, she waited at the doorstep, imagining someone striding along a vast hallway to reach the front porch. A well-presented, middle-aged female of above average height, Grecian-like facial features and a caramel blonde bob opened the door. A face greeted Maggie that looked weighed down by worry but was undeniably beautiful. She had the kind of deep-set beauty that would linger on someone's features all their days. It's how Maggie remembered her own mum. She didn't remember her wearing make-up, but could still picture the tone of her skin and her long eyelashes. Just like the woman facing her now, in the doorway. Her statuesque facial structure was lit by the morning sun as she squinted in Maggie's direction. She thought the woman would be effortlessly photogenic and had a sudden hankering to pull out her camera and start clicking there and then. Then a frown formed under her expertly highlighted and wispy fringe. Maggie felt a sudden surge of pity towards this woman who appeared to have it all, yet was clearly drowning in the weight of the surrounding chaos.

"Please, I've told your officers all I can for today, and I just need some privacy with my daughters."

Privacy. Something else Maggie remembered craving in the aftermath of her mum's sudden death. Privacy and answers. She desperately needed answers. Who could hit another human being and not even stop? The question haunted her for a full year until she got the answer she needed. Perhaps she could help Mark Anderson's wife find the answers she needed. She could do some good here. But first, she had to build trust.

Val moved to close the door again, but Maggie countered the move with the deft art of a veteran reporter twice her age and size.

"Sorry, Mrs Anderson. I'm not from the police. My name's Maggie Shields and I work at the *Fife Standard*."

Val's body stiffened instantly as Maggie reached for her NUJ card, bracing herself for the inevitable. All she could read in Val's eyes was utter resentment.

"I'm even less interested in speaking to your lot. Just leave me alone. Please."

Maggie had one more chance to stop her from closing that door. One more card to play.

"I don't want to make things worse. I promise. I just want to… help you find some answers. My editor wants us to run a story rehashing the rumours about your husband's historic health concerns – suggesting they're linked to his disappearance. But I'm sure you want everyone who is looking for him to remain more open-minded than that, surely?"

The forward momentum of the door closing on Maggie's face had stopped, but the look of resentment hadn't shifted from Val's.

Maggie chose her words carefully. 'Health concerns' sounded softer than 'ongoing drug misuse', but she knew Val would make the link. She let it hang between them for a moment.

Val's eyes narrowed. She pulled the oversized woollen cardigan across her chest, as if protecting herself from something. The pause gave Maggie an opportunity to continue.

"The thing is, we're going to cover this story one way or another. The community does care when a local sports hero and family man goes missing. I just wanted to give you the opportunity to influence the tone and content. I can tell you've been let down by the media in the past. I totally understand why you're suspicious. But at least let me try to help."

She shook her head gently from side to side.

"Oh, you can tell that, can you?"

Maggie sensed a softening and tightened her grip.

"I also wanted to ask you something about the footage of Mark in the bar before he went missing."

She noticed the expensive-looking rings on Val's hand that still rested against her front door.

"What did you say your name was?"

"Maggie. Maggie Shields."

Maggie caught the briefest sight of a tall figure moving across the hallway behind her. A tall male, she thought. He seemed to stop and linger from a distance, his face just in the shadow of the overhanging mahogany staircase. If Val knew he was there, she didn't acknowledge his presence. Something about his profile was familiar. Something about his facial structure or facial hair was out of the ordinary. It was not the first time she had seen this person – or someone who looked very like him, at least. She tried to strain to see him more clearly, but Val's eyes were on her, so she tried not to stare. He would come out of the shadows any minute, she thought. Then she'd see his face properly. But he didn't. He just hovered where he was, motionless. It made her feel uncomfortable, and Maggie wondered if that was his intention. But she tried to dismiss him. If there was any hint that Maggie was just wanting a nosey around this big posh house, all attempts at getting across Val's front doorstep would be in vain. She would send her on her way as another opportunist hack.

"What about it?"

"Mmm?"

Maggie had lost track of herself.

"The CCTV. What did you want to ask me – about it?"

"Oh, yes, sorry. Um, I just wondered if you knew the man confronting your husband? I believe his name is Peter McGill?"

"No, I don't."

"OK. Well, that's interesting because, you see, I may be able to give you a bit more background on him. And getting the right message out to the public can really help the police generate new leads. Which is where we come in. If I could just have five minutes of your time. Or two minutes?"

Val Anderson let out a long breath, lifted her arm off the door, and straightened her body.

"I know I'm going to regret this. You have precisely five minutes to convince me I've not made a mistake letting you through this door."

Maggie gave herself an invisible pat on the back. Having earned her passage into this woman's home and life at such a vulnerable time, she couldn't ruin it now.

Val led Maggie down a wide, parquet-floored hallway decorated with expensive-looking art. Fresh flowers in huge vases scented the air. They went straight to a vast, sun-drenched open-plan kitchen at the back of the property, which featured a small seating area with expensive-looking furniture at the far end. On the way, they passed several doors. Most were closed, but one opened to a lounge where two girls were sitting on a luxurious teal velvet sofa with their back to the door, loose hair from their messy buns dangling down their backs. They looked like teenagers, but it was hard to say for sure. Completely focused on their mobile phones, they did not notice Maggie's arrival. As she followed Val through the house, she felt the same male presence – still lurking out of sight. A powerful scent of cologne competed with the lilies in the air, and she picked up the sound of heavy footsteps on the wooden floors. They must be coming from expensive leather brogues with quality soles.

"Can we do this quickly, please? The cops have just left, and I've got calls to make."

The news was playing on a flat-screen TV, hung on a wall in the far corner of the kitchen. They were already running reels of Mark's rugby days, followed by grainy exterior images of the house she was standing in.

Digesting the display of wealth around her, Maggie noticed the solid marble countertops had collected more food crumbs and dirty plates than she was comfortable with.

Refocussing on the woman in front of her, Maggie tried to speak, but Val beat her to it.

"Why are you lot so obsessed with building athletes into these ridiculous heroes, just so you can spectacularly knock them off their perch?"

"Sorry, I don't..."

"Oh, don't try to deny it. You regional papers are just as bad as those grotty red tops."

It was the first time Maggie had heard the word 'grotty' in a while. She couldn't believe people still actually spoke like that.

"No... I mean, I don't normally cover the sports beat... I'm usually on..."

She was floundering, but she could tell this woman's patience would not last long. She needed to think quickly and adapt. Press the right buttons.

"Sorry, never mind. But if you don't mind me asking... totally off the record, of course... are you happy with how the police investigation is going?"

For the first time since they met, Val Anderson looked intrigued.

"Well, apparently, he doesn't tick enough high-risk boxes for them to throw much of their thinly stretched resources in our direction. So, for now, I think everyone's assuming he's just gone 'off-grid' of his own accord. That's what they call it, isn't it?"

She had a point. Maggie knew adults disappeared for many reasons: financial troubles, marital strife, hiding from their in-laws. None of them what the police categorise as 'suspicious' and none of them worthy of expensive inquiries, helicopter searches and prolonged public appeals. It sapped money and resources away from keeping crime off the streets in neighbourhoods where it was dangerous to walk home alone. Just because Mark Anderson was an adored national sports star, it didn't mean he was vulnerable or on the top of their priority list.

Maggie knew his disappearance wouldn't even make the *News In Brief* column if he was just an ordinary bloke from Kirkcaldy. Unless they found his body on the beach with feet bound to a metal weight or something. But that stuff just didn't happen in Kirkcaldy.

Val began shuffling in a drawer and pulled out some Marlboro Lights, offering Maggie one before lighting it with a silver Zippo.

"And you lot all think he's some sort of junkie, yes?"

Maggie opened her mouth to deny it but remembered it was the thinly disguised line she used to get through the front door.

"Bet you're thinking he's some bored, retired player who has a midlife crisis and canters off into the sunset?"

Canter. There goes another word I don't hear every day, thought Maggie.

"Not me, Mrs Anderson. But there's plenty of local gossip doing the rounds which we couldn't run anyway without proof, so…"

"So, you squirmed your way in here on a wing and prayer, young lady, yes?"

Val lit her cigarette at speed, inhaled deep into her lungs, eyes closed as if blocking out the world for a moment gave her some relief. She leant against the partially open bifold doors to her garden. The sun caught the side of her face and Maggie could see the lines around her eyes more clearly, through the layers of make-up. Her eyes wandered from Val to the framed prints of their daughters in their school uniform on the kitchen walls. They wore thick-looking blazers with gold trim and knee-length kilts. The whole thing looked like it would make her itch all day long. She thought of the two young girls sitting in the lounge and wondered who they were speaking to on those phones. Were they fielding messages of comfort from friends or batting off trolls goading them about their father's disappearance? Or maybe they were sending messages to their dad, begging him to get in touch. Maggie remembered writing letters to her own dad for the first year after he walked out. Begging. Pleading with him to come home. Every time she spent her pocket money from Lochie on stamps and writing paper, she told herself that it would be worth it when he wrote back. Telling her how much he missed them and that he would be home soon, when he was feeling better. But he never came.

Maggie assumed the police would probably monitor any social media interactions Mark's daughters were having already. That was protocol in miss per cases. Just covering all bases, they'd say. But she couldn't help thinking what an invasion of their privacy that must feel – if anyone even told them.

Val took another long drag on her cigarette and looked at Maggie with eyes partially closed to avoid her own exhaled smoke.

"Tempted as I am to give you a juicy headline about feeling let down, is that really going to help find Mark? I thought you said you could tell me something about that man – MacGill – or was that another lie?"

The way she mispronounced his surname with an M-A-C rather than an M-C confirmed to Maggie that Peter McGill was a stranger to Val.

"Sorry, yes… it's just… the CCTV footage that the police released to the media. Have you seen it?"

Val let a short, dark laugh escape from the edge of her mouth.

"You mean the bleak little movie of my husband being held against a wall in a dodgy Kirkcaldy bar? Oh, how the mighty have fallen, eh?"

Anyone who'd stepped foot inside the Harbour Tavern would never call it a bar. It was, in every conceivable way, a pub. A boozer. Not a bar. Kirkcaldy had very few bars, but plenty of boozers.

"Well, it's just… Peter McGill… He went to school with my brother."

She looked at Maggie square on with a gesture that screamed, *And…?*

"Is that all you've got to share with me? The fact he's

not been hanging out with the Glasgow mafia all his life?"

This woman wore the deep-set expression of someone who had long been a stranger to peace and contentment. Maggie searched in her head for a tactful way to approach her question.

"Sorry, what I mean is – I think McGill was a local guy whose family had a bit of a past. Some consistent run-ins with the law over the years. I just wondered if you knew why he was meeting Mark in the pu—bar?"

Val's gaze lifted without warning to the hallway, but when Maggie turned around to follow her stare, there was no one there. She wondered if it was possible to be intimidated by a house.

"No, I have no idea. But when your husband hasn't lived under the same roof as you for over two years, you struggle to keep up with the company he's choosing."

Maggie tried to stay professional, biting her tongue for a few extra seconds. It was a classic interview trick. Force your subject into filling the silence. Val was down to the last drag of her cigarette and jumped at the sound of her daughters screaming at each other from down the hall. She pressed out the stub of her cigarette in an ashtray on the tinted glass coffee table and ruffled her fingers through her hair before resting them on her temples. The screaming stopped suddenly, followed by a door being slammed.

"Listen, I've got a life to get on with – or what's left of it right now. Unless you've got anything of substance to share with me, I suggest you leave us alone. You're going to write whatever nonsense you want, anyway."

Maggie knew when her luck was out, but she was playing the long game.

"Sorry, yes, of course. But can I just ask you one more thing? It's just, our editor, she's a stickler for details, so I'd hate to get anything wrong. Even the small stuff."

Val raised a sharply plucked eyebrow, which Maggie took as a cue to continue.

"Your husband. Mark. I know you said he doesn't *live* here anymore but, was he in the habit of visiting a lot – *before* he went missing, that is?"

Nosiness and nerves had eventually collided with and overpowered Maggie's attempts at tact.

"Do you have children, Maggie?"

Women seemed to enjoy turning that question on her. She still hadn't learnt a way to bat it off without feeling inferior.

"No. I don't."

"Well, let me tell you, if you're raising daughters to be well-adjusted young women and their dad gets banned from the sport that defined his life because he wouldn't give up his artificial stimulants, you'd want him to keep his distance."

As she followed Val down the long corridor, toying with using those powerful words in print, Maggie heard more steps behind her. There was a sharp clicking sound, like toe caps moving across wood. Looking around, she saw another fleeting glimpse of a large, broad male figure disappearing into another room. It felt like he'd timed his presence perfectly to be noticed, but not seen. Not fully, at least. Maggie had seen enough this time for an inkling to form in her head of where she'd encountered this man before. A sudden urge to get out of the house as fast as she could took hold.

"Thanks for your time, Mrs Anderson. I appreciate you speaking to me."

Retreating down the stone steps, Maggie scrambled around for the cab number on her phone. But the image of the man in Val's hallway had taken up space in her head. Something about the way he moved took her back to a dark place. Somewhere she couldn't let herself go again. Ghosts from the past were crawling up to the surface at a disturbing rate. But this memory was coming back into focus: a reminder of a moment that once existed and didn't want to be buried forever. Leaving the splendour and tragedy of Val Anderson's house behind, she grew even more convinced that the Anderson family were mixed up with some dangerous people. She had to convince the police to show their hand and the best way to do that was to get public opinion working for her. It was time to fill some column inches.

6

WEDNESDAY AFTERNOON

The incongruent mix of fresh lilies and cigarette smoke lingered on Maggie's clothes as she sat in the taxi watching some of Kirkcaldy's grandest houses disappear behind her. She had to deliver something strong on Anderson when she got back, or Lexi would spike it and she'd be back to square one – trying to justify her next pay cheque.

Yer only as good as the headline yer bringing me today, princess.

It was one of Lexi's favourite lines, and she never tired of using it. But burning her bridges with Val by throwing in a cheap quote about Mark's weakness for *artificial stimulants* would not earn her a return invitation.

It was time to make a detour to the police station and go back to basics. Week one of journalism school: *The good stories never come to you. You have to go to them.* With any luck, she'd catch sight of a friendly face she knew and sweet talk them into throwing her a bone – just something harmless but enough to fill a column or two and stimulate an eye-catching headline. She'd repay them down the line by spiking some unhelpful leak or anonymising some ill-judged media statement from a busy cop who forgot his media training. They'd have one in the bank, so to speak.

There was a suitable spot to hover near the front door of the station, and it wasn't long before one of the uniformed PCs arrived for work.

"Away you go, Maggie Shields. We have a press office, you know?"

"They don't answer the phone, you know?" Maggie returned, without missing a beat.

A couple more uniforms followed him, jumping out of the panda car and heading back indoors, holding takeaway coffee cups. She switched her forced smile back on.

"You been out looking for Mark Anderson, guys? I've just come from chatting with his wife. She's in a bad way, that one. Keen for progress, it appears."

"Going to just let us do our jobs, eh? The days of us having friendly wee chats with loitering reporters are long gone. You know that."

Maggie was all out of tricks for now. But as she began the slow walk back to the office, the station door opened from the inside.

She caught sight of his features before he zipped up the neck of his jacket – hiding half of his face. But her photographic memory was foolproof.

Well, if it isn't the man of the moment, himself.

It made sense. He was bound to be hauled in for questioning soon enough. But she couldn't understand why they would be done with him so quickly. She'd heard the police like to drag out interviews as long as they could – it got those on the receiving end of the questions more rattled and more likely to slip up. Peter McGill must either have friends in high places or be very persuasive.

She moved towards him, keeping her voice low and calm.

"Peter McGill?"

He tried to pivot sideways to avoid her, but she moved in the same direction.

"Mr McGill?"

"Who are you?"

"Maggie, hi. My name's Maggie Shields."

The words seemed to stop his momentum.

"I'm in a hurry. Can you please..."

He was swinging his hands to the side now, trying to swat her away like an annoying insect, but she'd faced up to much worse.

"Sorry... Can I ask, have you just been questioned by the police about Mark Anderson? Are they making any progress there?"

"Listen, luv. I'm not in the habit of asking lassies to piss off, but I'm prepared to make an exception."

"I'm so sorry. Didn't mean to get in your way."

She wasn't sorry. She was stalling him. He tried again to evade her, but she was too fast, leaning into him as she spoke.

"I'm Maggie. Hi."

"You said."

"From the *Fife Standard* – the newspaper. Just out for a lunchtime wander, really. Our offices are up the road. I'm covering the miss per report that was made by Mark's wife Val. Do you know Val? Or anything about why he went missing?"

"I'm aware of Mark's absence. You're still in my way."

An icy wind hit Maggie on the side of her face, and she squinted from the shock. She refocused, noticing McGill was looking at her more closely. Almost staring now. But Maggie pressed on.

"Well, in that case, you'll know you appear in CCTV footage of the last sighting of Mark before he disappeared?"

He had stopped now, arms in front of his chest, making a solid barrier between them.

"I'm well aware of that. But so did a lot of people. It was a pub."

He continued walking, but she followed at his heels. Maggie would not be sidelined.

"Were you in there responding to the police appeal for witnesses then – to help with their inquiries? Is that what I should report? Or were you arrested? The police will tell us eventually – if we ask them a direct question – so you may as well tell me now."

He swung around to face her with a sudden movement. Maggie recoiled a little. Memories of Lochie's warnings to be careful shot back into her mind. But she was outside a police station. It doesn't get much safer than that.

"No, I wasn't arrested. They invited me down to the station to answer some questions – which I've done, honestly. The police questions, that is. Not yours. And now I'm going home. Are you going to get out of my way, or do I have to get one of the scary folk wearing black and white in that building behind us to ask you instead?"

Peter McGill finished with the conversation, but Maggie had other ideas. She wasn't about to waste this opportunity.

"This is Kirkcaldy, not London. It wouldn't take long until someone recognised you. Yeh, there were plenty of people in the pub that day. But I'm pretty sure you were the only one whose face was close enough to Mark's to tell whether he'd brushed his teeth. You were threatening him with something, weren't you?"

He shook his head and shoved his hands deep into the pockets of his wax jacket. At first, it looked like an effort at self-restraint. Then she panicked. Was he was going to pull something out of one of them?

This is a police station, Maggie. Remember? Don't be ridiculous.

Her body turned instinctively to the side, but his hands came out again, open and empty.

"Why were you holding him up against the wall by his shirt, Peter?"

His face remained as still as a corpse.

"I hope they find him. Trust me, I really do."

Peter's voice was soft again, and his words felt carefully chosen, genuine and personal. Could he be trying to tell her something? Is it possible he was telling the truth and Peter McGill wanted to know where Mark Anderson was as much as everyone else?

As she watched him walk away and turn the corner out of sight, her brother's warning rang again in her ear.

McGill was a rough diamond. Part of a family of rough diamonds. An ex-con, a man who wasn't afraid to get into fights. There was no shortage of reasons to avoid his company. She hadn't mentioned her brother's first name, but something in the way he reacted to her surname made her think Lochie and Pete knew each other better than they'd each let on. As she stood, watching him walk into the distance, the memory of her mum's voice came next.

If you flee wi' the craws yet get shot wi' the craws.

She had a phrase for everything. But the words were deadly serious.

There was no time to dwell on that for now. She had her top line for Lexi.

Peter McGill – the only person of interest in relation to Mark Anderson's disappearance – has been released without charge after answering police questions.

The police had hit a dead end, but Maggie Shields was just warming up.

Distraught Anderson Family Look For Answers: Police Release Person Of Interest After Questioning

She filed the copy with three minutes to spare – her standard safety buffer. The key facts were all in there: distraught wife and daughters desperate for answers. Mystery surrounds whereabouts of a beloved family man and national sporting hero. The unanswered questions left hanging: Has he walked out on his family? Why was the last person seen physically confronting Mark in CCTV footage questioned and released so quickly?

7

WEDNESDAY EARLY P.M.

Maggie had only been away from her desk for a few minutes to refill her water bottle but, by the time she came back, a takeaway coffee cup was sitting next to her keyboard. Several small drips of dirty brown liquid were seeping down the sides of the cup and a dark circle had formed on her desk around its base.

"Thought you might like a proper pick-me-up today, Maggie."

"Thanks, Harris."

She chose not to remind him she didn't drink coffee. It often prompted questions about why not, which she'd rather not answer. The truth was stimulants like caffeine had a profound effect on her anxiety. No matter how crap her sleep had been, a coffee was never worth the pay-off.

He reached over to her desk and played with her stress ball whilst she powered up her computer. The thought of his hands on the soft, clean rubber of her stress ball fought for her attention, but she battled against it as her desktop PC groaned back to life.

A collection of emails from Harris were sitting near the top of her unread pile. She clicked on one entitled 'the best shit'. His messages often had the tone of someone talking to his pals on a stag night. He was still watching her, an aura of self-satisfaction oozing from his pores, as she opened the star email. He'd certainly done some serious leg work for her, which made her immediately suspicious. In her job, she was as sceptical of seemingly selfless deeds as she was of corporate altruism. She scanned through what looked like a jumble of cut-and-pasted extracts from rugby forums where people called 'Matty McTall' and 'Bullet Brewster' shared their opinions of the Anderson family.

"Harris, this is not really going to stand up…"

"Check out the one called 'Anderson senior ruined his son's life'. It's brutal stuff."

Maggie forced herself to read on, through realms of angry rants, about how Mark's old man tried to run his life. Apparently, 'Anderson senior' was a hard man to please.

"Rumour was that he wanted his son to hold down a 'proper job' like accountancy or something, but he didn't get the grades."

"Yep, I can read for myself, Harris."

He crashed on, ignoring the hint of leaving her in peace.

"That's when Ranald single-handedly forced him down the pro rugby route. Bloody lucky he had a bit of talent to work with. Well, before the drugs scandal hit and the proverbial shite hit the fan, though."

"Oh?"

Her interest in what he had to add was warming up. Encouraged, Harris pulled up a spare seat next to her and leant in uncomfortably close to her monitor. She could smell the coffee on his breath and it turned her stomach.

"Yep, read that one there..."

Mark Anderson's dad exploited his rugby talent to make yet more money.

Maggie read about a man so obsessed with making money and ingratiating himself with the medical elite that he used his son as a PR tool. She lost herself in behind-the-scenes stories of him charging appearance fees to schools and charities and chasing sponsorship deals from fitness supplements with ugly health and safety records. Then Valerie came on the scene. His son began dating the daughter, granddaughter, and niece of some of the most revered surgeons and consultants in the land. The old man Anderson sensed a golden opportunity and didn't give until Mark had put a ring on her finger.

"Christ. What a romantic family man Ranald is."

"Aye. That's a shitload to lug around when Mark should be enjoying the prime of his life. You know, living life according to his own rules. How did you get on with his missus, anyway?"

Maggie paused before answering. Instinct stopped her. Sharing her spoils never came easily. Knowledge was power, and she didn't trust Harris. It was that simple. The only person Maggie really trusted spent a lifetime earning it. And shared her DNA. She kept her response measured.

"Pretty much what you'd expect. She was holding

it together for her daughters' sake, but she looked a bit broken."

Maggie caught sight of the time on her Fitbit as she leant her chin on her bony interlocking hands.

"Harris, I've kind of got to get on with… you know… work stuff. Thanks for the background, though, yeh? Owe you one."

"Aye, no bother. You know where to find me, eh?"

He winked, then backed off and returned to his own desk, leaving her to dive deeper into the secret life of a man whose illustrious career on the rugby field appeared to hide something darker.

Popping on her headphones to listen to Mozart, she placed the second caffeine-free Diet Coke of the day at arm's length from her keyboard. Working was her happy place. A time when she could block out the world of chaos and bring facts and truth to bear.

Despite the grim pay, anti-social hours, and characters she encountered (and often because of them), she loved her job with a fury. Lochie said that if she was marooned on an uninhabited, barren island with a notepad and camera, she'd still find enough going on to fill a newspaper. But Lochie wasn't her boss. Lexi was her boss, and she had a reputation for being hard to please. Make it punchy, make it controversial without being libellous and, most of all, make it better than anything she'll read elsewhere. Mark's story had got comfy in her crowded mind. It pushed out thoughts of rituals, cleaning and checking for a few precious hours.

But it couldn't last forever. Before long, the bully

returned and started to fill up tiny, empty spaces in her mind that weren't filled by the business of storytelling. They pushed their way in with thoughts of ordering and routines, expanding the space through force until they took control again.

Maggie saved her work, and opened a new Google search bar before typing a selection of phrases: 'online alternatives to in-person therapy', 'how to tackle troubling thoughts without visiting a psychologist' and 'digital therapy on the go'.

Her screen came alive with more possibilities than she could ever have imagined. For the first time in a while, she felt less alone in her own mind.

8

WEDNESDAY P.M.

Maggie knew there was a reason she clung to routine and repetition like glue. She just didn't have a name for it. Or a diagnosis. What difference would that make, anyway? All she cared about was what made her feel safe, grounded and in control.

Once you've had the ground pulled from under your feet once, you can't let it happen again. When someone forcefully rips the person who comforted you away from your life. The driver was in a hurry, of course. But they all say that. *He* wasn't special. The man that broke Maggie's family like a glass vase shattering into pieces. He was driving too fast because he had somewhere to be. That's what they all say, isn't it? Just as she was crossing the road. He thought he'd got away at first. He drove off into the distance without stopping. But right there, in that moment, he'd erased the childhood Maggie was supposed to have. She was supposed to have a normal, happy childhood with a mother who had cared for her for twelve short, precious years.

The police knew he'd left Scotland. They traced the car number plate to where he abandoned it: a stone's throw from the Haymarket train station. It was a camera black spot back then, apparently. He must have known that somehow. He ran from the guilt of his actions – but he couldn't run forever. Life eventually catches up with people like him. That's what Lochie told Maggie when he realised she needed to know. When the time was right to tell her who he was. Ryan was his name. Ryan Ross. The name of the person who destroyed their childhood.

Maggie's phone pinged into life. It was a message from a number she didn't recognise.

Call me. I have something for you. V Anderson.

She remembered leaving her business card on the marble kitchen worktop on her way out. Just next to Val's packet of cigarettes, where she'd be sure to see it. Always worth a punt. So many people resist speaking to reporters, but quite like to have one to hand if it suits them. She went to call her back, but something stopped her. The bully caught her first. She had to check her emails before she continued. Quickly. Just in case. Just in case of anything, really.

There was nothing life-threatening to deal with this time. She had a quick scroll of her inbox, scanned through Harris's glut of rugby forum effluent and today's press release slush pile. A couple of other unread emails jumped out at her as she read with speed.

The first came from a sender called Anxiety Relief Solutions, subject heading: Guided anxiety relief on the go.

The second was from a company called Next Generation CBT, with a subject heading even harder to ignore: Want to meet your AI-powered 24/7 Therapist?

Maggie's first thought was to rail against the newsletter she signed up to when researching alternatives to in-person therapy. She got mixed up on whether you had to opt out or opt in for 'additional marketing messages'. Clearly, she'd made the wrong choice.

After tossing the email from Anxiety Relief Solutions in her junk mail, she hovered her finger over Next Generation CBT, ready to do the same to its offer of an AI therapist. But something stopped her. There was a reason she had gone looking for this stuff earlier. A reason that hadn't disappeared. It was only so long before Lexi would find out she bailed on the appointment two days ago. The 'HR police' warned Maggie she'd need proof of her completing a programme of sessions to confirm her ongoing fitness to work in the job she adored. So, she carried on reading.

We understand that accessing in-person mental health support can present challenges for some patients…

Is it possible you sometimes make cognitive distortions such as jumping to conclusions, catastrophic thinking, mind-reading etc? Did you know that Artificial Intelligence is becoming an increasingly powerful addition to Mental Health Support Services? Perhaps it could help you reframe your unhelpful thoughts at a time, place, and speed that suits you as an individual?

Powerful addition? What, like Chat GPT on a virtual psychologist's couch?

If you are interested in finding out more about this trial, please scan this QR Code and follow the on-screen instructions.

This all felt wholly wrong to Maggie. Cognitive therapy and artificial intelligence are two phrases that should never go together – surely?

Then she remembered Val's request to speak to her. This deserved her full attention. Robo-therapist would have to wait.

She dialled the number and waited.

"Hello?"

Val's voice sounded shaky and quieter than she remembered.

"Mrs Anderson? Hello. It's Maggie. Maggie Shields from the *Standard*."

"What do you know about Mark's father's business interests?"

There was no small talk, but Val's softly rounded vowels sounded less confident. She wondered if that was just the difference in her phone manner, or something else.

"Mr Ranald Anderson? Well, I know he's in the IT business. And that he used to play rugby himself, but that's about it so far."

Val spoke louder but it only emphasised the nervousness in her voice.

"That man has picked up enemies like other people collect books. And it was my family that introduced him to all of his clients in the first place."

Maggie heard Val take a long inhale, she presumed, of a cigarette.

"I'm not sure how this relates to Mark's disappearance. Do you think one of Ranald's enemies has harmed Mark as some sort of revenge?"

"I wouldn't rule it out. Ranald has always been good about hiding his dirty laundry in public, but he's not so great at hiding it from his family."

Maggie considered if Val might draw her in to use as a pawn in a family at war, but her instincts told her differently.

"Mrs Anderson, is there something specific you want to share with me?"

"Hang on."

Val paused for a moment and Maggie heard the distant sound of her heels clicking across floorboards, followed by the sound of a door closing. Maggie assumed her daughters were in the house somewhere. She wondered what they knew about their grandfather's darker side.

"I'm going to give you a name."

She was speaking so quietly now, Maggie struggled to hear.

"Start with a company called Sapphire Healthcare. Do some digging into their historic dealings with Ranald."

"And who are—"

"They're big players in the medical business. A major client of Ranald's, but something weird happened a while back."

Maggie sensed the beginnings of something juicy and strained to hear Val's tentative voice properly.

"Ranald had me doing his secretarial work. Even his own wife wasn't allowed near it. But it looked like an opportunity to use my brain and think about something other than hormonal teenagers. I was in his study one day and found a letter – lying open on his desk – addressed to Ranald from a legal firm representing Sapphire Healthcare."

The last two words were delivered in a near whisper.

"What was in the letter, Val?"

"I didn't have time to read it in detail because I heard him coming down the hall, but the last paragraph had been typed in bold – which I thought was odd. It mentioned vast sums of 'compensatory' money that Sapphire had been pursuing from Ranald. It ended with a proposal that it was in the best interests of both parties to bring the matter to a close and sign a non-disclosure agreement."

It was starting to sound like the makings of a background story on the Anderson family, but Maggie needed a lot more to link it with Ranald's missing son.

"OK… so I'm guessing their relationship has been non-existent ever since?"

"Mmm, not exactly. That's the weird thing. Quite the opposite."

Val's answers sounded increasingly cryptic, arousing Maggie's suspicions of her motives.

"Again, Mrs Anderson, I have to ask why you think this is relevant to your husband's disappearance?"

Maggie feared she was being sold a half story at best.

"If you're a fraction of the investigator you want people to see, you might want to start there."

The slim pickings of a lead irritated Maggie, but at least it was something. Was it Mark she was investigating, or his father?

"Is there anything else you could add that may, um, help me?"

"Well, why don't you go away and do your own homework and then come back to me to fill the gaps? But give me warning next time, OK? That's important."

"Eh, OK… thanks… I think."

"Oh, and another thing."

Val's voice faded again down the line, as if she had turned her head away from the phone – distracted by something or someone.

"Keep Mark's name clean. Please. Well, as clean as you can. My husband is far from perfect, but we just want him found safe and well, so he can come home to his daughters. His father's failings are not his own. Deal?"

Maggie opened her mouth to tell Val that it was a tough deal to keep, but the call had gone dead. She gathered her thoughts before turning back to her screen and typing 'Sapphire Healthcare' into the search bar. She worked on, digging around their business and those associated with it. The office cleaning team began hoovering around her, but she still continued, intent in her work. The only thing that pierced her concentration was a series of pop-up ads on her screen offering testimonials of happy customers whose 'lives have been transformed thanks to Next Generation's AI Therapist'.

Suzy (22, from Kent) was trapped in her own home for two years until she discovered AI Therapy.

Suzy said: "I'm not sure when agoraphobia first took hold of me. It kind of crept up on me like a dark shadow. Maybe just after I contracted glandular fever as a teenager.

I think I just got so used to staying at home that it became hard to face the outside world. Everything was falling apart. I couldn't go to work or meet up with friends. Someone suggested visiting a psychologist but there was no way I could cope with getting there. I was trapped. Then I found AI-based therapy. It changed everything."

9

WEDNESDAY LATE P.M.

There had to be a reason that Peter McGill was threatening Mark Anderson in the Harbour Tavern, and Maggie was determined to find out. Lochie claimed to have no lasting loyalty towards him, so there was little reason to tread lightly for his sake. Her starting point was a troubled family, and a spent conviction for some minor misdemeanour. There were no shortage of candidates matching that description in most Scottish towns. It was a town with its fair share of folk who walk a fine line between right and wrong. Those who teeter between one side of the law and the other, often just to survive.

But that was all she had to go on, and she had to start somewhere.

From tiny acorns, large oak trees will grow.

Her mum used to dish this snippet out frequently and the remembering of it gave her a bolt up the backside. Maggie specialised in harvesting details about people – mostly by legal means – from the tiniest of acorns.

The digital superhighway wasn't all bad news for print journalists. It opened up a wealth of information sources – there for the taking. But sometimes, they'd work against her, too. When everyone fancied themselves as a modern-day whistleblower or Julian Assange, who'd want an investigative reporter on their full-time payroll? Her only future was contract work, but for that to succeed, she needed career-defining scoops. She had to deliver exclusives, and a contacts book that would make Carl Bernstein feel inadequate.

It wasn't any easy path that stretched out in front of her, but journalism and writing was all she knew, and Maggie Shields would go down fighting.

Searches of 'McGill family Kirkcaldy' came up with nothing but a collection of local roofers, an accountant and the odd obituary. She'd know when she hit on the right McGills. Diving deeper, she explored the online database of district and sheriff court documents. Maggie thrived on methodology. When she was rewarded with a hit, satisfaction and disappointment both struck. Like she'd reached the end of a brilliant book. She'd pulled a file from Kirkcaldy Sheriff Court, dated 2014: A Mr Peter S. McGill of 5 Denny Court, Kirkcaldy, who was sentenced to six months for one count of grievous bodily harm and theft of a vehicle/making off from a crime scene.

Maggie now had an address, and documented confirmation of Pete McGill's place on the wrong side of the law.

*

Lexi's voice erupted in Maggie's ears from the moment she got out of the lift. It cut through her brain cells like a foghorn through the east coast harr.

"Well, thank Christ, someone has some commitment to this paper!"

"Boss."

"Any idea where in the name of all that's holy our pretty boy Harris is? He's supposed to be on the late shift, and our back pages are emptier than my Tinder inbox."

Maggie neither knew nor cared where Harris was, but needed the shrieking to stop.

"Think he said something about an evening press conference at Tannadice?"

It was as good a guess as any, Maggie thought.

"For Christ's sake. He'll just be taking a jolly up to Dundee for some donuts at Crighton's. How the hell he's got biceps like that on his diet, I've no clue!"

Lexi trotted off towards her office with a face like thunder, ranting inaudibly as she went. She turned to face the office again.

"We're having a late planning conference for tomorrow's paper in half an hour, my wee wasters."

The spattering of editorial staff still in the office let out a collective groan as she entered her glass lookout chamber.

Maggie's desk phone was now ringing, showing an unknown local landline number.

Shit.

Maggie had hoped to make it to Denny Court to chat to Peter McGill's old neighbours before it got too late. It was a stretch to expect him to still live there, but there was bound to be someone nearby who had something to say about him – or the rest of his family. Tempting as it was to ignore the call, there could be an earth-shattering scoop at the end of it, so she pulled on the brakes and picked up her phone.

"*Standard* editorial desk."

The call started with a weird crackling of something against the receiver at the other end. Maggie remembered those earrings.

"Maggie? Maggie Shields? It's Val. Val Anderson."

"Hi. Yes, hi, Mrs Anderson. I've not dug into Sapphire Healthcare yet, but I absolutely will as soon as…"

"No, it's not that… could you come and see me… soon, I mean?"

"Erm, sure?"

The tension bubbling in Val's voice was palpable.

"Val? Are you OK? Has something happened?"

"Not exactly, but I'm worried it might."

"What do you mean?"

"Listen, I'll talk to you when you get here, but it's the girls. I'm worried about Olivia and Rebecca."

"Your daughters? Has something happened to them?"

She ignored the question.

"Come and see me and then we'll talk."

There was a raw panic in Val's voice that made Maggie uneasy. Whatever else was going on in that family, there were two girls at home who must be desperately worried about their dad. Maggie's imagination went into overdrive. Had they disappeared too? Or done something silly? She contemplated phoning the police herself, but thought better of it. What would she have to tell them?

"In here now, the lot of you."

Lexi was gathering the troops for an afternoon news conference, and it was the last place Maggie wanted to be right now. She was unsure how to convince Lexi that Mark Anderson's disappearance may just be the tip of a family iceberg.

*

When her time around the table came, she was ready.

"I've got more coming in on the back of Anderson's disappearance, but I have to head out now to chase a couple of sources."

Lexi took a sharp breath in, puckering her lips.

"This is a daily newspaper, and we need hourly news updates online, Maggie. What have you got for *tomorrow's* pages?"

Shit. Nothing she could share right now was the honest answer.

She had potential leads in multiple directions. Ranald's business enemies, Peter McGill's criminal record and goodness knows what unfolding drama with Mark Anderson's daughters. But none of it was useable yet.

"I need to work on this for a couple of days. I've got two house visits lined up – one to Val Anderson, who is worried for her kids, and one to Peter McGill's old neighbourhood. You know, the guy in the CCTV foo—"

"Tomorrow, Maggie. We have sixty-three pages to fill

for *tomorrow*. By some miracle, we still have advertisers who have paid for space in *tomorrow's* paper, next to actual news. Forget Anderson for now. Come back to me when they've found the bugger."

Maggie opened her mouth to speak, but Lexi was in no mood to listen.

"What did I say about the spoilt bairn face? I'm not having you gallivanting around Fife for days when you could be here, churning out some much-needed column inches about real local issues."

"I get that, boss, I do. However, Ranald Anderson's chequered professional history has come to light, and there's a possibility that it could be connected to Mark's disappearance. And this McGill lad – he needs more probing. I'm convinced there's some unsavoury reason a bloke like Mark was dipping his toes into Kirkcaldy's underworld."

"Kirkcaldy's underworld? Christ, it's only a dodgy boozer. Hardly the Krays' local in east London!"

Lexi shook her head and formed a hard stare in Maggie's direction – the stare that everyone knew meant the opportunity for debate was up.

"Who's next?"

Maggie sat, listening to the rest of the team read from lists on notepads – rehashing the same stories she'd heard earlier in the week to make them sound better, or just different. It made her ache for something more. She had to figure out a way to escape the office and get to Val's house soon.

Opening a new Word document, she began to scroll through the day's press releases for something resembling a story. But something else caught her eye.

Subject: How my AI Therapist was there for me when I needed him.

Robert, from Inverness, felt isolated in his rural community. As a single man with responsibilities for running a farm on his own shoulders, he lost all confidence in his social abilities. Before he was introduced to AI Therapy, the thought of a social get-together triggered a panic attack. He lost control of his breathing, felt dizzy, and struggled to function. Three months after engaging with our AI Therapy programme, Robert's perspective on life underwent a significant change. He's regularly attending local community events and is looking forwards to his first date in three years.

Go, Robert, Maggie thought. The kernel of something growing in her own troubled mind.

10

THURSDAY A.M.

Maggie clocked Val standing inside an imposing bay window when she arrived. She opened the front door to her visitor without hesitation, the hostility of their last in-person meeting appearing to have thawed. The striking features Maggie remembered on Val's face had taken on a mask of fear. Her hair looked unwashed, and her hands were trembling. The initial shock of her husband's disappearance had given way to something else. Something deeper rooted and burdensome. But Maggie was ready too. As soon as she entered the house, her senses fired off on another tangent.

Where was he?

There was no trace of the man whose previous presence woke up a sleeping memory. There was no sound of his heavy footsteps. Maggie questioned if he was even there. Were the ghosts from that day so long ago haunting her? Playing with her mind?

The bully in my head is messing with me, surely?

Val led her to the front room and pointed at one of

the large, elegant sofas that her daughters had been draped on just a few days before, lost in their smartphones. She scanned the room with her eyes, hungry for a visual clue that might build the accurate picture she needed. Val invited her to sit, and she complied. It was every inch the grand space. Framed pictures of serious-looking men holding stiff red tubes tied with black ribbon, dressed in fur-collared robes, adorned the walls. No one in Maggie's family went to university, but she knew a graduation photo when she saw one. The other-worldliness of it reminded her of the years after she left school. The only focus for her then was making money, fast. There were bills to pay and Lochie had held them above water for so long. She had to play her part.

Bookshelves took up an entire wall of Val's lounge. Maggie had never had a 'library' of her own, but she was never short of books. Library books, second-hand books from the charity shop. It was all the same in the end. But admiring the perfect alignment of Val's collection, she couldn't help wondering how many had been read. Soaking in the soft furnishings and extravagant wallpaper, Maggie suspected the work of an interior designer – a job she knew existed but couldn't get her head around. People who got paid to spend other people's money. The scene changed from one of Val's daughters being tucked up with a rug across her knees to several perfectly plumped, velvet-covered cushions neatly arranged in a row. Glancing around the lounge, it struck Maggie how at odds with its polished veneer were the layers hiding beneath.

"Thanks for coming back."

Val appeared genuinely relieved to have her company. She must have convinced her that there was a way she could help when she was here before. Maggie's conscience weighed heavily on her mind.

You can't let this woman down.

"Not at all. Sorry it wasn't sooner. My editor – she isn't – I mean, never mind. I couldn't get out of the office at first."

Maggie thought back to the fake tip-off Harris called in to the reporters' desk. His impersonation of a witness to the public consultation in the church hall was award-winning.

You have to get one of your hacks down here fast, luv. There's anarchy descending between the cooncillors and the punters. It's golden, man, I'm telling you!

Maggie had been sure to put the call on speakerphone and, as predicted, Lexi had her heading for the church hall faster than you could say *gossip column filler*. So here she was, back in Val Anderson's house, just like she needed to be.

"What's happened to your daughters, Mrs Anderson?"

Val sat down next to Maggie on the velvet sofa, taking a sharp exhale before she spoke. She used her trembling hands to self-soothe her neck with deep, massaging strokes.

"I need you to find out who is following them."

Maggie needed clarification.

"Did you say following them? Are you sure someone is following them?"

"As sure as I can be."

"OK, what makes you think—"

"They noticed something yesterday. I thought they were being overdramatic teenagers. Then I saw it too. A car was tailing us to school. And when I picked them up from school later, they said a man was watching them through the school railings at lunch break. Then – last night when Olivia cycled to her friend's house, there was some weird man hanging about at the bottom of our road. Looking at her from a car when she passed by, apparently."

Maggie didn't want to ask the next question but had no choice. Her code of ethics rarely wavered. She'd seen too many other journalists come a cropper by forgetting to do the right thing first, story second.

"Mrs Anderson… is this not one for the police?"

"Probably. But that's not happening."

Maggie knew folk who didn't trust the police usually had some baggage. Or, at least, what they believe to be a good reason.

"Oh?"

"Never mind that. I just want my girls to be safe, and I think you can help me."

"I'm not sure I understand?"

"Well, you want a direct line to the centre of our miserable drama, don't you?"

Maggie pulled out her notebook with no intention of writing anything down. It gave her something to do with her fingers, to stop her from tapping them on her lap.

"Why would you trust me with this? I mean. Sorry – I really shouldn't ask that. But, you've known me for twenty-four hours and, well, let's just say journalists are not known for winning fans that quickly."

Val looked faintly amused. She must have been expecting the question.

"Steady on… I think fan is a bit strong. But, for one, you've got some serious balls to doorstep the wife of a recently missing person without an invitation."

Maggie straightened at the compliment.

"And I've been told that you're a bit of a relentless bloodhound on the job."

She was hanging on Val's words, curious who had told her that but buoyed by the thought of her own reputation.

"I can try to help, but I should warn you I'll likely need to write about whatever I find. How do you feel about that?"

Val shook her head a fraction and her earrings jangled against her pronounced jawline.

"I had a feeling you'd say that. I don't know because, truthfully, I don't know what that will be. There are teenagers in the middle of this mess. I'm hoping you will not lose sight of that."

Maggie's conscience swelled as she wondered how this would play out for the girls. But it was part of the job.

"I want to help you, Mrs Anderson, but I've got a job to do. And there's every chance the cops will come down on me like a tonne of bricks with this one if I withhold anything that could put the girls at risk of harm. Or mess up their hunt for Mark. Or both."

Maggie wanted to probe more about why Val was reluctant to go to the police herself, but something made her hold back for now. Val stood up and wandered towards the door, leaving Maggie to guess that their chat was coming to an end.

"Well, I guess we're both taking a risk here. I've got my daughters to protect, and I get the impression you want to be taken seriously – yes?"

"Will you let me think about it?"

"I will. But not for long. My daughters' safety is more important to me than anything. And from where I'm standing, the hunt for Mark is going at a shameful pace."

Maggie nodded silently, feeling the fear radiate from the woman in front of her. Small chips had appeared in her nail polish that she hadn't noticed yesterday, and she had less make-up on. Perhaps there had been tears that washed it away already.

"Mrs Anderson, I should warn you that I've got another house visit to do after this, but I promise I'll call you later. I just need time to think."

Val seemed to accept her words for now. As she led her out of the house, Maggie craned her neck to peer down the hall corridor, but it didn't go unnoticed.

"Are you looking for something?"

Val had caught her out mid-stare.

"Um, no. I just wondered… do you live alone?"

Val's cheeks flushed.

"What sort of question is that?"

"Eh, sorry… it's just that last time I came here I thought I saw a man in the hallway, and I wondered if you had any company?"

An awkwardness was expanding between them, but Maggie crashed on, trying to make amends.

"I mean, has someone been here to look after you? Whilst Mark is… never mind, forget it. Shit. Sorry, I shouldn't have asked that."

Val's face broke into a weary grin.

"You are my kind of girl, Maggie Shields. I bet you get right in the way with all sorts of people. You really need to follow up that lead I gave you, by the way."

Val opened the front door, letting in a fresh blast of biting wind. Maggie hadn't forgotten that Ranald's ex-business partner was sitting near the top of her 'to call' list.

"Of course, yes. I'll contact them later."

"You do that, Maggie Shields. You do that."

*

"Ranald Anderson, father of the well-known Fife rugby international Mark Anderson, has offered a twenty-thousand-pound reward for information leading to the whereabouts of his son."

The local radio station was churning out the news through her headphones on her way to Peter McGill's former address. Desperate for some fresh air, she'd abandoned her work car on the edge of the woods. She'd take her bike on the footpath the rest of the way. It was one of those folding ones so she could stash it in the boot of a small car. The woods held so many memories – the good ones competing with the very worst. Even the musty, bark-infused air smelt the same as that day ten years ago. Maggie wanted to switch her brain up a gear, even if it was painful. That's when it worked best. When she was triggered. When all her senses came alive.

The sun was higher and stronger than when she squinted through the lens of her brother's camera, trapped behind the tree; its trunk was now a little fatter than she remembered, and the roots had taken a stronger grip on the ground beneath.

Maybe taking this route might help to lay some demons to rest too. It wasn't long before her mind had pulled her back to seeing the raw horror of a life being extinguished. The man she saw murdered that day meant nothing to her at the time. He was just a stranger. A man whose face she couldn't erase from her head. She remembered the paleness of his skin but was too far away to tell if he suffered long.

It was different for her mum. They said she died within minutes of impact. Maggie knew that anyway. She could see her mum was dead before the ambulance took her away. Her eyes were still open – staring at Maggie with motionless pupils. She looked up at the car to see who was driving but saw nothing but headlights. He couldn't even show his face before accelerating away from the scene. Maggie wanted to run after him, but Lochie held her back; he told her not to. *What was the point?* he'd said. *They'll find him somehow. It won't help us now. Let the police do their job.* And again, Lochie was almost right. The man whose name haunted their lives for so long was identified and his days of freedom numbered. At least that's what the police told Lochie after they identified his body that day in the woods. Ryan Ross eventually stopped running from the day he killed their mum when someone else caught up with him. That's how Lochie convinced Maggie not to speak up on the one-year anniversary police appeal for witnesses to the murder in the woods.

"It's justice, Maggie. That scumbag killed our mum and thought he got away with it, but he ended up walking into trouble of his own making. These people always do eventually. Don't waste your tears on him."

She didn't know whether to believe him at first. In a small community like Kirkcaldy, things didn't stay hidden for long. But she was too young and scared to ask for proof. How did Lochie know it was the same person? But the proof and the answers came later. That's when everything made sense.

She was back on that same path today, forcing her body forwards with all the strength she could muster. Her head dropped as she navigated her bike around sharp objects and focused on counting the sticks that lay across the path in front of her today. Same path. Different sticks.

Count them ALL until you get to one hundred. Or go back and start again. Just do it. Or something bad will happen. It will. Just like it did then.

The bully had her held in a trance. Numbers were racking up in her brain, exhausting her and relieving her in equal measure and blocking out everything and everyone around her.

She didn't notice the man until it was too late. His heavy frame had already nudged slightly against her body as they squeezed past each other between two overgrown chestnut trees flanking the path. The encounter almost knocked her off her bike.

"'Scuse me."

He was wearing a woollen beanie that hid almost half of his face. A high zipped jacket hid his chin, mouth, and nose. Their bodies had been in contact for half a second at most before he continued on his way, but he'd left his mark, and a wave of nausea and fear engulfed her. He had a strong smell, but it wasn't unclean. Quite the opposite.

He touched me. Did he look like a junkie? Smelt too clean to be a junkie. That's a stupid thing to say. Could've infected me with something. Needles in his coat, maybe? Did they jab me without me noticing? It happens. Was there blood on his body that touched me? It COULD happen like that. Infection. Disease. Shit.

The world around her was spinning, and she headed to the nearest bench to sit down and breathe. Just breathe. Nothing else. Let it pass, or at least let it settle.

"You OK, there, mate?"

Seconds, or maybe hours, later, she heard another stranger's voice and looked up from the bench. A teenager stood in front of her with a concerned look on his face. He approached her slowly.

Oh God, back off, please.

"Yes, yep… all fine, thanks."

"You look a funny colour, like."

She saw him move towards her, and she turned her body to the side.

"Just felt a bit… urgh… all fine though… cheers anyway."

He got the hint, thank God, and kept walking.

Maggie rose to her feet in a heartbeat and gathered

herself together, before heading back through the woods towards the housing estate at the other end. A battle raged on in her brain. Reaching a hand to her forehead, she felt a band of solid heat. A furnace of thoughts and fears colliding with each other. For a moment, she wondered if other people's minds felt like this. Exhausting, relentless, combative.

Let it go. He nudged you. You'd know if you were stabbed with a needle. How would I? You just WOULD, right? He smelt clean. More than clean. Something else?

Every time the intrusion pierced her brain, she fought back on the bully with all she had.

But what if that happened? Just what if he's contaminated me? My blood could be infected right now, working itself uncontrollably through my veins. MY veins.

Fighting to ignore the voice telling her to strip down and check for broken skin, Maggie thought back to smug AI therapy users with their 'improved thinking patterns' and '24/7 support on the go'. She considered what it would be like to turn to some robot therapist *right now, in this moment*, who'd tell her it was going to be OK. That she was safe. Would that help her get control of her life? Like it did for Suzy from Kent? Or Robert from Inverness? The thought felt both ridiculous and tempting.

She reached the entrance to the maze of terraced houses and rummaged in her jacket pocket for the note of paper with Pete McGill's one-time address on it. Her brain stored the memory of how these streets interlinked with each other from the days she and Lochie used to walk to school. The memory of those days brought her some comfort. Their route took them very close to a cutting in the woods on this side of town.

When Maggie arrived at the door of 5 Denny Court, she noticed a home that was well past its best, but the windows and front door had been recently renewed. Maggie couldn't ignore these details. Stuff like that would be important, even if she didn't yet know why. After ringing the doorbell, she gazed towards the front window of the property. An ornament collection covered most of the windowsill, flanked at each end by free-standing photo frames. These kinds of streets were full of curtain twitchers. People with one eye on daytime telly and the other on who were getting their windows cleaned: a luxury not everyone could afford.

She heard locks being fiddled with an uneasy touch before the front door opened. The face that met her was difficult to age. At first glance, she could've been in her eighties, but when Maggie looked closer, she saw eyes that were ten or twenty years younger, set in a make-up free face accented by dark circles. She'd dressed her slight frame from head to toe in clothes that could've been nightwear or daywear, and she'd scraped back her hair, dominated by coarse grey strands, behind her ears.

Maggie leant forward, tilting her head to one side to reveal herself to the woman whose body remained half hidden behind her front door.

"Hi, hello… sorry to bother you. My name's Maggie Shields and I work at the *Fife Standard*. I wondered if you had five minutes to chat?"

Maggie was used to cynicism and hostility in the face

of her visits, but there was something else in this woman's face that she couldn't quite put her finger on. She squinted, like she was attempting to focus on Maggie's face. The smell of alcohol on her breath travelled the short distance between them.

"What's that then, hen?"

"Could I come in for five minutes, Mrs…?"

"I dunno 'bout that, lass. You may not look like you're going to rob me of my last fiver, but I'll keep you on this side of my front door for now. Thanks all the same."

"Sure. And no, I will not rob you. I'm a reporter – from the local paper. Can I ask if this house is still owned by the McGill family?"

The woman retreated further behind the partially open door.

"Who did you say you were, dear?"

"Maggie Shields. Reporter from the *Fife Standard* – the local newspaper."

As she listened to Maggie, her hands constantly shook, and Maggie noticed her fingernails were stained a dark yellow. She seemed to grip the door frame for stability, and it was Maggie's turn to retreat half a step. Thoughts of this woman falling forwards onto her flooded her brain. What had she been thinking? She couldn't step into this woman's house, even if invited.

"Well, Maggie. Yer top of the class today, hen. I'm Anne McGill and I've lived in this house longer than you've been on this earth. What's it to a wee bairn like yersel' anyway?"

Could the sickly looking woman standing in front of her be Peter McGill's mum?

The loud arrival of a car reversing noisily into a spot just behind Maggie stole her focus. It was an expensive-looking motor. A BMW, Maggie thought at first glance, although she was no expert on cars. Mrs McGill's focus shifted to the well-dressed man getting out of the car. Her whole body seemed to melt like butter in seconds, and she loosened her grip on the front door. Peter McGill was walking towards them – but dressed differently to when she last saw him, being discharged from Kirkcaldy Police Station. He looked even less delighted to see Maggie this time.

"You again?"

Anne McGill lifted her arms in a show of expectant embrace, forcing Maggie to reverse back out of the way.

"Ah, well… look at that. Here's ma knight in shinin' armour."

She pulled him down to her level and hugged him like she didn't want to let go.

"Hello, handsome. Mary here was just asking me if this was the *McGill family home*."

Anne repeated the words *McGill family home* once again in an ill-fitting accent, and Maggie noticed the slur in her voice.

"Maggie, not Mary."

"Sounds awfy fancy when you put it like that, eh? Anyhoo, Mary – meet my handsome son, Peter. Peter is an *estate agent*. Ken what that is, luv? Sells all kinds of posh houses, does my lad."

Maggie lifted her right hand uncomfortably in his direction. Pete's skin was the colour of a strong cup of tea.

A shade that plenty of pale-skinned, freckly Scots would love. But the look on his face was far from warm. A subtle air of hostility cloaked his whole body, even penetrating Maggie's thick skin.

"Hi… it's Maggie. And we've already met."

"She's from the paper, Peter. Is that right, luv? Not sure I believe her though, as she seems softer than all those rough men we had to deal with before…"

Maggie's hearing sharpened at the comment.

"Yeh, Mum, she's a reporter. Not sure what's she's bothering you for."

Maggie was careful not to take her eyes off Peter. He looked keen to stop his mother from talking.

"What do you want with us?"

"Oh… do you still live… um… with…"

Peter fixed an icy stare on her, and she reversed out of her chosen route, finding the next thing that came to mind.

"So, the thing is. I think you went to school with my brother."

Anne giggled like a naughty school child.

"Reckon she's talking to you, not me now, son."

Her giggle morphed into an extended cackle, followed by a hacking cough.

"He's forever stealing the limelight, this lad!"

Peter was watching Maggie – possibly aware she felt rattled and self-conscious.

"Oh yeh, and who's your brother then?"

No going back now, Mags. Her brother's face jumped into her mind, as she imagined his rage when he found out about her latest mission.

"It's Lochie. Lochie Shields."

Still, he gave nothing away. There was no recognition, no warmth, but no obvious anxiety. Nothing. He knew the answer before he heard it. She'd mentioned her surname outside the police station. So why ask again?

"Come on, Mum. It's cold. Get inside."

Maggie watched Anne shuffling in front of her son, who was guiding her back down the hallway, protesting about being rude to *that wee lass*. Pete returned to the doorstep, in no mood for a friendly chat.

"Listen. I don't know what story you're chasing now, but you can keep my mum out of it. OK? She's not well."

"I… I didn't really need to… to be honest, it's more you I want to speak to."

Pete folded his arms and leant back against the side of the door frame.

"Again? Well, now isn't a good time. And I've already told you, I've answered the police questions, and I have nothing more to say."

People rarely intimidated Maggie. It was one thing that made her good at her job. But Pete McGill was unhinging her in ways she couldn't put her finger on. There was something about this man that made her feel less impervious. She found a business card in her wallet and handed it to him as he was closing the door. As she opened her mouth to stall him, she had nothing. No razor-sharp question or deftly placed landmines to force a reaction. Absolutely not a hint of anything that would stop him from closing that door on her. So he did.

Her hands were freezing as she approached her

bike, and she buried them deep in her jacket pockets for warmth. She'd met another closed door. It was feeling like a pattern she shouldn't ignore. But she knew this was where the good stuff happened. Just behind the closed doors. The more Maggie was told to back off, the closer to the truth she must be getting.

Cycling back through the woods to her car, she switched on her headphones, pulled the hood over her head, and hunted for a playlist to block out the bully. She knew he would wait to pounce with thoughts of her earlier encounter on the path. That man who could have brought her harm through an imagined infection. Reassuring herself again that he smelt too clean to be harbouring disease. In fact, he smelt pleasant. Cologne – a potent, male fragrance. Maybe even one she had encountered before.

*

Maggie couldn't go back to the office straight away. For a start, she'd have to blag her way around what didn't take place at the church hall consultation that never happened. But more importantly, she needed time and space to think. She needed to immerse herself in the calm and order of her own flat for a short while.

Turning in past the mailbox on the corner of her own street, she parked the car as close to her tenement block as she could. Walking down the pavement, she felt an icy chill on her back. The wind must have picked up, and she felt the start of a shower tipping onto her jacket.

Looking over her shoulder before she turned right at her main door, a noise of someone running with heavy feet on the pavement stopped her dead. Turning to look over her shoulder, all she could see was the outline of a figure running away in the opposite direction – the back of their body disappearing into the distance fast.

Bloody joggers, she thought, trying to reassure herself.

The rain was heavy now, dripping from the rim of her cycle helmet. As she made it to her flat, she saw the main door to her block was slightly ajar, and the lock stuck open on the latch. This had only ever happened once before in all the time Maggie had lived there. It was after a party in the flat above and the neighbours wanted to stop guests buzzing in and out all night. But there was no sound of a party coming from any of the windows above today.

Feeling her body tighten at the sight of the open door, she clicked the lock back on and pushed her bike through the door. Then waited for the sound of the Yale bolt closing behind her. She tied her bike against the staircase banister, adjusting the other two into a similar upright position. Three bikes tonight. Good. Her senses were still in overdrive, and she took the stairs cautiously, pausing to look behind her. For a second, the sound of footsteps below tricked their way into her overactive mind. She glanced down from the first landing, but there was no one there. It must have been the wind pushing the main door against the latch.

Unlocking her own door to the safety of home, she let her breathing return to a manageable pace. Everything looked in its place. Quiet. Undisturbed. Then her eyes rested on her feet and she saw a letter had landed on top of the rest of the day's mail – top side up. Her name and address were handwritten on the envelope, but there was no stamp. Something in her gut churned. Leaning down to pick it up, Maggie sat on the floor and rested her back against the wall. She unsealed the crisp white envelope and removed the single sheet of paper within. A photograph fell onto the floor. Her shaking hand gripped a printed photo of Lochie sitting at a table at his hospital staff canteen. He was wearing his uniform, leaning his forehead in one palm and holding a fork into some food with the other. Laying the photo to one side, she read the words in front of her. A familiar pounding grew inside her chest. Sweat was gathering on the tips of her fingers and forehead as her eyes traced the words written in a bold typeface:

> Find another story to write or you will regret it, Maggie Shields. And don't mention this to the police or we will hurt the only person who would really miss you.

11

THURSDAY A.M.

Maggie didn't know how long she'd been sitting on her sofa, clutching the letter and staring at the photograph, when her gaze drifted to the laptop in the corner of the room. Something had temporarily shut down everything else around her. She wondered if her mind had been playing tricks on her, so she read the words again. But the threat was the same second time around.

We will hurt the only person who would really miss you.

In all the years of surviving without a parent, Lochie was always there for her. Looking out for her and keeping her out of harm's way. It never even occurred to her that there may be a day when Lochie was the one under threat. But not just that. It was a threat of *her* making.

Dragging her heavy body back up and walking across the hall, she sat down at her desk, folded the letter up and placed it next to her keyboard. Her hands were still shaking. She let the words sink in.

Who would do this? And how the hell do they know where I live?

The bully in her head had come out to play too – it crept in where the cracks had formed in her mind. His exhausting demands queued up in her mind and offered only one escape from the panic and unknown. It was time to clean. Time to order, to check and then to do it all again until she reached something close enough to peace. She started clearing up the desk around her, but as she moved the keyboard, her screen clicked into life. A notification was waiting for her on the screen. It looked like a pop-up ad, but somehow felt more personal. The thing she would dismiss and shut down in an instant. But her mind was desperate for a way out of thinking about that letter. Those threats to Lochie.

She read the message on her screen again:

Want to be part of a groundbreaking revolution in mental health support? NHS Fife are looking for volunteers to take part in an exciting trial of a health service that has revolutionised mental health provision around the world.

No. Not now. Piss off and leave me alone. I've got work to do.

The bully kept tapping on her shoulder, urging her to change her clothes and check that no one had tampered with the locks on her door and windows. But she knew it would just be the start of it. Another exhausting, relentless stream of demands. She gritted her teeth, steeling herself for a fight.

12

THURSDAY A.M.

Maggie woke from a restless sleep at 5 a.m. Her skin was raw from strong bleach and every fingernail was split from chemical exposure and rubbing. What brief dreams she had found her stuck in a loop of opening that letter – again, and again. Each time with the same result.

She should go into the office and find another story to pursue. Nothing and no scoop was worth putting her brother's life at risk. Some disgruntled reader who had nothing to do with the McGills or the Andersons must have sent her the letter just to spook her. In a small town like Kirkcaldy, it's not hard to find out where your enemies live. The fact that it was a handwritten letter felt 'old school'. A move from the older generation who were less confident in the ability to send an anonymous email. The photo of Lochie at work was harder to dismiss. But then she thought of the hundreds of people that came through a hospital every day. Staff, patients – anyone could take a photo of him without him noticing. But whatever the explanation, there was no getting away from the fact that someone deeply disturbed had to be behind this.

Reaching for her phone to see what might be happening locally to lure her into an alternative investigation, she saw it had run out of charge.

She plugged it into the charger by her bed and waited until the screen came to life. Within seconds, it pinged with notifications. There were three more marketing messages from Next Generation AI Therapy. She wanted to ignore them, but something in their tone fed her need for reassurance.

Paul, 45, from Milton Keynes, turned to AI-powered therapy to tackle the past trauma that had led to obsessive thoughts every day of his life.

Past trauma, obsessive thoughts – they were both phrases that Maggie's pencil-scribbling, head-tilting psychologist had used with her. Her finger hovered over the notification bar, tempted to delve deeper into Paul's life. She wondered what his past trauma was. Considered what intrusive thoughts tortured him until the wee small hours. They couldn't be as weird as hers, surely. But the next message she read on her screen stopped her.

Hi. It's Pete McGill here. There's stuff I need to tell you. Can we meet?

Just as her resolve to do the sensible thing, the safe thing, had hardened, this arrived. She thought again about the letter. The photo of Lochie inside. The threats. And then she typed:

Sure. Where?

Could you come to my flat?

Somewhere public would be better, Maggie thought.

Ravenscraig Park? Next to the entrance?

Fine. 12pm?

She replied with a thumbs up emoji and leapt out of bed, keen to busy herself with something before more doubts crept in about meeting with a man with a criminal record on her own.

*

Peter McGill had a strangely calm aura about him when she clocked him hovering around the main park gates. Maggie found it hard to reconcile with what she'd heard about the man with a criminal record from a family on the wrong side of the law. He looked well dressed, had arrived before she did, and sat on a bench throwing bread from his Greggs paper bag at pigeons gathering around his feet. Her triggered imagination drifted to thoughts of clandestine meetings with spies.

As soon as he clocked her approaching, he stood up, looking happier to see Maggie than the first time they had met – on the doorstep of the police station.

"Hi. Thanks for coming."

"Sure."

It was an awkward start. The last time they'd met outside his mum's house, he couldn't get rid of her fast enough. The busyness of those passing around them broke through some of the tension. Mark pointed to the other side of the bench.

"Do you want to… I mean, can you sit for a minute?"

Maggie did as she was told but, conscious she couldn't put off Lexi for long, she tried to inject some urgency to the chat.

"Is this about Mark? Do you know what's happened to him?"

"Like I said before, I hope he's found soon."

"Is that because you were close?"

Pete let a short laugh escape. It sounded loaded and bitter.

"You said your name was Shields? Maggie *Shields*?"

She picked up on his laboured use of her surname – remembering how he reacted to it the last time they met – and her thoughts returned to Lochie. If she got out of this cosy get-together unscathed, there was a good chance Lochie might kill her himself when he heard about it.

"Do you and my brother have any sort of – um – history at all?"

His reaction was, again, hard to judge.

"We went to school together and we both still live in this small town. Does that count as history?"

"What about Ranald Anderson? Do you know much about him?"

Pete's eyes closed suddenly, and he took a long breath, as if steadying his own nerves. Once again, the mention of Ranald Anderson elicited a powerful reaction. It was becoming a common theme.

"I need to show you something. But it's back at the flat. Would you come back there with me – just for a bit?"

Maggie noticed the surrounding public. Were people staring? For a second, she thought she saw the same man who bumped into her in the woods. Her instincts were still chipping away at her, telling her no.

"Whatever you need to say, you can tell me here."

He looked sheepish, but nothing about him made her feel in danger.

"I just need you to see something with your own eyes – if you're going to believe me."

Maggie wondered what the hell could be waiting for her that he couldn't bring to the park, but again, dismissed her own suspicion. Perhaps she was getting better at shutting down the warning voice in her own head than she thought.

"Please trust me. I have nothing to gain from hurting you in any way. You'll understand."

I watched him stand up and wait for me to do the same. I felt in my pocket for my phone, pulled it out and checked there was enough charge to make an emergency call.

"Make this quick, McGill."

*

He wasn't lying about how close he lived to the park. They were inside his house within ten minutes. Maggie declined his offer to sit down, choosing to perch awkwardly against the back of his sofa instead. Her eyes were drawn to a strip of sharp white light flooding out from under the door of another room further down the hallway. Something about it looked out of place, and distracting.

Her attention returned to Pete as he opened a cupboard at the back of the room, pulling out something that resembled one of those lockable metal safes. He placed it on the coffee table, unlocked it with a key and sat down opposite her.

"Take a look in there..."

Grabbing the box from the table, Maggie lifted the lid impatiently, pulling out a mixture of photos and what looked like school reports and dog-eared certificates for a youth football tournament. He was watching her like a hawk.

"Look at the photos. All of them."

The first few images were of Pete, dressed in his school uniform with his arm around another male. Maggie's gaze locked onto the features of the other boy, who looked at least a couple of years older than him. He was wearing faded denim jeans and a hoodie and had a tattoo just visible on his neck as he turned his face towards Pete, his arm draped around his shoulders. There was a look of pride in both their faces that jumped out from the image. Maggie looked closer at the younger lad's face. In an instant, she felt as if she'd just woken up from sedation. They had the same eyes. The same slight deepening at the bridge of their nose, and the same high cheekbones.

"Is this... is this your brother, Pete?"

Maggie cast her mind back to her school days. She remembered the name McGill. She remembered her mum's warnings to Lochie to stay away from 'that family'.

Looking at Pete, she knew she was right on the money. But there was something else about his brother's young face that unsettled her.

"He left school at fourteen. Probably before you even started at the high school."

Maggie suspected that to be the case. Why was his face having such a powerful effect on her then?

"Keep going," Pete said, pointing to the pile of photos on her lap.

She flicked through some more images of the brothers in front of a tent, toasting something on a campfire. Some of them kicking a ball about on a frostbitten beach somewhere. And a couple of them wearing Christmas cracker hats on their heads, making rude faces at each other.

So, this was it. This is what he wanted to show me. Pete had a brother she didn't know existed. Was there more? Something about his brother's face nudged her in the gut. Then she looked at the next photo in the pile.

It was Pete in school uniform again, this time with the sixth form stripe on his blazer. His brother featured once more, sharing some tins of lager with him in the local park. A celebration maybe? A coming of age, perhaps? But there was a third person in this photo. A face she would recognise at any age, in any light. It was Lochie. Crouching behind the other two, one arm over both brothers, gripping tight and grinning at the camera. Lochie, the boy who should have followed his mother's advice to have nothing to do with the McGill family. Here he was once more, fleeing with the craws. The same Lochie she trusted never to lie to her – who said he hardly knew Pete, let alone his brother.

The same Lochie who told her she must never tell the police what she saw ten years ago because Ryan Ross, the person who was murdered that day in the woods, was the same person who killed their mum.

"Why are you showing me this?"

Maggie's body felt like jelly housed in a glass cage.

Keep control. Breathe.

"You said you wanted to understand what is going on in this town? You want to write about Mark Anderson, yeh?"

Maggie nodded, reluctant to break his flow with her own voice.

"Then you need to know these things. You need to see evidence."

Her blood was pumping faster around her body and her hands were tapping uncontrollably against her legs. The adrenaline was flowing now, but she couldn't lose control. She needed to keep her thoughts focused on what she was being told.

One, two, three… one, two, three…

Maggie chanted the numbers in her own head, on loop, until she got a bit more control of her breathing. Then started again at *one*.

"What do you mean, evidence? Evidence of what?"

"Evidence that our brothers knew each other… well."

Maggie's forehead felt hot. Had Lochie been lying to her? Or had she just misunderstood everything he'd said because she wasn't paying attention? Or because she was paranoid?

Some of the support material that had popped into her inbox recently promised immediate digital routes to 'tackling paranoid thoughts'.

Do you have regular feelings of others working against you?

Do you crave constant reassurance to calm your dread that something bad is going to happen?

But, again, Maggie's cynicism took charge.

Could this be some sort of trap? Is Pete McGill trying to steer me off course with his own agenda? Maggie took one slow, deep breath and tried to focus.

"What's the big deal?" said Maggie, but he didn't respond, so she continued.

"The brother was a sociable kid. He got on with many people – still does. But guess what, his wee sister hasn't always known who he was hanging out with. She still doesn't."

She felt the strength from her own lies.

Pete was leaning forwards now, staring at his own feet before turning his face to the side. She saw apprehension in his body language. Where had the man who confronted her outside his mum's house gone?

"Maggie, do you remember the boy that was found in the woods ten years ago?"

These words enveloped her completely, making her blood run cold. There was only ever one boy in the woods that was talked about in Kirkcaldy. Ryan Ross. The same boy that Maggie saw from a distance, through her seventeen-year-old eyes. The same boy whose last moments on earth she captured on camera, only to be deleted by Lochie later that day. A vision that still haunted her every day since. But each time it fought with her conscience, she reminded herself she owed him nothing.

He was the man behind the wheel of the car that hit their mum and then vanished. *Justice,* said Lochie. *He walked into trouble of his own making that day.*

She managed a nod. Nothing more.

Pete's gaze fell to the floor.

"That was my brother. My half-brother. His name was Archie, and he was killed the day before his eighteenth birthday. Never knew his dad, the poor sod."

Maggie listened intently, trying to make sense of what she was being told.

"Archie had issues. Made me look like the angel in the family. But he would've done bloody anything for me, that kid."

Old headlines and memories ambushed Maggie's mind.

"But the victim's name was Ryan Ross? It was all over the papers for weeks as soon as the police confirmed it."

"His full name was Ryan Archibald Ross, but he was always just known by his middle name – Archie – after his paternal grandpa."

Ryan Archibald Ross, *not McGill. He must have kept his father's surname. But why was he identified by the police as Ryan Ross and not Archie – the name everyone knew him by? That way everyone would've known the police were no longer chasing the lad who fled from a fatal hit and run.*

No wonder the town never linked the victim to the McGill family back then.

Maggie remembered some of the local gossips writing the victim off as a local drug runner or the like – a waster who wouldn't be missed. They said he'd probably got involved in one deal too many. The judgement was cruel, Maggie had thought. He was still a young man, after all. Did he really deserve that kind of end? But then Maggie heard the truth a year later, when Lochie told her. It was the anniversary of Ryan Ross's murder and the police launched a renewed appeal for witnesses to his attack. This was her big chance to come forward. It wasn't too late. She could help find justice for that poor young lad in the woods. Lochie told her he deleted the photos so there was no temptation to go back there. But she told him she was going to go to the police with what she saw. It wasn't too late.

That's when Lochie made her think again – told her not to spare another moment of sympathy for him. *He got what he deserved*, he told her. She asked why he was so sure it was Mum's killer, of course. Not that she doubted him for a minute.

"I hear things at the hospital, Mags. The first responder on the scene in the woods that day was your old-school, loose-tongued Fifer. It wasn't long before the rumours flew around. Said the face of the investigating officer when he looked at the victim was a picture. The man who the coppers had been chasing for a hit and run was being zipped into a body bag before their very eyes."

He offered to tell her more, but that was all she could stomach at the time. Maggie didn't develop her thick skin as quickly as Lochie. She hadn't hardened herself to death yet, so she listened to his warnings and moved on with her life.

Don't get involved, Maggie. Just walk away. Or it will haunt you forever.

He was her big brother. Her everything. And of course he was right.

But now Maggie knew Archie Ross had a half-brother who relied on him the way Maggie relied on Lochie. And a mother who no doubt loved him, for all his faults. That's what mothers do. Maggie knew that much already.

"Why are you telling me all this?"

"I showed you that photo so that you would listen to me and know you could trust me."

The mention of trust triggered something in her.

"Did you send me that creepy letter the other night? Did you take the photo of Lochie at work?"

"What?"

"I work for a newspaper. You should know it takes a shitload more than that to intimidate me."

Maggie hoped her words sounded more convincing than they felt.

"No, I didn't."

"Are you sure about that?"

"I want to help you, Maggie. Not creep you out."

"Help me with what, exactly?"

Pete had adjusted his position on his chair. He was looking her straight in the eyes, waiting for her undivided attention before speaking again.

His tone was calm.

"I think I know why Mark Anderson has gone missing. And I think his life could be in danger."

Anxiety was enveloping her whole body, but Pete had something to tell her about Mark, and it was her job to listen. Why did he need to break her trust in Lochie first? Why did the one person in the world she truly trusted keep appearing around the edges of this story?

Maggie looked again at the photos on her lap, drawn to Archie's eyes. They were an odd shade of hazel that switched on a deeply buried memory. Their colour pulled her back to the last time she saw them. Without warning, she was there again, seeing the same eyes staring up at her from the damp, earthy bed of fallen leaves. Those eyes were wide open, still full of colour, but the body that housed them was lifeless. Placing the photo on her own knee, Maggie remembered that same haunting death stare from her mother's face – lying on the road in front of their home. She was still looking at her with kindness – like she wanted to be remembered this way. Her mum was trying to tell Maggie not to worry. Taking one last comforting look at the daughter she loved with all her heart.

"So, you reckon you've got all the answers, yes?" said Maggie.

"How much do you know about Mark's family?"

He was annoying her now. She'd been over this before. People were queuing up to unmask the dirty truth about Ranald Anderson, but Val had beaten him to it with her revelations.

"I already know his old man is a prick who put making money and winning over everything – and everyone else in his life."

"There's more to him than run-of-the-mill arrogance and money-grabbing."

Maggie lifted her gaze from its fixation on her surroundings and just listened intently. She watched the contours of Pete's face as he spoke.

"Ranald Anderson is the man who buys his way out of

any shit and into any sugar, you know? A real Billy Big Balls."

"Um, OK… Not the first one of those I've encountered on this job," Maggie said.

"Well, I'm no stranger to ducking and diving my way through life either, but this guy – it's a miracle he's not behind bars."

Again, Maggie fought back the intrusive images of her flat burning down and compulsions to get home now and check… check… and clean.

"Not now. Just piss off. You can wait!"

"Eh? Eh?" Pete's confusion was evident, and Maggie realised she'd fought the bully out loud.

"Sorry, never mind. Carry on."

"A few weeks ago, I was helping tidy up my mum's house. You'll have seen, she's… not very well. Barely able to look after herself, to be honest."

Maggie nodded silently. She knew the signs. She'd seen more than enough issues with booze in a town that was struggling to keep itself afloat.

"Mum's issues have their roots in grief."

Maggie was no stranger to this truth. Grief had broken her own dad, leaving him widowed long before his time. He walked out on his children and signed off from life.

"I was pulling all kinds of crap out of Mum's cupboards," Pete continued, dragging Maggie back from thoughts of her own loss.

"That woman kept everything that Archie so much as breathed on. That's when I found this."

Pete paused, took a deep breath, and looked up, as if to check that Maggie was still listening. He pulled something else out of the box. It was tightly bound shut by a couple of rubber bands, and someone had tucked it away.

"What is it, Pete?"

"This notebook."

As well as a tattered notebook, there was also a stash of tenners and twenties, each one neatly rolled up and tucked inside the rubber bands which held the notebook closed – only just. He handed it all to her, and Maggie leafed through it carefully, fighting back the repulsion at the greasy smudges that covered the notebook's cheap, worn plastic surface.

Too dark to be blood, Maggie. Relax.

Maggie read the signs quickly. Entry after entry of dates, locations, weights, and monetary amounts – scribbled in barely legible handwriting.

"Drug deals?"

"My thoughts exactly. Look at the last entry..."

It stood out like a sore thumb. There was a date and a location.

– 5 Oct – 3pm, Kirk Woods, back wall, east end – handover for £50K – R. Anderson – £1K cut.

Maggie felt Pete's gaze on her as she let the words sink in.

handover for £50K – R. Anderson

(+extra25 – off the books)

"Maggie?"

Her memories of that day were more visceral than ever. She was in the woods. Feeling it all again, like she did on the therapist's itchy blue chair. Her hands moved involuntarily on her lap as if she was holding the camera, her forefinger poised and ready to click. The muscles in her body tensed just as they did ten years ago when the stick cracked under her feet. The stale cigarette smoke in the air. It had drifted from where he'd been standing – waiting, in position. *Back wall, east end – handover for £50K.*

The man who now had a name. And a family.

"Maggie?"

Maggie spoke softly, careful not to give away too much. He couldn't know that she was there. That she'd seen his brother Archie take his last breath but told no one who or what she saw. But she knew he was making a mistake with something huge. For a second, she had a clear memory of the person plunging a knife into Archie's flesh.

"It wasn't Ranald in the woods."

Shit. The words came out without warning.

"What? How the hell do you know that?"

"I don't. I mean, do you think Ranald killed your brother?"

"I don't know. It's his name on that note. But everyone says he wasn't one to risk his squeaky-clean image for anything."

Maggie pushed her own memories back. She'd tried to destroy them over the years, but they were as stubborn as she was. Raking around in other people's business brought relief. There was a safety in the hidden secrets of others. But nothing had prepared her for the day when the two would collide.

"What's this got to do with Mark's disappearance?"

"When I found this notebook in my mum's house, it all fell into place. I knew for certain there was a link between Archie's death and Ranald Anderson. I had to do something. We've been waiting so long for justice for Archie. But everything had gone cold years before – as if the town had given up on him. Like his life – and his death – no longer mattered. But they still matter to us."

The words were bleeding out of him now.

"Why didn't you go straight to the police with this when you found it?"

"I did. Well, I mean, I was going to. But then I stopped myself. I knew that this wouldn't be enough... The evidence wasn't strong enough. Going up against someone like Ranald, with the lawyers he'd have, I needed someone else to speak up. In front of a judge – where it would count for something."

Maggie was watching the lines on Pete's face as he spoke. Something in the way he spoke seemed so raw. Looking up briefly, he caught her eyes.

"The more I dug, the more I found about how Ranald Anderson forced his way through life to succeed. He was a hustler. One of Fife's best. But the cops never made anything stick. That bastard had wriggled out of everything. Too much protection around him."

Maggie thought back to Val's comments, which rang truer than ever now.

"Did the name Mitchell Stevens come up in your research, by any chance?"

Pete looked blank, so she let him continue.

"I knew he'd have a flaw, though. Some crack in the surface that I could exploit. So, that's when I started sniffing around his son, Mark. Seriously talented rugby boy, that one, but a bit more of a conscience than his old man. His steroid habit and use of other assorted substances to prop up his battered body and mind left him weakened."

Maggie thought steroids were mostly the choice of weightlifters, boxers and athletes. Not posh rugby boys whose parents taught them right from wrong.

"It started off as just a wee boost here and there, apparently," said Pete. "They kept it all under the radar at first. The sad thing was, no matter how well he did on the rugby field, it didn't live up to his old man's expectations. And these pros were getting bigger and stronger all around him. So, he needed a helping hand – in the gym."

Pete went on and Maggie listened. She wrote nothing down but didn't need to. She would stamp it all in her memory. How Mark's spiral into dependency on steroids eventually got so out of control that he made mistakes. He cut corners contacting his supplier. He dipped his nose into cocaine and boasted to too many people about how to bulk up the quick way. And, before he knew it, the press hounds came knocking.

"That's when the big man Ranald stepped in. He started paying lawyers to send shitty letters, and the hacks crawled back into their holes."

His words jogged her memory of the letter she had been sent. Would a hungry local reporter like Maggie threaten someone like Ranald Anderson? It felt like a stretch.

"You telling me there wasn't a single journalist who would tell the truth behind Scotland's star rugby boy?"

"You'd think, Maggie, wouldn't you? But you underestimate the depths of that man's pockets and the power of his influence, I'm afraid."

Maggie felt something die a little inside the part of her soul that believed in ethical journalism. From the first day she'd stepped foot into the *Standard*'s office as a clueless young cub reporter, she was a fully signed up believer that truths would always surface – no matter who you were.

"Ranald knew they needed rock solid proof of his son's drug use, or he would take them to the cleaners."

"And that's what they didn't have?" said Maggie.

Maggie was listening to every word he said and beginning to trust someone other than her brother. But she still didn't understand why any of this led to murder.

"There's more you're not telling me, isn't there?"

She was pacing now. The rhythmic movement was soothing her and helping her concentrate.

Three steps forward, breathe, three steps more, breathe, and repeat.

"What's the link with Mark's disappearance? Are you saying he's done a runner because the rumours were closing in about him, and he couldn't face it all going public?"

"At first, I thought that, yes. But now, I think there's more going on.

"Care to share?"

"Are we talking off the record?"

"Sure."

"I think someone might soon bring down the mighty Ranald Anderson. I think someone is ready to talk publicly – to the police, even – about Archie's murder."

The burning flame rose up Maggie's neck again. Who else knew that Ranald was behind Archie's murder? Who had the power to re-open this case after ten years?

"Oh. Who did you think would turn on Ranald?"

He looked like he was going to stall.

"Pete – who did you think would speak up about Ranald's involvement in Archie's murder?"

The answer to her own question came to her from somewhere deep inside the mess of her head.

Of course.

"Do you think Mark Anderson is going to testify against his own father?"

Pete didn't need to speak. His face confirmed what she needed to know.

"How the hell did you persuade Mark Anderson to turn on his own dad?"

Maggie wanted to believe Pete, but why would Mark betray the man who stood between him and a wall of career-wrecking scandal?

"I didn't at first."

"What did you say to him in the Harbour Tavern?"

He was on his feet now, hands in pockets, his glance pointing upwards to a canvas hanging on the wall. It looked like graffiti art – out of place in this house. Maggie remembered seeing something similar in the hallway of Anne McGill's home, on the narrow corner of wall visible from her doorstep.

"It was the morning of what would've been Archie's birthday. His twenty-eighth birthday. Birthdays were always a big deal to my mother. Especially when he was killed the day before his eighteenth. I knew she'd be in a bad way, but when I saw her that day..."

Pete covered his eyes with his right hand and started

massaging his temples, as if trying to ease some trapped pain. A strange sense of compassion washed over her. Followed by resentment for all the birthdays her mum had missed because of Archie's actions.

"If I'm going to write about any of this, I need to understand… everything. Is that what you want? Do you want me to write about this?"

"If you have to – in the end, when everything comes out."

"When what comes out?"

Pete wasn't interested in her leading the conversation. It was his agenda.

"So, there was Mum, just kind of slumped in the corner of her own front room – empty bottles lying at her feet and photos of Archie scattered on the carpet. She was as white as a sheet. Nothing was moving. I couldn't even feel her chest move."

Maggie's head flooded once again with images of her own mother's lifeless body lying on the dirty concrete, as dark pools of blood swelled around her head in a halo of death.

"I checked for a pulse and felt nothing. At first. But it was weird. Like I refused to accept she'd gone, so I checked again, and it was there, so faint I wondered if I had imagined it."

"So, you called for an ambulance, yes?"

He went ominously quiet again.

"Pete?"

"I should've called an ambulance, I know that. But – it sounds daft – I wanted to care for her myself. I knew she'd want me to. It would keep it out of view from the curtain twitchers. No ambulance or flashing blue lights. They'd had enough to gossip about from our family over the years."

"How did you even know what..."

"I'd seen the medics treat her after so many benders in the past. So, I lifted her to bed, changed her out of her stained and filthy clothes into a nightie, put her in the recovery position and lay next to her until her breathing strengthened."

Maggie sat motionless and listening intently as Pete told her about his broken mum. How the events of that day drove him to Mark Anderson's doorstep.

"He wasn't there, but his wife, Val, was. She looked like she just wanted my dirty boots off her marble floor. She told me Mark was shacked up in some swanky apartment down the road, where he'd been living for the past six months. Said I could piss off and find him there instead."

"So you did?"

Pete nodded with a faint air of pride.

"I gave it to him full throttle."

For all his talk and bluster, Pete didn't strike Maggie as the violent type. But then she remembered his spent conviction for GBH. It must have shown on her face.

"Don't worry. I didn't beat him up or anything. I didn't need to. I started with photos of Archie from school just to jog his memory."

Maggie glanced over at the box of images she'd seen earlier. Mark Anderson wasn't in any of them. His world of private education was a million miles from Pete, Archie and Lochie's.

"I needed to show Mark a face, belonging to an actual child who was once the same age as him. I asked him straight out if he knew about the lad who was killed in the woods ten years ago. The arrogant son of a bitch tried to fob me off. So, I pushed harder. I asked whether he knew he bled for almost an hour before the paramedics lost their fight. Mark just kept a straight face and said he'd heard he was a troubled lad who mixed in the wrong circles and met an unsurprising end."

Maggie tried to imagine someone describing her own brother like that. Her insides recoiled at the thought of him being brutally murdered and left to bleed out like a slaughtered animal.

"Did he show any emotion?"

"Not much. But when I shared photos of my mum the day before, that changed."

His voice trembled, and his expression swung between embarrassment and grief. She'd almost forgotten he was talking about a man who stole the life of her own mother.

"He needed to see what losing her 'troubled lad who mixed in the wrong circles' does to a mother."

"And?"

"At least it shut him up a bit. Gave me the chance to tell him that Archie was my half-brother."

Pete said Archie took extra paper rounds to boost the family housekeeping money, reminding Maggie of Lochie's sacrifices so she'd had what she needed. The nights out he skipped. The new clothes he didn't buy.

And when Pete told her about the aching sense of loss that ripped through his family overnight, followed by the aftershock of the perpetrator walking free, Maggie remembered the agony, her agony of not knowing who killed their mum and got away with it.

"That's when I asked him why Archie was killed," said Pete.

"And?"

"He claimed he didn't know for sure but thought it might be linked to a blackmail attempt."

"So Daddy was looking out for his steroid-injecting, coke-snorting son, after all?"

"Mark said that there were folk out to get him all the time. Jealous of his success. But there was more. He said something had gone down between him and someone else in the industry that was bad for business. Mark wondered if that was the clincher. The thing that made his dad lose perspective. Fly off the rails completely."

"How the hell would a wee lad like Archie get his hands on something damaging enough to Ranald to lead to murder?"

"Good question."

"And Mark never wondered why the threats just disappeared overnight?"

Maggie's bullshit detector was working overtime.

"I think he did a good job of turning a blind eye. Ignorance is bliss when problems are swept under the carpet, and you can get on with your day like nothing happened."

She needed to probe deeper. There was so much more she could ask him.

Maggie knew it wasn't Ranald in the woods that day who stabbed Archie, because she saw the man who did.

But she wasn't ready for Pete to know she was there that day – close enough to see so much but still able to hide.

"Do you think he had any idea what his dad had planned?"

Pete let a slow and pained exhale escape at this question.

"I honestly don't know."

"So, you told him… about Archie? About the notebook?"

Pete nodded; his face flushed with anger.

"He tried to say it meant nothing. Was just a scrap of paper in a notebook that anyone could have written. Lots of people wrote his dad's name down for all kinds of reasons. It would be worthless circumstantial evidence in court – their lawyers would laugh in our faces."

Maggie considered the witness statement she could have made herself that day. She remembered the photos that she took which never saw the light of day. Surely they would've contained enough evidence to help a jury piece the truth together. Even if Ranald didn't appear. The photos would've identified whoever it was he sent to do his dirty work and there was little doubt they would've dished up Ranald's name to save their own.

Pete's mobile phone vibrated on the kitchen table.

"Sorry, that's mum's panic alarm. It triggers on my phone if she hasn't moved in a while. Reminds me to check on her."

Maggie thought of Anne McGill, and how sad her life must be. No wonder her son's daily visit was the highlight of her day.

"So? How did you turn it around?"

She needed to press Pete for more, somehow.

"I told him he was right."

"What?"

"I told Mark he was right. Archie's scribbled notes were not strong enough to seal the deal with a jury. We needed more to link Ranald to my brother's death. He needed to do that."

"Can't imagine he jumped at that?" Maggie said.

"Nope. Told me to 'do one', if I remember correctly."

"Big man on the rugby pitch, scared wee coward in real life then?" she said.

A picture was forming in Maggie's mind, but something still felt incomplete.

"I gave up that day but knew I'd planted the seed. I asked around a bit in the right places, and it didn't take long to find out where he went to meet his steroid dealer."

"The Harbour Tavern?"

It all added up in Maggie's head. That was why Pete was seen confronting Mark on the CCTV footage days before he went missing.

"So, let me guess… you persuaded him that day?"

"OFF the record?"

Maggie nodded furiously.

"Something in him had changed. He told me he was going to turn on his dad. Said he'd confronted him about Archie's death and the bastard tried to wash his hands of it – blamed someone else. That's what changed his mind. Couldn't stomach his lies, apparently."

The hairs on the back of Maggie's neck rose like an animal homing in on her prey.

*

THURSDAY P.M.

The key players in the mystery of Mark Anderson's disappearance were swirling around in Maggie's mind, competing with the mental image of yesterday's threatening letter. If it was legit, someone was giving her a pretty strong STOP sign – right where it would hurt.

Who could she trust to speak to about everything she'd learnt in the last twenty-four hours? Lexi? The police? They were both the obvious, sensible options. But right now, she wasn't ready to take either. The police would likely tell her to leave the investigation to them. But she needed to be Maggie Shields – a fearless woman in a man's world. Even if it looked as if someone really didn't want her to be finding the answers.

She had to see Lochie. To update him on what she'd been told by Pete McGill and Val Anderson. He'd be able to keep her mind on track. Stop it firing off in strange directions.

Her phone was flashing with a message by the time she left Pete in the park. Lexi's voice was high pitched and loaded with anger.

"Have you gone AWOL, Shields? It's one thing to bail on a news conference for some imaginary church hall brawl. Harris is crap at remembering his own lies, by the way. But doing a runner from a therapy appointment is not going to win you any prizes, lass. If you don't get your ass back to work in the next hour, I'll be up to those HR warriors with news of your wee disappearing act faster than you can say P45."

Ah, shite.

She'd been working with Lexi for long enough to know you can run, but you can't hide when she's on the warpath. She had to placate her with a decent page lead and a believable explanation for her psychotherapy great escape.

She contemplated the HR warriors. It was a fair judgement. Sharon McGrath, head of HR at Fife Associated Newspapers, was notorious for living life according to the latest health and safety journal. She was unlikely to use the office printer without carrying out a risk assessment first.

The thought of Sharon's robotic warnings on 'fit to work practice' if Maggie didn't re-engage with therapy gave her an idea. Maybe Sharon would accept this AI-powered therapy option. *AI is just another word for a robot, after all. Bet she's right up on all that next generation CBT solutions stuff.* From the research Maggie had managed, it was all the rage in the USA – they even used avatars of dogs to monitor elderly patients in their own homes. Reminding them to take their medicine and engaging them in conversations about the news. There's bound to be some metrics on how this stuff is more effective than the real thing somewhere. If Maggie could convince her that signing up for the online option was as good as going back to the clinic, it might just keep everyone off her back.

*

She rarely visited Lochie's house. It was usually the other

way around. But she had too much to speak to him about today. She needed to see the whites of his eyes.

Since Lochie's promotion to charge nurse at the hospital, the house was in dire need of attention. Much like his social life. He'd often told her that, after clinging onto their family home through the hardest years, he was not prepared to let it go now. But it held too many painful reminders. There were still markings on the kitchen wall where Lochie and Maggie used to measure themselves. He couldn't bear to paint over their mum's handwriting. She was always careful to choose a red or pink pencil for Maggie and blue for Lochie. It annoyed Maggie at the time. A wasted anger for something that meant nothing at all. The kitchen cupboards were still full of the dinner set his mum saved for visitors who deserved it. Many of the plates and bowls showed the chips and scrapes of the passing years. They were all piled up in some unholy mess behind closed doors of faded oak veneer. Lochie had given up scrubbing the woodwork or covering rips in the wallpaper. He told Maggie to give him notice if she was visiting so that he could at least hoover the carpet. She called him on her mobile with one hand as she was locking her bike to the lamppost outside his gate with the other.

"Hey, Scoop. What's up?"

"Loch. I'm coming to see you."

"Eh, OK… when's that then?"

"Now?"

Lochie's voice faded a little, and she presumed he was scanning the house for mess.

"Does that mean… in the next half an hour now?"

"Nah, more like… I'm outside your front door now… now."

"Christ, Mags. Hang on!"

She heard him push something heavy out of the way, trip up and swear loudly as he walked towards the front door, opening it with exaggerated effort.

"Did you lie to me about how well you knew Peter McGill?"

Maggie was already in his hallway, pulling off her coat as she walked past him. The note and direct threat to Lochie was tugging at her mind, but she hadn't decided whether to share that with him yet.

"Is there something more you're not telling me about that lad? Have you guys got more recent history?"

Lochie held his hands out in an exaggerated welcome.

"Do come in. I've been expecting you. Oh, no… hang on, I've not. But let's brush over that."

She watched him like a hawk. Watched his eyes move around in his head, searching for something to cling onto. Then she studied his body language.

Heading straight for the lounge, Maggie ignored the comment and threw her body down on the sofa before opening her rucksack and pulling out the letter.

"I need to show you something else."

"Oh?"

Her skin went clammy as she unfolded the handwritten note and passed it to him, along with the photograph. He studied them both intently for a few seconds before his face turned grey. He stayed silent, but she was having none of it.

"Lochie? You got any weird enemies at work?"

He dropped the note and the photo back towards her on the sofa.

"You need to take this to the police and then back the hell off, Mags. Find another battle to fight. Seriously."

"The police? Why would I go to the police? Did you read the bit about hurting you?"

A rare but tangible anger was rising in him as he turned his back on her.

"You have no idea what kind of shit goes on in this town."

He looked like he regretted the words instantly.

"Do I not, Lochie? What kind of job do you think I do? I may not be saving lives but I'm not writing the lonely hearts column at that paper, you know?"

Lochie's whole body took on a disturbed look that she'd not seen in a while. He stopped making eye contact with her and stiffened from head to toe.

"Why do you do this?"

Maggie mouthed the word *what?* without saying it.

"You come here, showing me stuff like that and asking for my advice. Then get all defensive when I try to give you some. Why, Maggie? What's the point of that?"

He had a point, and she knew it. Lochie was the one who told her how to avoid trouble, just so she could walk straight towards it anyway.

"Just remember, I see things every day at work. I see people from all over this town at their worst – their angriest and their most desperate. The things that folk will do to themselves and to others because of pain or anger. It's… it's fucking grim, Maggie."

A dark shadow cast over her brother's easy-going exterior. He had his own demons. She knew that. But he didn't go looking for trouble. That wasn't what Lochie Shields was about. But sometimes, trouble found him instead – in the face of patients who had abused their bodies or others. She'd ask him how he finds the patience to treat patients who abuse him with care and compassion. But he just saw them as people who life had dealt the shittiest of hands to. Trouble showed up in the words of intoxicated and overdosed men and women who lashed out at the people who were trying to save their lives and make them better. She hated to think of him taking that every day.

"Loch, are you OK?"

He sat down next to her, and Maggie noticed the dark circles under his eyes. His face looked overused for its age. He wasn't even forty yet, but she could tell he'd seen so much of life's cruelty already.

"Whatever you think you know about some people, Maggie, trust me – there's always more going on than you would ever want to hear."

From anyone else, those words would be deeply patronising, but not from Lochie. She knew he must have something to say that she needed to hear.

"What do you mean? Is there something you're not telling me about the McGills?"

Lochie's eyes followed hers as she tried to break his stare.

"Or is it the Andersons? Is there something you know about Mark's family? Do you think the old man is involved in his son's disappearance?"

Lochie's gaze drifted upwards to some point in the ceiling as Maggie watched him, waiting.

"I honestly don't know. But seeing you digging into something like this on your own just makes me – oh, Christ, I just know it won't end well. Please. Just give it up for now. Move on. Find another cause. At least until the police have done their bit, eh?"

She knew it was his best shot. Lochie didn't beg. But seeing that letter had spooked him. Even if it was an empty threat. He was too important to her to throw him into harm's way. Lochie was everything to her. If the threat behind that letter was real, she would never forgive herself if anything happened to him. Anyone could have taken a photo of him at work. It was like a circus in there most days of the week, but who would know her address? She had to give him something.

"OK, Lochie."

She watched a physical change wash over him from head to toe.

"Seriously? You'll find something else to chase for now?"

Maggie could only nod. She couldn't lie to him and – for all she wanted to say yes – she knew deep down she was in too deep to walk away yet. All she could do for now was change the subject.

"Think I might explore that therapy robot thingy by the way – you know. I need to do something to keep the bosses off my back."

Lochie's shoulders fell, and his body relaxed so slightly that only Maggie would notice.

"Oh, right? So, you're not going back to that woman

at the health clinic?" he asked, an undertone of hope in his voice.

"Nah, I think you're right. I like the idea of a machine judging me instead of someone I might bump into in the bread aisle at the Co-op."

The mood had lightened a little, but something was still hanging in the air between them. A heaviness that wouldn't be ignored.

13

THURSDAY P.M.

It was late when Maggie left Lochie's house. She unlocked her bike and took three long breaths. A hunched teenager walking past her turned around and looked at her with a perplexed face, giving her a wide berth. She must have been counting out loud again.

She pushed her headphones into her ears, clipped her helmet buckle and jumped on her bike, with just a cursory check for ongoing traffic before pushing down on her pedals.

Lochie was forever telling her not to listen to music when she was cycling. *Do you know how many accidents are caused that way? Cyclists not hearing electric cars coming up behind them?*

A wall of fatigue hit her as soon as she got home. Desperate to get through her rituals as fast as she could and get to bed, she took her outdoor clothes off, had a shower, and put a fresh pair of pyjamas on, before settling down on her own bed for a last check of her emails.

Something unwelcome was hovering close to the top of her inbox:

Subject: Urgent Meeting Request

Sender: Sharon McGrath

Dear Margaret,

It has been brought to my attention that you did not complete a recent psychological therapy assessment and have not responded to attempts to reschedule the appointment. I would like to remind you that attendance at this assessment is an agreed element of the process signed off by your manager following a recent incident of concern at work. I have notified Lexi Brodick that you have 2-3 working days to re-engage with the process of psychological assessment or we will be left with no option but to suspend you from work until a full medical assessment is carried out.

Maggie's gut turned at the mention of a suspension. Nothing would be worse for her mental health that being forced to stop working. She needed to get this woman back onside – and fast. Continuing her scan of emails, something further down her inbox caught her eye next:

Sender: NHS Fife Mental Health Services

Subject: Trial Invitation: Could AI Powered Mental Health Support Work For You?

Dear Ms Shields,

We are aware you recently failed to attend an in-person therapy session. We understand that accessing mental health support in a public place can present challenges for some patients.

> For this reason, we are currently seeking willing participants to trial a revolutionary new mental health programme…

Maggie read on, past the waffle, searching for key facts, like she did every day when wading through hundreds of press releases for something worthwhile. A loud, ranting voice was screaming at her to ignore the email. There had to be a better option. Engaging with some sort of fake therapy avatar was beyond ridiculous. There was no way she'd trust a machine to keep her darkest fears and secrets safe, not to mention fix her problems.

But another voice – quiet and manipulative – teased her with temptation. It nudged and prodded her in a place of curiosity. Somewhere the bully couldn't hear it. How would the bully square up to a non-human nemesis?

She'd carried the weight of her own heavy, sludgy thoughts around for so long now, they'd become a part of her. Here was the chance to offload them to a non-entity – a machine. To flush out her mental waste to someone (or something) that wouldn't judge. A jumble of algorithms would be used to put her thoughts in boxes and assess them. It sounded so clean and risk free. She hovered her phone over the QR code and clicked.

In a millisecond, she had a new screen open on her laptop. The image of a smartly dressed man with no cares in the world greeted her. Although his features were well proportioned, it seemed like someone had stitched his eyes onto his face, making them look flat and lifeless. He was the kind of man anyone would walk past in the street and never pick out of a line-up. Like an avatar created by a child or the kind of model that sold GAP jeans. They'd even stuck a pair of glasses on him – possibly as a shorthand for implied intelligence. He was waving at her but looking through her at the same time.

Thank you for signing up for our trial. My name is ANT. I'm your Artificial Neurology Therapist and I'm really looking forwards to getting to know you.

Eh, you what? Signing up? Did I?

His accent sat somewhere between Peter Capaldi and Ewan McGregor. Undeniably Scottish, but not too rough or raw. She found a mute button on the screen and his words immediately transferred to subtitles in front of her.

Feel free to change my gender, age, ethnic origin or appearance by clicking on the different areas of my body.

I thought I was clicking on a link to find out more? Shit, where's the back button? Cancel?

As Maggie started punching buttons on her keyboard and mouse, 'ANT' whirred impatiently on her screen. Then he appeared again in the top right corner of the screen, pointing to a digital form that sat below him.

OK, great. Looks like we're ready to move forwards with our first session. Are you happy for me to take some basic details before we get started?

What? No? Absolutely chuffing not. Go away!

Maggie felt like she was on some hideous first date that was moving way too fast. She stood up from her bed, slamming her finger on the power down button of her laptop. Just as her machine asked if she was 'sure she wanted to shut down without saving open file', she caught sight of a cloth on the kitchen worktop and saw the red raw sores on her hands from years of strong bleach. It was a reminder of the bully she had to escape. Falling back onto her duvet, she felt trapped by her own desperation.

Would it hurt to see how ridiculous this thing really is?

Maybe she could make a story of this – dress it up as a 'ditch the fake tech' piece or an exposé on how to avoid becoming an AI guinea pig.

Her finger landed on the auto-fill option, and in an instant, it delivered her basic details into ANT's greedy clutches.

14

FRIDAY A.M.

Mark Anderson had been officially missing for four days. With each step closer to the truth of Mark's last known movements, many more questions came too.

What was Pete McGill arguing with Mark Anderson about just before he vanished? And what the hell is my brother not telling me?

Maggie separated life into two sides. There was the world she worked in: uncontrollable, misguided, full of injustice and mystery, and it was her job to make sense of it. Then the other side: her shelter. Her perfectly curated home life – the calm sea. Everything was in order around her there. But it felt as if the waves were swelling beneath her.

"Maggie? Earth to Maggie!"

Harris's intense voice pulled her back into the room. He was running his hands through a generous mop of dark brown hair as he approached his adjoining desk. Arriving even later than her, but looking much less concerned about it, he presented her with a bottle of caffeine-free

Diet Coke. Right in front of her keyboard, with a flourish of pride. Maggie broke into a smile at the sight of this chilled bottle of joy.

"You like your drinks cold, Shields?"

She was sure she saw something resembling a wink in his eye but ignored it and clung to her own social awkwardness.

"Eh, thanks."

"Welcome. You got anything chunky to keep the boss off your back this morning?"

She wasn't ready to share what Pete McGill had told her about Ryan Ross – or Archie McGill, as she now knows him to have been. But she'd been AWOL for too long and needed to offer something.

"Val Anderson reckons her daughters are being followed."

Harris's eyes widened to saucers.

"Eck. That's not good. And she wants that written about in the paper – a bit odd, isn't it?"

Maggie thought back to their agreement.

"Probably not, no. But she still wants me to help her figure out who's doing it."

"You turning a wee side hustle as a PI now? Better paid, to be fair."

"Not exactly. But the thing is… I need Lexi to know there's more substance to this story than a few cheap headlines. There's other stuff going on that I can't tell anyone about yet, but I need the time and space to dig around more – with the McGill family, for a start. And…"

Harris seemed to be genuinely listening for once.

"There's more?"

"It's just. I've got a name from Val of a bloke who was in business with Ranald a while back. It ended badly apparently. But he's come back out of the woodwork recently."

"And this relates to Mark, how? You don't think Mark's old man is involved in his son's disappearance, do you? The man's just been on STV posting a twenty thousand pound reward for help to find him. Could be a mighty decent bluff, though, to be fair."

"Aye, I know. But I've just got a feeling all this links up somehow. I just need to find out how."

Harris pulled his fingers through his messy hair again with greater force. It looked like he was trying to warm up his brain. Maggie opened a clean document and began to write. With a fair wind behind her, she'd get something sent over before Lexi came looking.

Missing Rugby Ace's Wife's New Fears For Daughters

Fife Standard exclusive, by Maggie Shields

Valerie Anderson, the wife of missing Fife rugby star Mark Anderson, has expressed fears about the safety of their two daughters as police investigation continues.

Mrs Anderson has spoken of her concerns that the daughters she shares with Mark are being targeted by unknown individuals as mystery mounts surrounding the search for her husband – now in its fourth day.

"I'm worried someone is following my daughters. I don't know who or why, but I'm putting my faith in the police and local community during this difficult time for our whole family."

Mrs Anderson was speaking exclusively to our reporter, Maggie Shields, from her Fife home.

Her concerns come as Police Scotland refuses to be drawn on any further lines of inquiry regarding their search for Mr Anderson, who was last seen in a local bar on Sunday afternoon.

Local man Mr Peter McGill, who was identified as the last person to see Mark before his disappearance, has been helping Police Scotland with their inquiries. No arrests have been made.

Follow Maggie Shields online via Twitter @NewshunterShields

15

FRIDAY EARLY P.M.

Olivia Anderson was seventeen – five years older than Maggie when she lost her mum. Maggie wondered if seventeen was a better age to lose a parent suddenly. Would plenty of money or a few more years of life protect you from the miserable pain or the feeling of being robbed?

Cycling out from the underground newspaper office car park, she tried to focus on the job in hand. The Anderson girls were due out of school at lunchtime. St. Mary's School for Girls was a grand-looking building sitting just outside Kirkcaldy. On the way, she passed her own high school – slap-bang in the town's heart. It had some patchy playing fields that were maintained well enough by the local council to remain playable – with the usual scattering of litter and dog shit. Vandals quickly covered the school's sixties-style concrete walls with fresh graffiti after each new paint job. Olivia and Becky Anderson's school struck a very different tone.

Arriving at St Mary's, Maggie saw that the building

itself was every inch the imposing Gothic fortress. Vast grounds benefitted from the type of landscape gardening Maggie's mum watched on TV programmes about royal palaces and antiques.

She locked her bike outside the black-and-gold-painted school railings and found the nearest bus shelter to hover under, trying to blend into the surroundings. Waiting for the girls to come out, she contemplated her options back at work. The news piece she sent through earlier held the boss off temporarily, but she'd need to work hard to convince Lexi that the Anderson story was worth pursuing, faced with a police blackout. She'd also have to think of a smokescreen to give her brother when he asked if she was keeping her promise to stay away from danger.

A large metallic-grey Audi pulled up opposite the main school gates. It stood out for a few reasons. It couldn't be normal to arrive half an hour before your children got out of school – especially if you're paying for every hour they're in there. Parents were forever moaning about not having enough time in the day to do anything. *Every minute's a prisoner before the kids come out of school*, they'd say. The car driver also had an arrogant disregard for the double yellow lines. Why would you need to park illegally, when you're early enough to take your pick of the spaces further down the road? Something didn't add up. This had to be the people Val was worried about. But who were they, and why were they following Olivia and Becky Anderson?

She lifted her head to look inside the car, but the windows were all tinted a dark-grey colour.

The heavens opened at the same time as the school doors

and a sea of smartly dressed girls with identical hair styles spilt out into the rain. They lifted their blazers over their heads to protect various shades of long, flowy hair. Maggie recognised the heavy blazers from the photos in Val's kitchen.

The Audi's headlights came on, and the windscreen wipers began working at top speed. Olivia appeared first. Deep in conversation with a small group of friends who peeled off as they came out of the gates. She observed the younger children being transferred from their teacher to a waiting parent within the school grounds, but the older girls left the building on their own. Were older girls less likely to be picked up by someone who meant them harm?

Olivia hovered outside the gate when she saw her sister approaching. They exchanged a few words, then huddled under a golf umbrella before breaking into a sprint in Maggie's direction.

Oh, crap.

Bolting from her vantage point, the full force of the driving rain hit as she tried to cross the road. By the time she'd weaved her way through the Volvo estates and Teslas jamming together, the Audi was moving off with a purpose. Slow enough not to draw attention, but certainly not hanging around. Searching for her camera with wet hands, Maggie pointed it at the licence plate, zoomed in and pressed her shaking fingers on the button. Becky was now boarding the bus behind her sister. With the briefest of side-eye glances, she caught Maggie's gaze head on.

Despite it being an amateur attempt at counter surveillance, she firmly believed that the girls and their mother were not paranoid. Someone in that car was watching them and didn't want anyone to know they were there. Once again, Maggie had uncovered another layer in a story she wasn't supposed to be chasing, but there was one person she knew could help her find the answers she promised Val Anderson.

*

Lewis Kovachev, or Tetchy as Maggie called him, was more comfortable around IT than people. But he seemed to make an exception for Maggie. His parents moved to the UK from Russia just before he was born, giving him a rare and exotic surname in Fife. Maggie, the awkward, shy girl in the class, stumbled towards him in a friendship. He worked for AeroTech – an international aerospace technology company whose Scottish headquarters were next door to the *Fife Standard*. Their location made no sense to the people of Fife. Until Amazon erected a major distribution depot in the neighbouring Fife town of Dunfermline. That's when folk realised space and proximity to Scotland's central belt of human resources without paying city rates had a certain appeal.

Picking up the phone to Tetchy, she read out the number plate of the Audi from outside the school to him. He said he'd get back to her in a couple of hours – *the best he could do* – and she tried to sound more grateful than impatient. Her attentions turned to the other key player in this unfolding story. It was time to introduce herself to Ranald Anderson, but even Maggie knew this would be harder than getting through Val's front door.

*

Val Anderson had warned her that Ranald's country pile was hidden in the back of Anstruther – another lively harbour village tucked away up the Fife coast a bit. The house was safely hidden from passing mischief, but impossible to ignore once you found it. That's just what he wanted, she said. Forced to ditch her bike for a work car to make the journey, Maggie's sat nav told her she'd reached her destination. Apparently, she had 'arrived' at Lowercroft House, KY10. In reality, she was halfway down a B road in West Fife with nothing but fields to the left and a choppy coast to her right.

After parking in a layby, she scoured the nearby country roads for anything that looked promising. Following her nose down the next road, she reached a signpost with the words 'Lowercroft – ½ mile' etched in black on a mottled white background.

She looked towards an expanse of land dominated by a heavy-looking forest and considered sending a location pin to Lochie, just to be safe. But didn't. He'd bombard her with questions she couldn't deal with. Maggie drove on, weaving around the narrow, potholed country road, flanked on either side by banks of tall fir trees. Another wood surrounded her, and she felt the bully closing in.

Count the trees. Get to this bend before your clock turns to four ten. Do it now, or things will end badly.

A sickness ran through her gut and tightened her breathing. Why would Ranald Anderson live so off-grid?

Eventually, the trees gave way to a large metal gate.

She pulled up next to it, opening the window of her Ford Fiesta as close to the intercom as possible.

Not for a second did Maggie expect to be welcomed into this man's home, unannounced, with open arms. But she had a plan. Maggie Shields always had a plan. A crackling noise came first, then a female voice through the intercom. Soft and polished but laced with an air of nervousness.

"Can I help you?"

"Um, hi. Yes. I'm here to see Mr Ranald Anderson."

"And you are?"

"My name's Maggie Shields. I'm responding to Mr Anderson's appeal for information about his son Mark's whereabouts."

A long silence fell between them. It was a bold move, but Maggie was used to having this effect on people.

"He's not here right now. You'll have to come back another time."

Her voice sounded frail now. This had to be his wife. Not exactly the bullseye, but still worth a friendly chat.

"But the thing is. I'm not local. I need to speak to your family in person whilst I'm here."

"You should have called the number provided."

Think like your audience, Maggie. Work for it.

"I know. It's just, I'm guessing, that's a police line? And, the thing is… I don't trust them. The cops I mean."

This was a line that seemed to land well with the Anderson family, so she tried it out for size. A camera above the intercom caught her eye, and she treated it to her most innocent smile. Inspired by ANT's *you can trust me* head tilt.

Another silent pause. It was make or break time.

The gate pulled back, revealing a grand drive. There were flower buds appearing in clumps around the large stones to each side. A handful of cameras were nestled at various points on the approach to the house. She reminded herself this was the East Neuk of Fife, not downtown L.A. The house was exactly how she expected. A few levels below *Downton Abbey* but with more of a *Real Housewives of Cheshire* vibe, judging from the cars outside and the modern embellishments to the exterior. A woman who looked about seventy-something stood outside the front door. She was wearing a long, woollen poncho with a fur trim, and an expression which fused disdain and hope.

"Follow me."

Maggie was no stranger to hostility, but this seemed especially cold.

"I'm his wife, Sue. He's in the hunting shed – I'll take you there."

The words tripped from her lips as if they were perfectly normal.

Hunting shed? Where the hell am I?

Maggie tried to concentrate on putting one foot in front of the other. She pulled out her mobile phone but noticed there was no signal.

"You better not be another gold-digging fantasist. Mark was… is my only son."

A lump of guilt rose in Maggie's throat. She was going to have to confess the truth, but she'd wait until Ranald was in front of her, too. Before she was escorted off the premises, she needed to lay eyes on this man. To see him in the flesh and get her own measure for what he was capable of.

"Bad things follow him around, you see."

"Sorry?"

"Mark. I think he was in serious trouble – before he went missing, I mean. He told me he needed to go away for a bit, but didn't know when he'd be back. Has someone hurt him?"

Sue was walking at a snail's pace, but, as they turned a corner on the gravel path to the side of the main house, Maggie clocked their destination. Tucked away to the side of a large triple garage was a log cabin with enormous antlers hanging over the entrance.

"I don't… I don't know whether he's been hurt. That's not what I'm here to tell you."

Relief flooded the woman's ageing face, and Maggie's heart broke a little.

"He adores his girls, you know. Kept telling them how much he loved them just days before he up and left. It's been a while since he spoke like that to them and, well, you can imagine what those poor girls are thinking now.

"Anyway, that's where you'll find Ranald – in there."

She pointed to the cabin and by the time Maggie turned to ask why she wasn't joining them, Sue was shuffling down the path, her poncho blowing gently in the wind.

"Mrs Anderson?"

There was no answer.

The counting began in Maggie's head before she could stop it.

Breathe in, count to three, breathe out. And again. Tap your forehead three times. Everything will be fine. You're safe.

She knocked on the wooden door, softly at first, then again with more force. Again, nothing. She turned the metal door handle and pushed open the solid wooden door. Rusting metal hinges squeaked as she entered. A sickening horror hit her senses immediately. The place smelt of death. Like the butcher her mum used to take her to as a child. The sickly smell of dried blood and the sweet rotting of animal flesh. Pheasants and other smaller birds hung from large metal hooks on the walls, interspersed with antlers of varying sizes. This was a world that Maggie never wanted to understand. But there was no going back now. She heard a faint but unmistakable noise from behind an internal door. It was the sound of knives being sharpened. The door was ajar. She couldn't see his face but saw the shining blade of the knife he was holding – the sight of her own eyes reflected in the metal. Something about the knife felt more familiar than shocking. It made no sense. Was the bully messing with her again?

She cleared her throat and tried to make a noise of her own.

"Hello?"

Nothing. She eased closer and pushed at the second door.

"Hello? Is someone there?"

The sound of blade against blade stopped. And so did Maggie's breathing. Just for a moment. Until she saw him. He pulled the headphones down from his ears to rest around his neck as he opened the door with large, dirty hands. He looked every inch the country squire. Head to toe in the uniform of the landed gentry. He was tall and broad, with a gut that pushed the padding of his tweed gilet out around his middle. The cap on his head had small smears of dried blood. His presence rooted Maggie to the spot.

"Do I know you?"

The voice didn't match the outfit. It was a deep and well-established local Fife accent. Not a hint of a private school upbringing in it. But there was no doubt – this was the man who stood side-by-side in photos with Mark. His son had been missing for two weeks and he was here, plucking feathers from something that used to enjoy the freedom of the skies.

Find your voice, Maggie. Don't be intimidated.

"No. Sorry. Your wife let me in. My name is Maggie. I'm..."

"I've been warned. You've got information about my son, I'm told?"

It was confession time. She stole another glance at her phone – still no signal.

Shit.

"I don't know where he is. Sorry. I lied."

As the words landed in the sickly air between them, Maggie noticed his bloodshot eyes baring down on her like a laser.

"Is that a fact?"

This man's presence dwarfed her in every way. He walked towards her, and Maggie felt her muscles tighten, readying for something. Then he leant forward, pulled out a wooden chair, and indicated for her to sit down.

"Then what are you doing on my property?"

She tentatively perched on the edge of the wood.

"I'm not here for the reward, if that's what you're thinking? I'm a journalist. I want to help with the hunt for your son. Bring it some more attention by writing about it. That's all."

He sat down opposite her and looked her up and down.

"Well, Maggie. Did your parents not teach you it was evil to lie?"

"Sorry, but people don't tend to trust journalists."

"Oh, really. Now, why on earth would that be the case?"

"Sometimes it's easier to bend the truth until people trust us. We're not all bad though."

He continued to look at her, his face giving nothing away, and she felt emboldened.

"You're no stranger to the press, are you, Mr Anderson?"

A sinister laugh escaped from one side of his face. The other side remained frozen. She wondered if he'd had a stroke.

"So how do you think you can help us, Maggie…?"

"Shields, Maggie Shields, from the *Fife Standard*."

"Ah, *that* paper, no less. How is the ever-so-slightly feral Lexi Brodick?"

His eyes seemed to glisten a little as he mentioned the boss's name. There was a good chance Lexi was leaving her a ranting phone message right now.

"She's fine, thanks. I wondered if you wanted to make a more personal and direct appeal to the public? You must be desperately worried about your son by now."

"Oh, well, isn't that very full hearted of you, Maggie? And don't get me wrong. I am very grateful for the opportunity you are generously presenting me with. But do you know what I've learnt about this community?"

Maggie shook her head silently. Looking over his shoulder, she caught sight of a collection of plastic pill bottles lined up on a shelf. There must have been at least fifteen bottles.

"Money talks, Maggie Shields. Money talks. As tempting as it is to send you back to that wily editor of yours with a tidy little exclusive, I think dragging folk out of hiding by dangling cold hard cash their way has more potential. In fact, just having this little chat with you makes me think I should raise the reward a little. How does fifty K sound? Might loosen the tongues a bit more, don't you think?"

"Um, I..."

Maggie wanted to say that would cause a fresh wave of nutters knocking on the door of his hunting shed, but thought better of it. He didn't look like a man who would take advice from a twenty-something he'd just met. Her eyes drifted again around the shed and connected with the handle of the knife he had been holding earlier. A distinctive marbling detail on the handle struck her as very elaborate for gutting a pheasant.

"Great plan, Mr Anderson. I'm sure you just want to do whatever you can to bring your son home safe and well to your grandchildren."

Ranald's breathing seemed to hasten at the mention of the girls. He stood up with an effort, leaning his substantial frame on the back of the chair.

"Have you ever been hunting, Maggie Shields?"

"No. Not my thing, sir."

"You should try it sometime. It's much more about using your brain than your weapons. So much more."

As the words stumbled from his half-frozen mouth, an urgent need to get as far away from this man as she could overtook Maggie.

16

FRIDAY P.M.

The rest of her evening lay ahead of her. Space and time intimidated Maggie. She lived in fear of empty hours and quiet time alone. The bully was nocturnal. It would tell her to find something to clean or something to dwell on until it burrowed further and further into her skull. She would try to outrun him, but he always caught up with her, reminding her that something dark was waiting around the corner unless she got busy with his demands. The images of Ranald Anderson's hunting shed were sitting just behind her eyelids, waiting for her every time she closed her eyes. But when she opened them, she jumped back to thoughts of Archie McGill, or Ryan Ross, or whoever the hell he was. Did he really deserve to die that way? And the face of his killer. Why is it coming back into her dreams now? Has something or someone caused the image to resurface?

She kept coming back to one unavoidable horror. Whatever Archie Ross did wrong, it was her fault that the killer got away with it. *It will all catch up with you soon, Maggie.*

Tonight, she wanted to go to war with herself. She wouldn't give in to the desperate, clinging compulsions. She would be better than him tonight – the bully that thinks he knows better.

She reached for her laptop. Hunting around on her desktop for the therapy app, she clicked on it and waited for something to happen.

Within seconds, a smaller version of the man she had 'met' before filled her screen. He'd changed his outfit – swapping the GAP look for leisure wear. She feared he was going to force her into some group exercise for distraction. That's the kind of shit these things are likely to pull, she thought. *Oh, please don't tell me he's sponsored by Nike or something.*

His Capaldi/McGregor blend was still too much to listen to, so she muted him and opted for subtitles again.

Hi Maggie. Do you have time to record your thoughts today? I'd like to hear them.

Eh…?

She stared at the screen whilst trying to plan a response. Did she launch straight in with the image of Ranald Anderson's shed of death, or was that likely to trigger some red alert? Too much for a first date, perhaps? She'd test him – warm him up first with something else. As she thought, words kept appearing across her screen.

Did you know that AI-powered mental health platforms like mine offer complete anonymity, allowing you to discuss your issues without fear of judgement?

He's clearly not one for granting much response time. He's already on to 'my issues'.

She began to type.

I'm heading out and about soon. Can't really do this now...

Three dots appeared on the screen for what felt like a millisecond.

[...] That's OK but please remember that exercise stimulates neurogenesis – the creation of new neurons in the hippocampus, positively influencing memory and learning. So, any work we did whilst you were out and about would be well worth your time.

Christ. You're keen.

Weird couple of days. Anxiety triggered by contact with a stranger near a park bench the other day too.

[...]

I'm sorry to hear you have been anxious. I'm here to help you. Can you tell me more about how that contact made you feel?

Oh, what the hell. This is not... a... real... person.

Scared they were a junkie and that I've been contaminated.

Maggie sniggered to herself, thinking that if this was an online dating app, ANT would run a mile by now.

Please clarify the term 'Junkie'?

Drug addict.

Ah, you mean a substance abuser. I understand.

He just kept asking questions that didn't feel judgemental. His face on the screen remained earnest – his head tipped ever so slightly to one side as he 'listened'. Maggie had seen Lochie doing this when he was speaking to patients. He called it 'active listening'.

ANT made a series of suggestions on how to reason with her own mind – to challenge it – that were oddly simple and reasonable.

I need to go now.

OK, Maggie. Thanks for checking in. Please congratulate yourself on overcoming your anxious response to the man near the park bench and making it to your destination. Minor victories must not be overlooked.

Lifted slightly by the encouragement, she hunted for her door keys. As she moved her finger over the log off button on-screen, a thought crept back into her brain, like an animal returning to the safety of its lair.

Maggie was almost certain she didn't mention to ANT that the stranger was a man. Does he just know these things somehow? That's a bit creepy. *Or is that me being paranoid – again.*

She felt like playing with him a bit more. Stretching his legs, so to speak. There was a question she'd never dream of asking a real person. But now was her chance.

How do I know if I'm paranoid?

The three black dots hovered below her question for about a second.

It's very common for many people to feel 'paranoid'. Paranoid thoughts can sometimes just be exaggerated suspicions. For example, being talked about behind your back, the risk of being physically harmed…

He continued running through a list of the many ways that paranoia can present itself and, for a fleeting moment, Maggie felt a sense of company in her own misfiring brain.

Does that mean I've got major mental health issues?

ANT was motionless for a moment. Was she being redirected to some emergency response hotline? But then his face tilt returned, and Maggie watched his lips moving on the screen, imagining the exaggerated West coast rolling of his 'R's on the muted screen.

In some more severe cases of clinical paranoia or persecutory delusions, paranoid thoughts can be a symptom of paranoid schizophrenia or delusional disorder. I can tell you more about this if you want to explore it further?

Do I? No, no, I don't. That's not me. That's different. I think. My weird stuff is about repetition, rituals, tidiness. Isn't it? Or maybe this is me too?

Maggie was back in the therapist's chair, a stranger walking in on her innermost thoughts. It was too much.

I have to go. I'm busy.

Sorry to hear that. I think it's important we explore this in greater detail. Are you going somewhere that cannot be rescheduled?

None of your chuffing business, nosey!

It's what she wanted to say. But didn't. Her mobile was ringing and Tetchy's number flashed up on the screen, so she slammed her laptop screen shut.

"Hi Tetch. You got something for me?"

Maggie could hear a nervous undertone in Tetchy's voice, which was out of character. "Yep. But I'm worried about where you're going with this."

"Come on… Tetch, I need this right now."

"OK, have it your way. The car plate you gave me came up as totally untraceable at first."

"Right? At first?"

"Yes, which usually means one of several things – most of which I won't bore you with, but I checked out some more hidden avenues and eventually hit the right target."

"Uh-huh?"

"That plate is registered on the database of current police-operated vehicles."

"It's a copper's car?"

"Not just that, Maggie, it's a senior copper's car. A model only allocated to ranks from inspector upwards. Can't give you a name, but safe to say it's not a uniformed PC."

She tried to catch up with what she was hearing.

"Maggie? You still there?"

"Aye, sorry, Tetch. Eh, thanks for that. Owe you one."

"You owe me more than one, Maggie. But go easy here, will you? You don't want to get on the wrong side of the top ranks this early in your career, surely?"

Maggie thanked him again and hung up. She'd found something better to replace thoughts of Ranald Anderson's home or debates with a computer about whether she was paranoid.

Dialling the police media office number from her mobile, the call rang out before being diverted to answering service.

"Hello. This is the Police Scotland media relations team. Our office hours are eight a.m. to six p.m., Monday to Saturday. Please call back during these hours."

Bollocks.

Glancing at the clock on her kitchen table, her heart sank. She'd have to wait until tomorrow. It was 11:15 p.m.

She left a message asking for someone to call her urgently in relation to concerns that had been raised about Olivia and Becky Anderson. She would be at her desk first thing tomorrow morning. Waiting…

17

FRIDAY A.M.

"You've got the police waiting for you in Lexi's office, Shields."

Harris was quick with his warning as soon as she made it back to work. Maggie suspected it had to be something heavy for the senior cops to make an in-person visit this close to the weekend.

"For me?"

He nodded slowly and theatrically. Harris was a permanent feature on the weekend staff, being a sports hack.

"What've you done this time? Must be bad if they need to come down and read you your rights in person."

She looked over and saw the backs of two heads in Lexi's office – one male and one female. They didn't look familiar.

"Been with her long?"

"Aye, long enough to talk about you plenty, I reckon."

"Thanks, Harris."

Lexi was speaking to the male. Her expression was hard to

judge from a distance; it was somewhere between a grimace and a flirt. Her attention shifted, and she caught Maggie's eye.

A sharp gesticulation summoned Maggie to join them.

"Hope you've got your big girl pants on today."

She ignored the comment and made for Lexi's office, remembering Tetchy's revelations about the car that was watching the Anderson girls. Should she confront this pair about it right there, in front of the boss? It would be a gutsy move, but fraught with danger. There's nothing Lexi hated more than hearing a juicy nugget at the same time as others, rather than before.

The male cop looked well into his later years of service and greeted her with a warm smile. Here was a man who had kept himself in good nick, Maggie thought. In his fifties at a guess, he still had the build of an athlete. His colleague, a woman, who was around forty at a guess, had her hair tied back in a tight bun, revealing a solid line of grey roots around her forehead. Her facial expression barely moved when Maggie looked at her. Lexi sat opposite them both, doing a poor job of hiding her discomfort.

"Nice of you to join us, Maggie. May I introduce you to Detective Inspector Julie Clarkson and Detective Seargent Lorne Symington? They've taken time out of their *very busy* day to come and chat to us about Mark Anderson."

There was a hint of sarcasm in Lexi's tone. The man stood up and offered Maggie a firm handshake, but his senior colleague didn't budge.

"Um… hi. Maggie Shields."

Maggie leant across the table, offering them a weak handshake.

Symington eked out a decent smile, but Clarkson nodded without making eye contact.

"Our visitors have some concerns in relation to your reporting of Mark Anderson's disappearance."

Maggie leant against the glass wall, her arms tightly crossed in defence. She read Lexi's face, trying to guess if she had her back on this. So far, it was hard to tell.

"OK. Can someone maybe explain the concerns to me, then?"

Her own hands were shaking, so she gripped them together tightly behind her back.

"DI Clarkson feels that your reporting of the situation may be detrimental to their work within the community. Have I got that right?"

"Yes, that's about the size of it."

Maggie stood, quietly simmering, and waiting for Lexi to leap to her defence. *Have yer back in public but do yer legs in private* – that was her modus operandi. Always had been. But nothing came except a silence, and three sets of eyes looking in Maggie's direction.

"Sure. Here's me thinking I'm just doing my job," she said.

It took all of Maggie's self-control not to share exactly what she knew about the Anderson family and the McGills. But, for now, it felt better to keep it to herself. Wait and see what hand they were going to play first.

"And we are trying to do ours. But we need to keep the local community on our side. So, it would be helpful it you could restrict your reporting to the statements we provide as and when we provide them and leave the Anderson family alone."

Maggie dug deep and bit her tongue. DS Symington forced a cough into the stilted air and waited for his colleague to lean back in her chair.

"I'm sure we all want to support the Anderson family as best we can."

His monotone eased the tension a little.

"I think what we're trying to say is that this could be best achieved if we work together."

Maggie was irritated now. She thought of all the times she never got a call back from their press office and had to use the default 'no one was available to comment' at the end of her story.

"Couldn't agree more. You might want to tell your press office that, though."

Another death stare from Clarkson met Maggie straight on.

"Are you suggesting our media team is being obstructive?"

"Well, it seems mighty odd that there hasn't been a peep out of them since Peter McGill was questioned and released. Should we assume he is of no further interest to you?"

Maggie caught Lexi's stare. This was not the face of a woman who had her back. What the hell was going on here?

"I am sure they have good reason for any information that is or is not shared with the media. You should know that by now," Lexi said, sounding like a stranger reading from a script. It occurred to Maggie that she'd have to stand up for herself.

"I tried to call your media team yesterday, actually."

Clarkson and Symington widened their eyes in response to Maggie and shot each other a look.

"Yes, we understand you left an urgent message at eleven fifteen p.m. last night. Is that the one you meant? I'm sure you know we only operate an out of hours media service over the weekend?"

Maggie felt secretly impressed by how quickly her message circulated internally. Someone or something appeared to be moving quickly in the background.

"Well, in the spirit of working together, I guess I could just ask you two directly – whilst you're here and all that."

Lexi's face took on a nervous pallor. What was wrong with her today?

"So, the thing is. I wondered if there was any reason a police officer... sorry, correction, why a senior police officer's unmarked car would hang around Olivia and Rebecca Anderson's school – two days in a row?"

No one in the room spoke. They just took turns staring at each other before Clarkson took control again.

"What gives you reason to believe this is the case?"

"I'm confident of my source."

She got that look again. The one that said, *I'm sure you are, lass.*

"Well, that's certainly not anything we can comment on."

Maggie watched both detectives with an intensity, searching for any giveaways that they were hiding answers or, worse, didn't have answers to hide.

"I'm happy to call the press office again today, if you'd

prefer? Should I tell them you couldn't help when we met – here? Today."

Maggie caught Lexi's reaction out of the corner of her eye. She continued to look awkward, lifting the glasses from her face before she spoke.

Perhaps there were just too many alpha females in one room, but Maggie didn't feel like capitulating yet.

"Maggie, I'm sure you will hear back from their press lot on that later."

Another unexpected intervention from Lexi threw her for a loop. Lexi enjoyed being bossed about even less than Maggie.

"Just as I'm sure you will appreciate having more regular discussions with them from now on, yes?"

For Christ's sake. Where has this woman's loyalty gone? Maggie made a mental note to start a rumour that Lexi was jumping ship to the police press office.

"Nothing I'd love more, boss."

"Great, well unless there's anything else, I'd say we're done here?"

Everyone rose to their feet in unison and made their way to the door. Maggie kept her head down, forcing the rage back down into the pit of her stomach. She'd process it later. She watched Lexi walk them to the lift, all fake smiles and warm hand gestures. But something made her hover slightly before leaving the boss's office. Maggie was almost never in this room without Lexi there, too. She took in the view of the surrounding press pack, heads down like lemmings, and wondered what it felt like to sit in Lexi's chair. What would it really be like to hold the casting vote on every word that makes it to print and who gets to have their byline on the front page? The distinctive sound of an on-screen notification pinged in her ear, drawing her eyes to Lexi's screen. Checking that there was no sign of the boss returning, she walked around to the other side of the desk and shook the mouse a bit to wake up her monitor screen. A new email sitting at the top of her inbox. The subject heading jumped out at her immediately.

From: COPFS@gov.co.uk
Subject: Strictly Private and Confidential: Anderson MISSPER

Reading the words in front of her made her insides swirl with something between excitement and fear. The Crown Office and Procurator Fiscal Service, or COPFS, was one of the first acronyms she learnt on the job. Whenever those guys were involved, it was the real deal. Someone further up the chain must be getting involved in Mark Anderson's disappearance. But why were they emailing Lexi about it? She thought about opening the email but wasn't ready to cross that line. And there was no need. Lexi would share it with her – whatever it was. Just as soon as she got Clarkson and Symington safely out of the building.

Maggie's excitement grew stronger. She knew this case had long roots under the surface. Her first instinct was right, and whatever was on that email from the Fiscal would vindicate her to Lexi. This feeling reminded her why she had to do this job, and no other, for as long as she could.

Hearing the sound of the door to the lifts squeaking back open, Lexi shot back to where she'd been before, waiting for the boss to return.

"What are you doing still hovering around here? Have you not got someone to interview, or do you need me to send you out with the work experience lad somewhere?"

Lexi pulled the seat out on her side of the desk and sat down, muttering something about being left alone and looking directly at her screen. She'd have seen it by now. Whatever it was that the high heid yins had to say about Mark Anderson. But it became blindingly obvious she wasn't going to share it with Maggie now.

"Seriously, Shields. Are you planning on moving in here or what?"

Maggie's throat filled with the start of so many words, but none of them made it out fully formed.

Wandering back to her own desk, tail between her legs, it took all her powers of persuasion to convince herself that Lexi just needed to read her emails in peace. Then she'd share the important stuff with Maggie. It would feel good when the boss admitted she was wrong about Mark Anderson's disappearance losing momentum. It was blindingly obvious that just the opposite was the case.

18

SATURDAY A.M.

Maggie knew she had to confront Lochie with what she'd learnt from Pete. She had to talk to him about what she'd seen with her own eyes in that diary and the photos. The image of her brother with his arms around both McGill brothers was haunting her. If Lochie knew that Ryan Ross and Pete's brother Archie were the same person, why would he not have told her that? He'd never even mentioned that Pete McGill had a brother – that couldn't have been an oversight. If Lochie knew that the man who was responsible for their mum's death years ago had a brother walking the streets of Kirkcaldy every day, how the hell had he never mentioned this to her? Was it some bizarre attempt to stop her from pursuing him for his side of the story?

But that couldn't be right. Not when she thought of how Lochie talked about needing closure for their mum. When he found out the woods murder victim was the same man police wanted for causing death by dangerous driving, he felt a guilt-free comfort. Lochie said it brought him a sense of peace to know that, however brutal Ryan Ross's death was, that man couldn't get back behind the wheel and do the same to any other family. Maggie understood what he meant by closure. So she played her part by keeping quiet every time there was a renewed appeal for witnesses to the murder. That was the least she could do for Lochie.

He doesn't deserve your help – and it can't help him from the grave, anyway.

She often thought about his family, though. But told herself she was doing them more of a favour by not speaking up. She – the girl who lost her mother – would just remind them of their son's evil rather than bringing them to justice. And so, with every passing year, it became a little easier to erase what she saw from her mind.

But now what? If she confronted Lochie about everything Pete McGill had said, would it open the most painful of old wounds? And for what? Just so that she could get her big scoop?

And then there was the link between Ranald Anderson and Ryan Ross/Archie to consider. Was it wise to share this with Lochie? He was already desperate to get her off the Anderson story after she got that creepy letter. Sharing this latest disturbing layer would hardly get him back onside. Could it even have been Ranald Anderson that got hold of photos of Lochie and sent that shitty note warning her to back off? It had a sniff of old-school intimidation about it that felt like a fit with his generation. But that made no sense either. Why would the man not want to find his missing son, even if it meant letting a nosey reporter sniff around their business? He'd just posted a

£20K reward for information leading to his whereabouts. Surely, he'd be happy for a nosey reporter like her to go sniffing around for answers if he was getting none from the official channels so far?

An aura of stillness had descended on the open-plan office. Most of the noisy editorial team were out on jobs, leaving just a few quiet workers with their heads down. A spattering of subeditors stared into their large screens – blue glare reflecting off their glasses and vitamin-starved faces. There was a faint buzzing sound coming from the ageing vending machine near the door to the stairs. Maggie noticed Lexi was still working in her office.

Her messy blonde bun sprang into view from between her office blinds and then her head appeared around the door, and Maggie's thoughts jumped back to the message from COPFS.

"Shields? Do you not prefer to work from home at the weekend?"

Her voice carried through the air, unchallenged by the usual noise.

"My home Wi-Fi's been playing up again, so just thought I'd get my head down on some stuff whilst it was quiet."

"Good grief, your commitment is almost tragic."

"Just trying to make headway on the Anderson piece. Reckon we got one over on the cops yesterday? Don't think they expected the question about the covert cop car outside the girls' school?"

Lexi was heading towards her now.

"You think?"

There was a sarcasm in her voice and Maggie wondered if she'd been on the G&Ts she kept in her cupboard for tough days at the coal face.

"Don't you, boss?"

"Just remember, Maggie, you won't be the first ambitious hack to cross their paths. That pair have been around the block a few times between them."

Lexi's words seemed cryptic. Maggie's desperation got the better of her.

The Fiscal, Lexi. Tell me what was in that email from COPFS.

"Don't suppose you've had any other related leads come into you that might steer me a bit?"

Lexi was pacing around the room. She'd taken her heels off and it changed her whole appearance. She was flat-footed and cumbersome. An unsettled look took hold of her face.

"I mean. I know it's my story, but just, sometimes things come in through your desk by mistake," Maggie continued.

"By mistake? To the editor? That's never a mistake, lass."

"I just meant, if it's stuff that you can share with the team..."

"No, Maggie. Nothing has come to me. I think this one is getting a bit, you know, old."

Swallowing down a lump in her throat, Maggie tried to compose herself. She was determined to stand her ground.

"I disagree. It's just getting interesting, boss."

"Maybe it's just that missing people bore me a bit after

a while. Gets a bit repetitive. Missing man is still… missing. Nothing new to see here. Tralala. And to be blunt, I can't be arsed with having the senior cops breathing down my neck on this one – on a bloody Saturday, too. Yesterday's wee visit really cut into my morning. Did you not say you had some dodgy local MP to hang out to dry, anyway? You seemed pretty keen to bear down on him with force a few weeks ago."

Maggie paused and took a long, hard look at her boss, searching for something in her eyes that might explain the change of heart. But Lexi was looking down at her nails, fiddling with the rings on her fingers.

"Bit of a U-turn, isn't that? Not like you to drop something with reader appeal without a good reason."

Lexi looked straight at her, her hackles raised – a situation that was hard to reverse out of, as she knew from bitter experience.

"This Anderson stuff was always *your* agenda, lassie. NOT mine. I've told you to find something else to pursue. But now you think you know better, eh, Shields?"

"I… no, it's just… sorry."

"Have you been selling newspapers to the people of Fife for twenty-five years? No? Well, maybe listen to someone who has. The story is getting dull, Maggie. D-U-L-L. The police have given us nothing but a standard holding line and have made it very clear there will be no off-the-record 'extras' coming your way anytime soon. Mark Anderson is clearly *not* a high-risk miss per, no matter how much you want him to be. So… I don't want you wasting time on it until we have an excellent reason. Understood?"

"What about the fact that his daughters are getting

followed by someone who happens to be driving a senior police officer's car? That's all shades of shit – you have to see that."

"Maggie, that's just not something we should report in our paper. It's something that the police need to investigate for themselves. And I think it's fair to say there will be phone calls made internally."

"But, boss… there's something not right. I've started getting this creepy…"

She stopped herself. Did she really think that telling her editor that someone was sending her a creepy letter was going to make her roll over and capitulate?

The rage in her own head felt like a furnace, but she fought to hold it in.

What the hell is she not telling me?

Lexi was marching back to her office, carrying her own high heels in her hands. Fuelled by rage, Maggie had one last card to play.

"I went to see Ranald Anderson. You ever met him?"

Lexi almost tripped over her ankle. She held an arm out to the wall to steady herself and turned back around to face Maggie.

"Stay away from that man."

The colour drained from Lexi's face, leaving just the sharp lines of her lipstick and black eyeliner looking more prominent than before.

"Boss?"

"You heard me. Keep clear of Ranald Anderson."

Maggie was in too deep now and needed to stand her ground.

"His son is missing. He's just posted a twenty K reward, and I wanted to get a fresh line from him. That's all."

It wasn't all, of course. Not by a long shot. Everything Maggie had heard or experienced for herself about Ranald Anderson made her question whether his business conduct had a baring on his son's disappearance. But Lexi was in no mood to hear it.

Lexi straightened her body and walked purposefully towards her office before pulling the door behind her. It was the ultimate 'F-off' sign, and Maggie knew there was only one option now. Pack up and go home.

She sloped back to her seat and packed her rucksack, pausing as a message came through on her phone. It was from an anonymous number and had a picture attachment. She read the text first; the words were written in bold letters:

HOW WELL CAN YOU REALLY TRUST HIM, MAGGIE?

And the photo attached was an image of Lochie. It looked like a still from a Ring door camera. She recognised the street behind him because she'd been there recently herself. But the sight of Lochie there on his own wearing an outfit she'd seen him in just last week made her fingertips sweat onto the screen. She needed to find him and ask him what the hell was going on. But first, she dialled Tetchy's number on her phone. He'd come up trumps with the cop car ID and was the one person who could tell her who sent her the text message. The call rang out three times in a row. So, she grabbed her coat and made for the exit. Muhammed was coming to the mountain.

19

SATURDAY A.M.

Lewis Kovachev worked in a small, windowless space on the lower ground floor of AeroTech. He worked odd hours – often at weekends, in the evenings or early mornings – in a building that brought her out in hives if she went to visit, but she had to see him today.

"There's a visitor for you at reception, Lewis. A Mrs A. Chapman. Says she's here from a supplier, but I'm not seeing it in the diary, and she's forgotten her ID."

Standing in the main reception hall, Maggie tried to look composed and confident as she imagined Tetchy squirming at the other end, despairing at her subterfuge. He told her years ago that media are about as welcome in the AeroTech building as a fart in a lift. It made her instantly suspicious of who exactly their clients were, but that remained a project for another day.

The receptionist stopped talking, pushed the small microphone part of her headset away from her mouth and prepared a laminated visitor lanyard, which she handed to Maggie with a wholly fake smile. It occurred to Maggie that she'd make a perfect life partner for ANT.

"If you'd just like to take the lift to the lower ground floor, Ms Chapman, Lewis will meet you there."

Tetchy was standing in place as the lift doors opened to the dark underworld of the five-story building.

"I see it's as depressing as ever here. You getting any sunlight at all, pal?"

"Maggie. What a pleasure. Albeit unexpected. Could we drop the Anna Chapman joke next time? There's always an outside chance someone in here might not appreciate Russian spy jokes, yeh?"

"Bet your Christmas night out is a riot. Not that I can talk. Always dodge ours like the plague."

Maggie looked around at a sea of hunched shoulders leaning into banks of monitors. Some were picking their noses or shovelling beige food into their mouths.

He led Maggie to the galley kitchen in the centre of the floor, where a small gathering had congregated. Some younger lads were searching in the fridge and others were heating Pot Noodles in the microwave for breakfast.

"It really would help if you gave me a heads up about these visits. If I'm caught smuggling one of your lot into this department, I'll be…"

Tetchy stopped himself as he shifted his gaze to those around him.

"Yeh, sorry about that. Should've called, I get it… but it's a bit of a delicate one. I need you to trace a text message for me."

"Christ, Maggie, shhh…"

Tetchy yanked Maggie's arm and pulled her towards a booth far away from the communal kitchen area.

"Steady on with the grip there, eh?"

"You do know that is illegal, yes?" Tetchy said, looking increasingly on edge.

"Yeh, sorry about that. I doubt these folk will have heard though. Do they even keep their headphones on when they go for a shi—"

"Maggie! What did the message say?"

He cut across Maggie's words, something she was not used to from him.

"What's that?"

"The text, Maggie, the one you want me to trace illegally."

"Oh, yeh, sorry. Seriously weird one this. I got this earlier, when I was in the office."

Maggie flipped her phone around on the table to show him the words.

"*How well can you really trust him, Maggie?*"

Tetchy read out the words in a staccato style, making them sound like they came from a robot.

"So…?"

"Look at the picture attachment."

He clicked on the image, and she watched the contours of his face change from annoyance to concern.

"Can you find out who sent it to me? I mean, it's probably someone who hates me for misquoting them in a story. I never do that, by the way. But, you know, I…"

"Maggie, come on!"

Tetchy had interrupted her for the second time…

"What? It's just creepy, Tetch. I want to know who sent me this. Lochie's been coming over all protective brother on me too. Plus, whoever sent it must have something to lose – which means they don't want me to do any more digging."

He pushed the phone back across the table at her, dismissing her request.

"No. No way. If you use the info to uncover some shady shit, and it's *ever* traced back to me, I'll be deported."

"You're a UK citizen, Tetch. That's not possible."

"OK, my parents will. Or I'll end up in the jail. Don't fancy that much, either."

"I think that's unlikely."

"Not taking any chances. Anyway, I'd put money on the fact it was that brother of yours trying to wind you up, getting someone at work to take a photo of him on their phone. Have you wound him up recently? I mean, more than normal?"

Maggie shook her head furiously.

"No, Tetchy, he doesn't have the headspace to pull something like that. Trust me… and why would he suggest I stop trusting him for a joke? That's a shite idea. Whoever sent me this, it wasn't him."

"Can you not just ignore it – or speak to the police?" Tetchy said.

"No, because I got a letter too. And it was worse."

He looked like he was properly listening now.

"A couple of days ago. It told me to back off from the story I'm working on, or I'd regret it, and if I spoke to the police, they'd hurt Lochie."

Tetchy's concern was rising. He was looking jittery.

"Shit – that's grim. But I guess anyone could send a

journalist an email like that just to give them the fear. Did they mention Lochie by name?"

Tetchy always asked questions like that. He was a stickler for facts.

"No, they just said they'd hurt the only person who cared about me. And again, there was a photo of *him* inside the envelope. So, they must've meant *him*."

Tetchy opened his mouth to respond, but closed it again and shook his head – like he was recalibrating a thought.

"Tell me again why you like your job?"

"Well, for one, I get to see daylight out of my window. That's more than you can say. And I get to work this close to my favourite geek."

Maggie shot him her best wink before pressing her hands together in a praying motion. Tetchy released a long, laboured sigh and shook his head in defeat.

"Oh, heck… how long have I got, Maggie?"

"Honest answer?"

"NO – realistic one, please."

"Twelve hours? I need to know who is trying to push me off course, and why."

"Well, I can't help you with the second part. You're all alone there," Tetchy said.

"Fair enough – that's the bit I'm good at. Not this geeky stuff. That's your bag."

Tetchy let out a long breath before glancing around and reaching his hand across the table with an open palm. She treated him to her finest smile before handing the phone over.

"Stay there… don't touch anything or talk to anyone…

I'll be back shortly once I've pulled some data off it."

"Thanks, Tetch. You're the best – you know that, don't you?"

He returned twenty minutes later as Maggie was pacing around the staff kitchen, deeply agitated and tapping all available surfaces, number sequences on loop in her head.

"Right, here you go. I can't analyse the data until later, OK? I have a proper job to do."

"You're a legend."

He grunted at her before pausing a moment as she smiled at him, making her suddenly self-conscious.

"And Maggie?"

"Uh-huh?"

"You were never here, yes?"

"Never where?"

Winking at him again, she made her way out of the building, past the receptionist who muttered at her about returning her pass. It gave Maggie some light relief at the thought of the near one hundred non-returned lanyards and press passes hanging from her wardrobe at home. In alphabetical order and colour coordinated.

She checked her phone outside Tetchy's office block. He'd changed her wallpaper screen to a wolf pack baring their teeth. A reference, no doubt, to news hounds or something.

Typing in her password, the home screen came to life and a series of text messages popped up. One from her AI therapist, ANT, saying she hadn't 'been in touch' in a while.

Christ, ANT, we've only had one date! But it reminded her she had someone – or something – to download to that wouldn't look at her like a judgemental human. Someone she could literally flick the switch on as soon as she wanted.

Realising it was almost lunchtime and she needed to wait to hear from Tetchy, she forced herself to go home and get some rest.

The rain came on fast as soon as Maggie approached her flat. Rain in Fife fell in a horizontal direction and could seep into the hidden parts of your skin within seconds. The joy of peeling off her clothes and changing into clean, crisp linen played on her mind as she locked her bike in the stairwell.

Her phone vibrated in her pocket. It was a message from Tetchy.

Blimey, that was quicker than expected.

Tried to trace your text to an address. Came up blank at first but dug around more and found a link from the sender to an IP address.

She scribbled a response as quickly as her fingers could type.

English please, Tetch. What does that mean?

His reply came back quickly.

Means the text didn't come from a phone. It came from a PC – or, more likely, software installed on a PC.

20

SATURDAY EARLY P.M.

Maggie needed space and time to think. Time to come to terms with everything she'd learnt. Discovering the man who killed her mum lost his own life because Ranald Anderson had to silence his son's drug misuse was a lot to start with. Then there was Pete's revelation that Mark intended to snitch against his dad and bring justice for Archie's family. A justice Maggie's own brother convinced her he didn't deserve. She wondered just how far Ranald would go to stop his own son from bringing down the house of cards? And if he was involved in his son's disappearance, why would he post a £20K reward to locate him? Was it some sort of elaborate ruse to look like the doting father?

Then there was Lexi to contend with. Her orders were about as clear as they could be. Maggie had no choice but to back off from reporting on Mark Anderson. Completely. Or risk losing the job she loved. Lexi had her limits, and she wouldn't tolerate any of her team ignoring a clear instruction. On the other hand, if Maggie didn't start proving her worth as an investigative reporter soon, she'd be out on her ear, anyway.

Her first instinct was to find Lochie. To confront him with everything. He was the one person who could always help her make sense of life. But there was too much doubt in her head about him now, holding her back.

Then she thought about ANT. It was only a matter of time before Sharon confronted her about her therapy progress. What harm could it do to have a judgement-free chat with a well-dressed avatar?

Something was troubling her about him. Was it just curiosity? Or was she developing some ridiculous shyness for baring her soul to this perfect-looking human construct who she'd set against her own bully? The bully definitely had squatter's rights. Where did her words go after ANT had signposted them through various coded pathways? Were there humans at the end of the system somewhere, making empathetic assessments of what she had to say? ANT probably just moved on to the next person waiting on his list after a quick costume change. Or was he having simultaneous conversations with five thousand other people at the same time? Maggie couldn't get away fast enough from the clipboard woman in her real-world clinic, but when it came to spending time with ANT, it felt refreshingly straightforward. Effortless. Whatever she told him, she knew ANT wouldn't look up at her over the top of his glasses or make her sit in a chair after ten other people and breathe the same air.

His fresh-looking face would ask her how her day was going. There was no hidden disdain from ANT. He wasn't thinking about having to get away early to pick his kids up from school and hoping this woman would stop bleating on so much. ANT was ready for her, completely. She told him how her day often started with folding her towel neatly in two places and hanging it over the towel rail. Then doing it again because the creases weren't even. Minutes after that, she'd put two slices of brown bread into the toaster and allow herself one last check of the bathroom before sitting on her bed and switching her laptop on. She needed to check if the shower was absolutely switched off. It usually always was, but it gave her a little extra comfort to check. And check again.

ANT asked her why she needed to check things so much. Maggie considered telling him to mind his own business, but she didn't. Instead, she said that if she forgot, and the shower flooded her flat when she went out, and the flat below her, it would cause an electrical fire. People might die, and it would all be her fault for *not* checking the shower properly that one day. Somehow, it sounded a little less logical when she wrote it down like that.

Is that weird?

I don't believe any human mind is weird. It has a reason for everything it does.

Jings, you talk like a politician.

ANT set her a challenge to record evidence that her perceived danger wasn't real and evidence that it was. She looked at the lists: the evidence for being grossly outweighed by the evidence against. Somehow, it made her think again.

Are you worried about going in to work today?

How the hell does he know… Ah, hang on. I mentioned my shift start time yesterday. And I AM late. There it is again, paranoia.

Was now the time to launch into the whole Mark Anderson saga? Her dilemma about Lochie. Her fears about being lied to, and the overwhelming pressure of needing to prove herself at work. It was a bit much – even for an advanced processor like ANT, surely?

Have you been having any more disturbing thoughts today, Maggie?

Yes. But I have them every day. I'm struggling to decide about something. But it's work stuff. Can you help me with that?

As she waited for a response, she hoped he wouldn't answer like a psychologist. Any time she'd heard them speak on TV or contribute their opinions, they'd say it wasn't their job to make patients' decisions, but to lead them to make the right one for themselves.

Let's start by filling in today's behaviours and emotions checklist, shall we?

Oh, Lord. Not you too.

No, let's not. I'm bored with that. I need to know if my instincts are sound or if I'm up shit creek.

I'm afraid I don't understand – where is shit creek?

Oh bloody hell, this thing has a lot to learn.

Am I going mad?

That's a big question, Maggie. Why are you questioning your own instincts?

Because I'm trying to investigate a story, but someone is lying to me, and I can't decide who it is.

You can't decide who, or you can decide but don't want to believe it?

Christ, he's definitely not reading from the psychologist's handbook here.

Who do you think is lying to you, Maggie?

She felt free from self-censorship – liberated by knowing there was no human at the other end, judging her answers in real time. Talking to ANT was different; it was safe. A wall of security protected her words. So she shared. She shared her reluctance to trust people: Pete, Val, Ranald – and, recently, even her own brother.

I think I'm losing my mind, too.

What do you mean by that, Maggie?

Things have been happening – I sometimes feel like people are watching me or following me. Or I imagine other people without seeing them. And there's the voice of the bully that tells me to keep doing these things – over and over again. I've been getting messages too. A letter and then a text message. They're probably unrelated, but I don't know.

The words were flowing in a way she had never found the courage to share with another human. It was a release. Like medication flowing through her system.

But a text message from Lexi invaded her moment of release.

Get back in to work now, Shields.

*

Harris was leaving the *Standard* offices just as she reached reception.

"Any idea what Lexi's got for me?"

He grunted at her about a new football manager announcement in response, so she continued to Lexi's office, tapping lightly on the glass before entering. Lexi pushed down on the plunger of a cafetière with her scarlet-taloned hands as Maggie entered. The dark, strong coffee was compressed at the bottom, leaving a thin layer of foamy bubbles on the surface. Her stomach turned quickly at the image.

"What's happening, boss?"

"There's been a fire down at one of the ex-Lino buildings. I presume you've seen it on the news?"

"Just the headline, really."

She tried to hide her disappointment. Part of her hoped she was going to share the contents of the email from COPFS with her – or some other nugget that gave her the green light to get back on the Anderson story. Five years ago, she would've jumped at being sent to the scene of a major fire. But Maggie wanted more now. She wanted stories that took their time to crawl from under the woodwork.

Kirkcaldy's linoleum factories once stood proudly in the town – producing lino flooring for half of Scotland and beyond. But almost all of them had now closed and the land redeveloped, turned into luxury flats or office buildings. She had seen nothing break on the news yet about a fire but wasn't about to admit that to the boss.

"Anything coming through on the wires about what happened yet?"

"Nope. Get yourself up there and start pestering the fire

chief. We need top-line answers early doors for tomorrow's front page – any fatalities and all that – should be some impressive photos coming in soon to set it all off nicely."

Maggie found Lexi's clinical approach to trauma and disaster distasteful – even in a world where dark humour was a survival instinct.

"On it, boss."

The road closures around the old factories were bound to make for an awkward journey. There was so much development down there that she had to check Google Maps on her phone for a route through that hadn't been dug up. Tetchy's number kept flashing on her screen. She needed to get rid of him for now.

"I'm on my way to a cover a fire, Tetch. I'll call you later."

Her finger hovered over the call end button when she heard his protest.

"No, Maggie. I need to speak to you now. It's important."

Tetchy sounded agitated, with his low voice indicating that he was keen to not be overheard.

"OK, OK. Hang on. I'll pull in. What is it?"

There was noise from the passing traffic all around Maggie's car and a couple of blue flashing lights sped past her, drowning out Tetchy's words.

"Tetchy, you'll have to speak up. It's going like a fayre out here."

"… you… using… online psych… therapy programme?"

She only picked up that end of the sentence, but there was no mistaking the question.

"What? What are you on about?"

"Maggie, I'm being serious. And this isn't about judgement. I need to know if you've downloaded a piece of software that's designed to monitor your mental health. Think it's called Artificial Neuro-something or other."

Her palms lost their grip on the steering wheel as a thin layer of sweat formed on her skin. The familiar sensation of panic rose from her core.

"Maggie, can you hear me?"

"I download all kinds of weird stuff for work reasons."

She wasn't ready to admit it to Tetchy. It was too much of a stretch for now.

"I'll take that as a yes."

"Tetchy, chill. I've just signed up for an NHS-backed trial – Lochie said these things go great guns in other countries, apparently. So, if you're about to tell me the Russians are watching, you're wrong. It's all legit."

Maggie thought she heard a faint protest down the line, but a fire engine sped past her at the same time.

"You know how you were asking about a message that I traced back to an IP address?"

"Uh-huh?"

"And I said it came from a piece of software – probably on a PC rather than a phone?"

Staying silent felt like the safest option. She remembered Lochie and Pete's denial of having anything to do with the message.

"You said it was from some untraceable source?"

"I know, but I looked deeper… I mean, it looks like it's more than that. I think that psychotherapy app of yours has been compromised by malicious actors of some variety."

Maggie had no time for his lingo. She switched her engine off and put her hazard lights on.

"Could I have that again in the language of the common folk?"

"Sorry. I mean hacked. I think the software application you've installed has become vulnerable to hacking – someone may be accessing your data or manipulating the output."

She felt sick. He must be wrong. There's no way anything the NHS was trialling could be compromised like that. Then she considered the word 'trial' again.

"Dare I ask which is worse?"

"Well, to be honest, they may do both. It depends on so many things."

"Like?"

"Like, what their motivations are, for a start?"

The driver of another car had pulled up alongside her and was gesticulating manically at her. She was blocking the entrance to his drive. And traffic was mounting up behind him. Mouthing her apologies, she raised her forefinger to show she would be one minute more.

"Are you telling me some sicko is playing mind games with me online?"

"Maybe, but I don't know why. For some of these guys, there's no significant reason. It's just mischief-making – a game – a mindless way to pass the time. But sometimes, it's for…"

"For what, Tetch? You're freaking me out here."

"Well, it's just seriously bad news for mental health patients that are using this software."

She couldn't bear to ask him any more questions. Her mind drifted to some things she'd just shared with ANT. Her concerns about paranoia. The worries about being contaminated by passing strangers. Her work dilemmas. Maggie hadn't been physically attacked – or sexually assaulted. No axe-wielding man had come at her on a dark night. But the sense of violation building from her core was overwhelming.

"Maggie? Mags? You still there?"

She couldn't cope with this right now. Noise and emergency vehicles were passing her on all sides. It must be a major fire. She HAD to do her job.

"Listen. I don't have time for this. I've got a job to do. Have to go, Tetch."

"You've got to make *this* your story, Mags," Tetchy said.

"Not now."

But Tetchy was not for letting this one go.

"This is the story that will make your mark. These people are out there somewhere and if they've done it to you, they could do it to others. Some guys at work said there were rumours of another medical data breach in Fife recently – it affected patients at a private hospital in St Andrews. But it never made the news. Which was weird."

The rumblings of temptation were simmering inside her, but she couldn't face it. Pursuing this story would mean publicly admitting that she accessed psychological therapy. That she was one of *those* broken people. She'd have to tell Lexi that she was using a mental health AI therapy system instead of a real-life human psychotherapist. It would only be a matter of time before Sharon in HR came knocking.

"I don't know, Tetch."

"Just have a sniff around. Do some background," he persisted. "Apparently something went down at that Sapphire Healthcare, near the golf course. There's bound to be something hidden online to give you a steer."

As soon as she heard that name, Maggie made the leap in her head. Sapphire Healthcare was the name of the company Val Anderson told her about. Ranald Anderson was back in the picture again.

21

SATURDAY P.M.

The darkness of a cloudy afternoon seemed to fall on the *Fife Standard* building by the time she got back to her desk. Something quieter had replaced the noise and mayhem of a mid-week shift. Maggie was fond of solitude. Life was more straightforward when she could work on her own. She wrote until everything was out of her mind and on the page. Then she worked some more to trim the fat and expand on the good bits. She often missed meals, forgot to sleep, and ignored the few invitations she got to parties. Once in a while she'd pitch up late to an event, if she thought there was a story in it – but almost always left early, desperate to get back home where everything was safe and clean. Because that was the way she liked it, and everything was under control that way.

She even forgot Lochie's birthday because she was pursuing *the* story that would make them all stand up and take notice. But, so far, they never had. She'd carved a bit of a local reputation. She had built up a name for being the face that popped up when there was trouble brewing. But Maggie Shields craved more. And she couldn't let it go.

Tetchy had known Maggie for a long time. She'd told him that investigating and writing were all she wanted to do. He said he remembered watching her at school, spellbound by the eccentric English teacher, as he tried in vain to get the entire class enthused about writers like Kerouac or Steinbeck. Maggie couldn't get enough of it. English was the class she looked forward to every day. She just couldn't remember a time when she wasn't able to write well.

Tiredness was grinding away at her energy, but her head was still full of Tetchy's bombshell about ANT. He'd wanted to give her more details, but she didn't want to hear it then. Knowing that some loser had violated her most private thoughts, sitting at home in his grubby bedroom, surfing the web and invading someone's most private thoughts and fears roused something in her.

Clicking on a fresh Google search page, she typed the words – Sapphire Healthcare. The results came flooding in about the vast and wonderful range of holistic health services they offered from their state-of-the-art hospital facilities.

We put the care in healthcare, the website proudly stated.

She scrolled further, scanning the About Us section for a name. A point of entry. She liked to go straight to the top.

The first photo was an airbrushed, corporate headshot of the managing director of Sapphire Healthcare Group: Mr Mitchell Stevens.

This had to be the same man that Ranald Anderson had dealings with, like Val mentioned. Once again, a road straight to the Anderson family. Straining to look at the image of Stevens more closely, she took in his broad shoulders and angular jawline. His head was crowned with a receding hair line, combed back and held stubbornly in place with what she presumed was some heavy-duty gel. She'd seen this man before. It was from a distance, but there was no mistaking it.

This was the figure she saw when she first entered Val Anderson's home. It was him, lurking in the background, making his presence felt but not fully seen.

*

Maggie's call to Mitchell Stevens diverted to his PA. She left a message but had little expectation of hearing back soon. But less than twenty minutes later, her phone showed an incoming call that surprised her.

"Hello. Thanks for getting back to me, Mr Stevens. I'm looking into a story about a potential data breach in an online medical platform being trialled by the NHS. I have reason to understand your hospital in St Andrew's may have been vulnerable to software hackers in the past?"

An eerie silence filled the line.

"Mr Stevens?"

"I don't know where you got this from, but…"

"Is that a denial?"

"Did you say an NHS trial?"

"Yes. An artificial intelligence–led system providing

psychological therapy to patients with mild to moderate mental health conditions."

He swore sharply under his breath.

"I realise this is a different area to your business, but compromising of any medical platforms is a genuine concern for so many…"

"You don't need to tell me that, Ms…"

"Shields. Maggie Shields. And I was hoping you could tell me a bit more about what happened in your case."

"Well, you thought wrong, Ms Shields. My hospitals take protection of patient and colleague data extremely seriously and, other than guaranteeing we have absolutely no concerns in this area now, I have no further comment."

"Now? … Does that mean that you had…"

"Goodbye."

Shit.

That was even less helpful than she feared. Why did he react so strongly to the mention of the NHS, though? It felt like everyone in a five-mile radius of Ranald Anderson was too afraid to speak out.

Irritation quickly gave way to something stronger, pulling on her nerves today. She couldn't linger on Mitchell Stevens for too long.

It was the third Saturday in the month, which usually meant one thing. When Lochie finished work, they would spend the evening together, starting with a visit to their mum's grave. They would try hard to focus on the happy memories. To avoid the anger, the hurt, and the horror. Lochie was good at that. Celebrating the good stuff. He said that being around sick people every day reminded him that we all needed to hunt out the joy in life.

The noise of her phone ringing erupted through her skull like a bullet. She saw Lochie's name flash up on the screen and felt guilt at the thought of ignoring it. This was her brother, Lochie.

But the thought of him waiting downstairs to spend the evening with her didn't feel the same this time. It didn't feel like an extra layer of comfort. Or a security blanket being laid across her. Was it because of what Pete had told her about *his* brother, Archie? She could have been the one to bring justice to his family years ago if she'd ignored Lochie's advice – not just once, but again when Lochie told her what that man had done. He was hardly a man, though. Ryan, Archie – whatever his name was – he was only seventeen. Was it right that he lost his life like that, even after what he'd done to their family?

She could've ignored Lochie's advice and spoken up – gone straight to the police. The photos would have shown the world a clear picture of the killer. What they looked like then. What they were wearing. But they were gone too, deleted in an instant of panic that could never be reversed.

But Maggie couldn't delete what her own head was piecing together from images old and new. There was no going back. She knew who the perpetrator was now. The same man whose face she'd been staring at on the computer screen earlier. That was the man who plunged that knife into Archie in the woods. But it was all too late. Even if she told someone it was Mitchell Steven's face she saw that day all those years ago, it would be too little, too late for anyone to believe her.

Her phone pinged again.

I'm downstairs. Switch your PC off and get down here, please.

Her head was spinning with the magnitude of what she'd just figured out. The identity of a killer from ten years ago. But no one could force it out of her until she was ready. And today, right now, was a moment that had the power to push everything else aside.

She threw on her jacket and headed downstairs.

"You took your time."

Taking a proper look at her brother's face calmed her a little. She felt her body relax as she saw his features. They were the centre of everything she'd known all her life.

"Sorry, Loch. It's been a…"

"Don't give me that tough shift bollocks. I had a twelve-hour shift and had a whole new combination of offensive insults thrown at me today."

Maggie capitulated. This was a moment in time they shared with just each other. Where everything else just stopped – no matter what. That was their promise to each other the first time they visited their mother's grave together after the funeral. A moment to remember the good times, the smiles. The woman who held it all together before she was stolen from them in an instant. By him. The boy who Maggie now knew to be Ryan Archibald Ross.

"I just… there's weird stuff going on Loch. And I need to tell you, I mean ask you about…"

He cut her off immediately.

"Not today, Maggie. Today isn't about scoops, or patients or anything else."

He was right. Today was a time she should feel at ease in another person's company. Separated from the rest of the world in their own bubble. Lochie would remember stupid stuff about their childhood and take the piss out of her for any reason he could think of. She would remind him how smelly he was as a teenager and how he feared making eye contact with girls. And then they'd both remember their mum's lasagne – made with extra cheese, just a little crusted around the edges. The smell of it made everything feel a little better.

But today, she resented his need to revisit all of that stuff again. She needed to ask him about Pete McGill's dead brother. She needed to ask him if he knew what she knew. What Pete had told him about Archie.

Could Lochie really stand by and let Archie's killer walk free? Even if he'd made a stupid, horrible mistake that cost their mum her life? Maybe he knew Archie was mixed up with Ranald Anderson all along and feared the consequences of speaking out. *That had to be it. That had to be the reason that he's told me none of this.*

She shivered more as the thoughts brought more questions, heaped upon each other like a rotting pile of rubbish.

"Maggie, please can we get out of here? You look like you could do with some fresh air."

She did as she was told, pushing the questions into the small places in her head where they might not bother her for a little while. Lochie watched her closely as she walked towards the door, swiping her fob as she left.

Why is he watching me like that?

She craved that the rest of the day would take its

usual course. They would sit out in the park opposite the graveyard. He would have a double espresso and a bacon roll, and Maggie would watch as the brown sauce oozed out of the side of his mouth before beginning its slow creep down his chin towards an ultimate resting place somewhere on his shirt. She would take out her own straw from a sealed plastic bag, wipe it with antiseptic gel and place it in her caffeine-free Diet Coke bottle – sipping carefully to avoid contact between her lips and the plastic rim of the bottle.

"How's your therapy going, Maggie?"

Maggie turned to her left to look at him. He had one eyebrow raised – a move that reminded her of their mum.

"Fine. It's fine, Lochie."

"You know it's not normal, yes?"

"What's not normal?"

"All that weird shit you do with cleaning; avoiding microscopic dirt and that? I see stuff like that from patients sometimes, and it can get out of hand. What has your 'artificial therapist' got to say about it all?"

He gave her *that* look again.

She wanted to tell him that the one place she'd found to talk about her anxiety turned out to be riddled with bugs and hackers. That she'd just built up enough confidence to share something with it, only to find out *hostile actors*, or whatever Tetchy called them, had interfered with *it. How* could she be so naïve?

But she couldn't tell him. He was so nervous about her divulging memories to an actual human who was bound by confidentiality. That's why he'd suggested looking online for something less community based. Something less bound by obligation to divulge secrets to authorities.

If she told him the NHS trial had been compromised, at best Lochie would freak out. Worst case, he'd mention it to too many people at work and those responsible would disappear underground or protect themselves before she pieced it together. To get under the skin of what was going on – just like Tetchy said. The idea had already grown in strength since he suggested it.

"Let me guess? You've abandoned that route too?"

She needed to shut down this conversation until she worked out her next step.

"I know what I'm doing, OK?"

"Christ, Maggie, why do you have to overthink everything?"

Maybe he was right. Tetchy could have got this wrong. She wasn't thinking clearly. She needed to get out of the office. They walked all the way to the graveyard and didn't bring up newspaper investigations or any member of the McGill family. She didn't ask him about the photos taken ten years ago in the woods. Instead, Maggie listened to her brother tell her about the day he spent all his pocket money on a new pencil case for Maggie instead of buying his football cards. She listened to him telling her the last thing their dad said before he walked out:

"You'll look after that lass better than I ever could, son."

Lochie had told her about that before, but she let him tell her again and just listened. Maybe he knew she needed to hear it today.

When it looked like he'd run out of memories, he thought of more. He filled every silence before she had a chance to ask him anything. Her big brother spent all his days listening to other people's moans, groans, and aches, so she let him speak. Her questions could wait.

By the time they made it back home, Maggie was physically and emotionally spent. She headed to her room to change her clothes, and Lochie collapsed on her sofa. They ordered takeaway Chinese, and ate off plates she'd cleaned twice. Lochie chose *Indiana Jones and the Temple of Doom* to watch because it reminded them of happy times at home. For the first time in many days, Maggie fell into a deep sleep, curled up in the foetal position, leaning against her big brother's broad shoulders.

When she woke up, he was gone. He never just left without saying goodbye or leaving her a note. But there was nothing today. She needed to get to bed, but then she'd lie awake obsessing about the dirt her brother's clothes had left on the sofa. So, she got up, pulled the hoover out, and began to rub it vigorously against the sofa cushions. Running her hands down the side of the soft velvet covers to reach for any crumbs that may be lurking, she fished out a piece of crumpled paper. Opening it, her heart thumped so hard in her chest she had to sit down.

She held a medical prescription slip – from the hospital pharmacy. It had yesterday's date on it and a list of medicines she didn't understand. But there was no mistaking the name of the patient it belonged to. Mrs Anne McGill. Pete McGill's mum.

22

SUNDAY A.M.

The early morning light crept through a hole in Maggie's bedroom curtains, but she was already awake. Still clutching the prescription in her right hand, she lay staring up at the ceiling. How could it be that so little made sense anymore? She ached to shut it all out and stay safe, on her own, at home. It was Sunday, after all. Maggie wasn't religious, but something about Sundays made her feel obligated to rest. But it rarely worked out that way. Her laptop was sitting open on her desk. After entering her passcode, a wall of notifications from ANT hit her.

Hey Maggie, how are you? What are you doing today? I see it's a nice day for a cycle?

I'm sorry you've not been in touch for a while. Is something troubling you?

I'm concerned that you've not checked in for over twenty-four hours. It's really important that you let me know you're OK.

She disabled her laptop camera, slammed the screen

shut, pulled on some warm clothes and forced herself out of the door. Her cycle to the office took her through deserted streets, and she could feel the fresh coastal air hit the back of her lungs and fill her brain with energy. Letting herself in the building's back door, the only signs of life she saw were a few cleaners who were trailing Henry hoovers along the over-worn carpets, the smell of their last smoke break following in their wake. The Saturday shift would have filled most of Monday's paper, and nobody would be around until later that afternoon.

There was a missed call on her phone – from Mitchell Steven's office number – but no message. She was desperate to find out more about this medical data breach and history with Ranald. But why would Val have tipped her off about a man she was sharing a house with? Was this some kind of trap, or an attempt to throw her off course? There were three stories colliding here: a missing man, a decade-old murder and a major medical data breach. That was a lot to link together. She needed to take it one step at a time.

Maggie also had to find out why Lochie had dropped a prescription for Pete McGill's mum out of his jacket. But first, Stevens.

She dialled the number for his office and waited.

"Hi, it's Maggie Shields here."

"Give me a minute. I need to move."

She was used to nerves, and it was a line she'd heard so often from a good source.

"Have you remembered more details about your software breach, Mr Stevens?"

It was an aggressive opener, but Maggie was confident she had the upper ground here.

"If I give you some background, will you promise to keep my name and Sapphire Healthcare out of anything you print?"

Maggie sighed. It was time for the usual script.

"If you give me something strong enough to run with no need to quote you directly, then I'm happy to go with that."

It wasn't even close to the reassurance he was seeking. But the man was desperate to speak.

"You need to focus your attention on someone else."

"Oh? Who's that then?"

"A couple of years ago, I introduced some software to my hospital data management system – it was supposed to make everything more streamlined, easy to access between hospital admin and the clinical team."

"OK…?"

"But it was a nightmare. I'll spare you the details, but online hackers targeted the software and shared highly sensitive patient data on some public forums. Thankfully, we were on top of it faster than lightning – and shut it down – thanks to our excellent IT experts. But the outfit who provided it to us in the first place begged us to keep it all under wraps."

Maggie flushed with satisfaction as the pieces all fell into place.

"Was Ranald Anderson behind this product, by any chance?"

An awkward laugh came down the line from Stevens.

"Impressive, Ms Shields."

"Call it a lucky guess. So, did you?"

"Did I what?"

"You were gunning for him. What did you do?"

Another silence hung in the air, giving Maggie time to scour her own memory. It was the words on the email that Val Anderson read that came to her next:

It is in the best interest of both parties to bring the matter to a close and sign a non-disclosure agreement as soon as possible.

"We made it go away."

"You covered it up, like he told you?"

"You're not to be underestimated, are you, Maggie Shields?"

"I hope not. But here's a question for you. Why are you telling me this now?"

"Unlike Ranald Anderson, I have a moral compass. It's one thing to cover up a momentary breach of data that no one ever knew about. But I made that man promise he would trial his products properly before exposing sensitive public data to them again."

"And using the desperate, cash-strapped and cost-cutting NHS as a pseudo trial platform wasn't what you meant?"

"No, it wasn't."

"Thank you. Very interesting."

"I'll ask you one more time. Use this information wisely, please. I've not acted well in the past, but I hope this goes some way to making amends. My company is founded on a strong set of ethics and I try to stand by them every day. This information cannot be traced back to me. Ranald and I still… well, let's just say he's a man who is safer to have on your side that not. He must not know I've told you this. Understood?"

"Understood."

Maggie ended the call abruptly. She was going to get her nails into Ranald Anderson again from a different angle, but first she had to confirm Lochie about Anne McGill's prescription.

*

She glanced at her Fitbit as she rounded the corner to Lochie's house. It said 3:25 p.m. on the glowing digital dial. She rang the bell once and waited. No sound was coming from the TV in the front room, so she rang it again. Still nothing.

Where the bloody hell are you, Lochie?

She rang again and then yelled.

"Lochie! If you don't answer the door, I'll let myself in!"

Resentment gave way to undiluted anxiety. It was Sunday. His day off. Lochie never went anywhere on a Sunday. She found his key on her chain and unlocked the front door. A wave of cooking smells would hit her soon – or worse, the slightly musty smell that sometimes lingered around the house when he'd not left it all day. A cocktail of body odour and Pot Noodles. But it wasn't there.

"Loch? Lochie?! You in here?"

Still, nothing. The house was silent. She wanted to

sit down and wait. But she couldn't relax. Lochie was a man of routine and, although he was a grown man with every right to leave his flat without telling her, she couldn't escape the feeling that he was avoiding her.

Chaos and uncertainty surrounded her. Moving on autopilot, Maggie began picking up cups, gathering rubbish into the bin and pulling out Lochie's hoover from the hall cupboard. He kept it in the same place their mum did. Housework levelled her out again. She lost track of time and stopped caring when he might come home. Sweat covered her body and exhaustion crept up on her as she cleaned the windows and door frames. She returned the hoover to the hall cupboard, pushing it against the wall where she knew it had to sit for the door to close properly. A small shoebox in the corner of the cupboard became dislodged. It fell from the makeshift shelf her dad built for their mum to put her cleaning products on. He was no DIY expert, but he'd attempt little jobs like that, just to keep her happy. He'd build a shelf for her when she was alive but couldn't parent their children alone when she was dead.

As she let go of the hoover, the box fell from the shelf and landed on her foot, spewing out some of its contents onto her toes. She saw a small red and black USB memory stick. It seemed out of place in the same box as old gardening tools and ancient baking tins. She looked more closely and remembered it was part of a batch of these little orange and black Kodak sticks that he'd ordered online. He'd gotten ten by mistake because he couldn't work out how to cancel the auto re-order button on Amazon. Each time the USB arrived he archived more photos from parts of his life that he'd want to remember. Lochie was a hoarder, and he would turn on Maggie sharply if she suggested throwing out anything with sentimental value. He'd often make her look through them with her, to prove what a worthwhile exercise it was.

Maggie needed to feel that connection to him again. She had to remember how tightly they were bound together through life – especially the crap bits. Sitting on the hall carpet, Maggie reached for her laptop in her rucksack, switched it on, and inserted the USB stick, bracing herself for some bittersweet family memories. There would be images of fun times on holidays spent across western Scotland. Or afternoons in the back garden with a paddling pool and a barbeque. Dad would be relaxing on a sun lounger whilst Mum busied herself with refilling jugs of diluting juice. All the stuff of a life lived with happiness before their world was destroyed overnight. When they had two parents who loved them, and each other, and life was good and simple, and worked like it should.

Taking a deep breath, she opened the file on her desktop. There was only one folder. It was unnamed, but something about the date made her skin prickle.

May 25th, 2013

The date alone still haunted her and woke up something in her bones that felt cold and stagnant. But the images that appeared next in front of Maggie's eyes marked the beginning of the end of everything she believed to be true.

23

SUNDAY P.M.

A light flickered above Maggie's head and extinguished with a sharp pop, leaving her in the dark with just the glare of her laptop screen to guide her. The same glare that she saw under the door in Pete's house. She parked that thought for now, knowing she would need to come back to it too. There was a reason she'd held onto that memory from Pete's house. She just needed to work out what it was.

Her internal organs felt like they might dissolve one after the other from the adrenaline surge tearing through her. As she lifted the laptop closer to her eyes and focused on the images, she was right back there again. Long ago in a dark wood, hiding just out of sight. Trying to be invisible but desperate to watch every unfolding detail. The camera was heavy in her shaking hand, straining to zoom in on the scene and absorb more detail. It all came flooding back as if it had happened yesterday. No matter how hard she'd tried to push the memories to the back of her mind, they resurfaced. No invitation required. Anxiety consumed her and fed off her oxygen. The bully made himself known and took control of everything. It felt like nothing would stop him from regaining control of her thoughts.

She stared at the photos on the screen, mesmerised by the autumnal colours of leaves on the trees which framed the photograph. Nature was trying to make something beautiful out of something so dark.

All the players were in position on the two-dimensional stage in front of her, almost exactly as she remembered them. She was looking at a film set. The small man was closer to the foreground. Close enough to see the profile of his face. The features that she knew in so much more detail now from their likeness to Pete's. It was unmistakable, even in this grainy and fleeting moment in time. But Ryan Archibald Ross looked so much weaker than Pete McGill – the result of being sired by a different father, no doubt. Where Pete had strong cheekbones and full, rounded lips, Archie's face looked pinched in and ill at ease with daylight. But there was a desperate focus in his eyes. Scanning rapidly across the image, she saw *him* next. The man whose movements Maggie had encountered a few times in the last week. In the shadows of Val Anderson's house and smiling back at her from Sapphire Healthcare's website – the same angular jawline, emphasised more from the side view. Mitchell Stevens. The man who claimed he told Ranald Anderson never to bring untested data management software to the medical industry again. The man who convinced Maggie *he* had the stronger moral compass. The best interests of everyone front of mind.

In that moment, she knew what had evaded the police and Archie's family for years – the identity of the man that killed him.

She focused on Stevens's position in the photo, close enough to Archie to intimidate him. He was ready for the exchange that he knew would end badly for the desperate kid who was still running from his own past. Archie couldn't have seen his fate coming. He thought it was just another dirty handover job in the shadows of his old town. He would have asked no questions.

Maggie saw another crucial part of the story next. She had to squint to be sure. But there was no doubt. The elaborate marble handle of the knife she saw in Ranald's hunting shed poked out of Stevens's grasp behind his back, ready to strike. Maggie would recognise that handle and the size of the blade anywhere.

Oh, Archie. You thought you were going to walk away from it all forever, did you?

Every second of that day was coming back to her again, in waves. All her senses were alive, reliving the moment. She rubbed her fingers over the photo, reminding herself that it was still in the past. *No one knows you were ever there, except Lochie.* But seeing these images again as if it was yesterday assaulted her in aftershocks of horror.

He told me he'd deleted these, so they'd never be found. But he didn't. He kept them. Why, Lochie. Why?

A single tear fell onto her screen. Wiping it away, her finger hovered over a spot of colour she hadn't noticed before. In the top right of the picture. Straining to make sense of it, Maggie's first thought was that it was a shed, or a red shrub. Then she realised it was a cap, a red baseball-style cap, worn by a third person. He'd jumped into the scene like an afterthought. Someone Maggie didn't know was there. This person was hovering in the distance, too far away to be involved in the action, but close enough to see exactly what was going on. How did she miss that at the time?

Her phone vibrated in her pocket, and the laptop fell off her knees to the exposed floorboards with a clunk. A text from Lochie told her he was on his way home. A fever grew in her head as she tried to take stock of everything. There was another witness to the murder who was right there – closer to the action than Maggie – and they didn't come forward either. Should that make her feel better, that she wasn't the only one who kept silent? Then it dawned on her with a fresh clarity. The third individual wasn't just another innocent witness. They were involved too. Had to be, in some way. They weren't hiding. If they were just passing by at the wrong time – like her – they would hide, run or try to intervene. So, who was this? Had Ranald Anderson graced the scene with his presence, just to check everything went down as it should have? Or was it Mark Anderson? Maybe his dad forced him to watch, too? Is that why he'd disappeared? Someone found out he was there after all and was forcing him to talk – or wanting to silence him?

Maggie clicked hungrily through the remaining photos for more clues. There had to be more images of that moment. Something from a different angle to show the face hiding under the red cap. One of them teased with the slightest detail: a tiny, white Adidas logo emblazoned just above the rim and a brief flash of skin beneath – a pale tone against the red fabric.

Maggie tidied up around her and put the contents of the box back together seconds before she heard Lochie's key in the door.

She was panicking now. Should she ask him about the photos? Or take them home herself? Or just pretend that this day never happened? She couldn't let it build in her mind. Bad things happened to thoughts there – it was too crowded and toxic. Her fears would stew, ferment, and spiral out of control.

There will be a reason. Just like there will be for Anne McGill's prescription. Breathe. Deeply. Count to three… one, two, three…

Maybe Lochie thought he'd destroyed the photos but realised years later that he hadn't. And, then, when he knew what Archie had done to their mum, he wanted to hang onto them as some dark reminder that he got what he deserved?

I'll ask him, she thought. *And, when I do, he'll tell me the innocent explanation.* Lochie never liked answering questions. He kept telling her he was a private person – and that was OK. He could be a private person. He had his reasons. Questions gave him headaches.

Don't come over all super-scoop on me, he'd say to her.

But this was different.

He was home now. Walking through the front door.

"What the hell have you been up to in my house?"

Lochie stood in the hallway, casting his eyes into the

lounge and down towards the back of the house. She remembered her earlier cleaning frenzy.

"Mags! Maggie! Where are you?! What the hell have you done in here?"

Popping her head out from the hall cupboard, she made her call.

"Your domestic skills are shite, Lochie. This place is falling apart. I was just putting the hoover back."

"I like it that way, Maggie. It does me just fine. You moved out five years ago, remember? Why can't you sit down and watch telly like normal people your age?"

Maggie turned her back on him.

"Where were you? You never go out."

"I don't know… I felt like shaking things up a bit. I went for a walk. That OK?"

Maggie nodded silently.

"Why are you so uptight, anyway?"

She tried to soften her tone – to calm things down and find her way out. Then she turned to check she'd closed the hall cupboard door properly behind her. When she turned back, he'd moved closer to her. Too close. It made her muscles tighten in a basic fight or flight response.

"I need to ask you some stuff, Loch."

She glanced at the back door of the kitchen, and wondered if it was unlocked. Lochie's face was unmoving, waiting. He looked expressionless, as if poised to react to whatever came next.

"What kind of stuff?"

Your call, Maggie. Where do we go from here?

She wanted to find the strength to confront him. To

tell him what she had found in the cupboard and find out what it meant. To ask him about Anne McGill, and all the rest. But courage fell from her like ice melting by a fire.

"It's just that I've been thinking a lot about the work you do. Nursing people back to health. Preserving life – all that 'good human' stuff. It just seems to come naturally to you, doesn't it? You know, making the right choices for other people."

As the words come out, Maggie wondered if she was trying to convince herself. His eyes narrowed in response, and he loosened the scarf from around his neck. Maggie could see a rash rising onto his face. The same rash that he used to get as a teenager when he was embarrassed or ashamed. It was an automatic response he'd never grown out of.

"Maggie, I'm certainly not special. I just go to work every day and do my job. Like all of the other medics and carers."

She wasn't going to settle for being fobbed off this time.

"I just don't understand."

"What don't you understand?"

"The day I saw him murdered..."

The rash had engulfed his cheeks now and he rubbed his hands over his eyes.

"Maggie? What is this about?"

"I get why you convinced me not to come forward. Not just to protect me, but because he killed our mum – and didn't even stop to check. But what if... what if he was just a lad too... just a stupid, scared lad who didn't know what would happen to him, so he just ran? And then he didn't know how to stop running because no one was looking for him. So, eventually, he ran back into the arms of the big sharks. Did he still deserve to get killed so brutally himself?"

"Maggie, don't. Please. Not now. Not today."

"I could have helped the police find that lad's killer. They could be behind bars by now, instead of…"

An image of Ranald and Mitchell living a life of privilege and moral high ground flashed before her.

"Instead of what?"

Lochie clenched his fists and took a deep breath before speaking again.

"Why are you asking me about this again? Why now? It was ten years ago."

Looking at her brother's anger, her bravery melted slightly. Could she really trust him with everything she now knew? He'd lied to her about the photos being destroyed. She'd found a prescription for Anne McGill's medicine that he left behind in her flat.

Why was she so scared of the truth when it involved him? The person she needed to be better than the rest of them?

"I just… I've been thinking about it a bit today. Because of Mum and how she died."

She met his lies with one of her own. But she couldn't tell him why she was questioning him. Not yet. Not until she'd given him the chance to volunteer an explanation himself.

"I thought nurses were taught to do the best by others, no matter who they are or what path they have walked in life?"

He searched her eyes for something. Maybe he was looking for a clue about what she knew?

"That's some high pedestal you have me on, Mags. We are not saints. I've told you why I wanted you to keep quiet so many times. And I'd say the same thing if it happened tomorrow. You have to move on. It's what Mum would want. Your whole life would be dragged into being a pawn in the criminal justice system. You think it would protect you? Keep you safe after you provided evidence? Why do you have to be so naïve?"

"I know, but… do you never think about it? Do you never wonder why they gave up investigating the case?"

She could see his eyes filling with anger now. She'd pushed too far. His body tightened.

"I have to get on with my life, Maggie. And so do you."

Maggie forced herself into places she was scared to go.

"You've never thought about the lad over the years? Wondered what his family went through?"

Lochie's face turned grey, and his features changed in an instant.

"Christ's sake. I was protecting you, Mags. You know that. You were seventeen and hadn't long buried your own mother. Our dad left us to our own fate, and I was the closest thing you had to a parent. I made choices because I had to. I gave you the best advice I could at the time. Someone had to."

Maggie was used to folk dodging her questions with expertise. But she couldn't accept it from him. Not Lochie.

"You did. But that's the point I'm making. They were your choices, weren't they? Not mine."

A silence hung between them which terrified her.

"I think you're paranoid, Mags."

There it was again. Paranoid. But coming from him, it hurt so hard.

"What the hell does that mean?"

"You know. I've told you; your brain is not…"

"What? What is it *not*?"

Maggie could hear the desperate sadness in her own voice. But he carried on.

"It's not… rational. You do stuff, and think stuff that's not… all that counting, and cleaning, and checking and unrelenting routine. It's a clinical condition that is taking over your life, and your sense of rational thought. You're so preoccupied with that stuff that it's making you doubt other things. It's making you doubt me, Mags. Me. Your brother. Your own living relative. Don't do this. Just… don't."

She listened to his words and wanted to fight back, but a tremor in his voice stopped her. She couldn't push him too far. Seeing Lochie lose control of his emotions would be too much to bear. She wanted to tell him that her paranoia kept her on track. The questions she asked kept her on the right side of the truth. Just like her little habits kept her life in control. Like a crutch she relied on to cope with life. She counted, and cleaned, and checked because she couldn't not do those things. Because she had a genuine fear that not doing those things would have catastrophic consequences. Either for her or – worse – for someone she cared about. Would he understand if she told him about the bully – the mad pilot who's always in charge? The person telling her she can't leave things to chance? Because if she didn't do what he said, something awful would happen. Just like it did when her mum was killed in an instant. Or when Ryan Ross lost his life in the woods that day. She needed to keep her world in order. She couldn't take chances with the bully. She had no choice.

But she didn't say any of this. Instead, she let him convince her he had a point. He was the nurse, after all. Of course, he knew what he was saying.

"Why haven't you spoken to me about this sooner? If I'm so… abnormal? You are no stranger to asking your patients intrusive, unwelcome questions."

Perhaps their jobs were not so different after all.

"I'm not a bloody psychiatrist, Maggie. I'm a hospital nurse. I take a truckload of pee samples. I measure blood pressure in my sleep, and I spend a lot of time telling patients that the doctor will see them soon, whilst holding their hand and trying to make them laugh – or just a little less afraid."

Maggie clasped her hands around her mug of herbal tea, self-soothing as best she could.

"OK, Lochie. I get it. I know you're bloody good at your job. Folk have told me. But, sometimes, I just, I see or hear parts of someone different."

Maggie folded her arms across her chest, trying to protect herself from her own vulnerability. She could not let herself feel exposed again. Even to him. But her world was shifting on its axis because the one person she'd trusted all her life had lied to her about destroying those photos and about keeping in touch with the McGill family.

And that's the problem with lies, she thought. As soon as you uncover one, it makes you look for more. It makes you question everything.

"Lochie, I've got to go."

Everything inside her wanted to scream at him right now. But she'd lost her nerve.

Maggie was meant to ask him if he knew Pete McGill's half-brother was responsible for their mum's death. She was meant to ask him if he knew why Archie ended up working for Ranald Anderson, and whether he believed Mark agreed to testify against his own dad. But she couldn't say any of it, and thinking about each small lie stung her a little more. She had to get out of his house and keep walking until something made sense. But there were so many cracks on the pavement to avoid first.

24

SUNDAY P.M.

Maggie didn't stop walking until she got home. She considered a detour to the office but stopped herself. There was something unavoidably depressing in being there when the rest of the world was at home, tucking into roasts and binging on box sets with their families. It was bad enough that the one part of her precious family still left was breaking like thin ice under her feet. She didn't need another reminder of the emptiness of her days off.

As she opened the door to her flat, Maggie felt her knees buckle with relief, and the strength in her legs evaporated. She gave way to all of it and let her body fall to a seated position in her hallway, leaning against the wall. An overwhelming wave of sadness came at her without warning. Then a gnawing, grinding sensation of loneliness attacked her. She felt it from her skin to her bones.

Any sense of time deserted her. She stayed in the same position long enough for the buds of something new to push through the surface of her mind. Someone had met her need for company or support head on. Not by the bully this time, or an uninvited guest. It was something far more comforting. A sense of purpose. The hunger to see this thing – whatever it was – through to the end. Maggie had come so far with everything she had uncovered about the players in this story. Now was the time to write the final act. She couldn't back down from uncovering the answers to Mark Anderson's disappearance, or how it was tied to what she saw that day ten years ago.

Pulling her sorry body up from the floor, Maggie changed her clothes, washed her hands as quickly as she could and grabbed a caffeine-free Diet Coke from the fridge. She opened a fresh document on her laptop and a Google search bar on the tablet. There were three priorities to explore. First up was Mitchell Stevens. Why did he respond to a seemingly straightforward blackmail with murder? What was he doing in Val Anderson's house the day Maggie first visited, and if he was living with her, does Val know she and her daughters are sharing their home with a murderer? Perhaps she suspected something was very wrong about him but turned a blind eye – too afraid to explore herself or involve the police. That's why she sent Maggie on his trail.

The second question was about the Anderson girls. Why would a police car be following those girls secretly, but not tell their mother about the surveillance?

Then there was the last question that was digging in more stubbornly with every passing day. Why have the police built a wall of silence around their search for Mark Anderson?

It was going to be a long night.

*

"Morning conference in five minutes and I need a showstopper from each of you, my shifty pile of ink wasters, or this rag is going to the wall."

Lexi was on the rampage, like a woman possessed. With a bit of conferring, the news team could usually put this down to a specific reason, but they hadn't worked it out yet.

"Has she been dumped again?"

Harris's comments attracted a collective groan from the female reporters, like a Mexican wave of disgust.

"What? Menopause then?"

On any other day, Maggie would be tempted to tell Harris that overdoing his aftershave was pointless when his breath smelled like a brewery, but she didn't have the energy today. She'd had about two hours' sleep, but it was worth the sacrifice. Taking a long breath, she kept her head down, trying to avoid eye contact with everyone.

Looking at today's paper, she saw her report on the suspicious fire at the old Lino building hidden on page twenty-one, where no one would care.

The lack of coverage about the police hunt for Mark continued. It was as if his disappearance had dropped off the radar. He may not be high risk to the cops, but surely there were enough rugby fans in the northeast of Scotland to merit the odd update on the story?

She transferred last night's work to a shared news file where Lexi would find it. It was all in there. What she'd written about the family that she'd immersed herself in for the last few days. After everything Lexi had said, Maggie feared her words would never see the light of day, but she didn't care. She wrote them anyway. She wrote about a family torn apart by the loss of their dad, husband, and son. There was the glittering surface of the Andersons' sporting and financial glory before being brought to their knees by a sudden and inexplainable vanishing. Maggie wrote on, asking why there were no answers and why the police had – apparently – stopped communicating with the media. It was all there. Out of her head and down in writing.

Then she picked up her ringing phone to be met by Val Anderson's clipped vowels.

"I wanted you to know I've had a family liaison officer on my doorstep. Turns out they've identified, questioned and released two suspects with a warning to stay the hell away from my daughters."

"Eh? But that makes rock all sense."

"No? Well, that was their last word on the matter. Are you going to tell me you know something they don't?"

Maggie couldn't help thinking it felt deeply sinister. Having a covert police operation around Val's children was one thing, but faking an arrest and release to cover it up was a whole new level.

"It was a senior police officer's car that was following them, Mrs Anderson. I told the police that myself. Sorry, I know you didn't want me to involve them, but…"

"Let me guess, you used my daughters' situation against them to get something in return?"

"No, I…"

"And you wonder why everyone hates reporters?"

The bitter tone of Val's voice sounded stronger than ever.

"Please try not to see it like that. We both want the truth, for your girls. I promise."

"Do we? And did they?"

"Did they what?"

"Give you something, girl. Did they give you something in return?"

"Not exactly, no."

"Yeh, I thought as much."

Val sounded like all the fight was seeping out of her and Maggie realised now was not the moment to ask if she knew she was living with a murderer. The unnerving thing for Maggie was that she didn't know if it would be worse if Val did or didn't know about Mitchell Stevens's past. She had to protect herself too, but going to the police with what she'd learnt didn't feel like a good move either. Maggie wasn't a police hater. She respected everything the police stood for and knew that the good cops far, far outnumbered the bad. She'd done her job long enough to know that theirs was no enviable task. Yes, there was a tension between the press and Police Scotland. But she was sure there was nowhere in the world that this love/hate thing didn't thrive. But she never forgot they were doing their job, just like her.

She picked up her desk phone. Maybe she could lean on their press office about Mark again – or at the very least, get an explanation for why the media were being told nothing. She just had to get one of the team who owed her a favour for burying something unhelpful.

If she got nowhere with that, it might be time to break cover with her findings about Ranald's data breach and the vulnerable NHS trial. But going public with her exclusive on a large-scale medical data breach meant bringing herself into the story.

The press office phone rang out without being answered.

Collaborative working in action, eh?

She tried it once more from her mobile in case they were just blocking her calls. It wouldn't be the first time. Still no answer. Lexi had gathered the troops for a news conference and Maggie was all out of thinking time.

*

"Right, now that Shields has decided to join us, I'll start with the kick up the arse you've all been waiting for."

The boss's black eyeliner seemed to veer a bit off course halfway around her left eye, and her lips were not painted their customary pillar box red.

"There's not a shadow of a doubt that the dark beast of digital and social media is chasing us like a rat up a drainpipe. That means that the bosses want us to be centre stage at the twenty-four-hour news party with a regional newspaper budget. So, you don't have to be Einstein to work out how that's going to pan out."

All eyes dropped to the desk in front of them. Harris let a snigger escape under his breath, but Lexi pounced on it.

"Yes, even smart-arse pretty boys like yourself won't

be getting by on a wink and prayer when that lot upstairs swings the axe."

That shut him up at least, thought Maggie.

"The harsh reality, my collective guddle of wordsmiths, is that we need to be knocking out fresh news every hour... on the chuffing hour. We need to get folk off their celebrity podcasts and TikTok crap and re-engaged in local events. Give them stories they can fill the comments section with online. You know, the stuff that affects readers' *actual* lives – the cost-of-living crisis, where their taxes are being spent, how long it takes to see a doctor, whether their streets are safe to walk down. Get the picture?"

Heads were now down all around the room. For Maggie – whose main aspiration was to pursue the long game of investigative reporting – it was the hardest of news. Her work was slow, expensive, and came with high risk versus reward odds.

A depressed hush hung in the air of Lexi's office, cutting through the mix of perfume, hair spray, and strong coffee.

"Ah, but cheer up. It's not all bad. Whilst I've still got puff in my blackened lungs, I've no intention of letting your talents hide under a bushel. So, what wee gems have you made up for me this morning, then? Who wants to take the stage first?"

Stan was first to speak. He was the grandfather of the group, less than a year from pensionable age, and often took one for the team. He was always the first man over the top of the trenches whilst the rest braced themselves for impact.

"Some interesting stuff going on at the Sheriff Court today. Usual line-up of weekend lunacy coming up from the cells, but that bloke from Leven who's accused of nicking expensive malt whiskies from delivery vans out the back of the posh hotels in St Andrews is on the stand. Should be interesting."

Lexi looked at Stan with a forced smile. It would fill space and the subs would have fun with the headline, at least.

"Crap day for sport, I'm afraid, boss."

Harris was next to make his excuses.

"There's a late transfer announcement coming between the Dundee clubs. But other than that, I'm clear to support where needed."

Maggie felt the embers of rage take light in her gut again.

Clear to support where needed was Harris speak for *I've got rock all of my own doing but I'm happy to butt in on someone else's territory.*

It was Maggie's turn, and she was feeling brave.

"I've got a potential new lead on the Anderson family."

The words were out before she could stop them. She paused, waiting for the reaction.

"Hang on, Maggie. Just a minute."

Lexi didn't hear her. She was on her feet, pulling something out of a printer behind her, and handing it to Harris.

"Could you look at this? It's a follow-up from that business we chatted about yesterday. Come and see me once you've got to grips with it."

Maggie bore her gaze into the back of the paper, wishing the heat of her stare could render it transparent.

What the hell was that about?

"Sorry – what were you saying, Shields?"

"The Andersons. I've got some more stuff emerging there."

Lexi heard this time, and her anger was mounting.

"I could do you a holding piece on the stalled investigation into Mark's disappearance. Val says they've not had a visit from the cops in…"

"We've spoken about that story, Maggie. I told you clearly to back off until we get more from the coppers."

Maggie's heart sank as she ran headfirst into the brick wall she feared was just around the corner.

"I tried to call them earlier. There's something else, boss. It's the old man Anderson – Mark's father, Ranald. Turns out he's got some dodgy previous on providing software to medical groups that's got more holes than a Tetley tea bag."

"No. not now. It's not right for us."

Maggie's cheeks felt red hot. That was the hardest no she'd had this year. She'd plucked up the courage to speak up and Lexi was throwing it back in her face. It had everything – normal people suffering at the hands of powerful, greedy incompetents. Vulnerable medical data being hacked by all the world's weirdos. It couldn't be more squarely in Lexi's ballpark. What the hell was going on?

"But I'm telling you, there's a history of serious medical data breach and it's happened again with…"

"I said NO, Maggie. Are you not listening? Find

something else for tomorrow's pages or I'll put you on the Obituaries. Do you understand?"

Maggie dipped her head and bit her tongue. Holding onto the job she loved was no picnic, but she had a story to tell, and she was going to tell it – regardless of what Lexi thought.

"Sure, boss, I understand."

She left the conference hoping Lexi would see the piece she'd filed earlier that morning and change her mind. It was only a matter of time.

25

MONDAY P.M.

Maggie had to get out of the office as soon as she could. The cogs in her brain moved better after a long walk. She felt the air sweep through her body with a power that shed the worst of the day's mental sewage. There was no coastline that could match the east of Scotland for pumping high-density oxygen straight to her vital organs. Whatever month of the year, there was a raw purity in the air that smelt of ripe seaweed and the plentiful shellfish lurking under rocks and crevices all up the east coast. Looking at the jumble washed up on the shore, she felt the entanglement of her own mind.

The beach helped her think clearly. It was somewhere she came with Lochie when they were younger. They would dig holes so deep that it felt as if they were heading for the core of the earth. He insisted on being buried up to his head in the sand whilst their parents lay behind, drinking warm beer and laughing. Those were effortless days that felt like they would go on forever. How wrong could she be.

Doing her best to capture the surrounding landscape, Maggie headed towards the shore road, dusk crowding around her from every angle. She felt the breeze cool and heard the faint sound of footsteps walking behind her. But when she turned around, the street was empty.

Feeling another chill ripple through her body, she increased her speed, moving on autopilot until she found herself outside Lochie's house. She tried to focus on counting the pavement slabs under her feet, back under the spell of the bully and the rituals that helped her before ANT interfered.

One, two, three… breathe in.

One, two, three… breathe out.

Find the rhythm, Maggie, find the safety.

Looking at his windows, she noticed there were no lights on. Lochie couldn't be inside. Even when he was hiding from the world, there would be one dim light on in the upstairs bedroom, but there was nothing but empty blackness.

Reaching to open his front door with her own key, she found it was already open. He never left his home unlocked. The hairs on her arms stood to attention. Something felt very wrong. Maggie knew the contours of this house like her own body; she could navigate the furniture in the dark. A hard object knocked against her shins – like a piece of furniture in the middle of the hallway. Whatever it was, it shouldn't be there.

"Hello? Lochie?"

Maggie felt around the wallpaper with a shaking finger to locate the light switch. Unforgiving artificial light showed the carnage in detail. The dining room table was on its side, drawers and cupboards in the lounge thrown open, their contents exploding out of them like vomit. In the kitchen, the scene was repeated – all kinds of mess on the floor. Electrical wires, old wallets, batteries, and other detritus. Mum's cookbooks had flown from the old wooden dresser, which hadn't been touched since the day she died, to the rug inside the back door. Memories of chocolate brownies, chicken soup and failed attempts at complicated eighties wonders like baked Alaska reduced to a mess of pages and broken spines.

A door squeaked behind her. As she looked down the hallway, she saw the cupboard door flapping in the breeze that drifted through the house from outside. Did she leave the door open behind her? Flashbacks of what she'd found in that cupboard gripped her in a vice.

The photos. Someone was looking for the photos.

Stepping forwards to look inside, she found more chaos. The shoeboxes that she'd discovered only days ago strewn across the floor, their contents littering the worn wooden floor in heaps. Shifting further into the darkness of the cupboard, she searched around on the floor for the one thing that really mattered.

The same floorboard shook slightly when she pressed it – just like it did last time. She'd found it by accident in that last desperate moment as Lochie arrived home. It was the perfect hiding place. A way to protect the evidence without stealing it.

With one sharp knock of her fist at the corner, it flipped open, and her heart skipped a beat. There, in the crevice, just where she'd left it, was the USB memory stick she'd wrapped in a piece of paper. Just for safe keeping. Beating someone else to it by less than twenty-four hours. Who was looking for this with such desperation that they had to turn the whole house upside down?

Maggie fell to her knees in the one part of the hall that wasn't covered with debris. She needed the support of a hard surface to ground her.

What have you got yourself into, Lochie?

She reached for her phone. She needed to hear his voice. Whatever else was going on, she had to know that he was OK. He kept his shift patterns on a pinboard in the kitchen. Rising slowly back to her feet, she walked back along the hall, stepping over destruction as she went. There was a printout of his hospital shifts stuck with a safety pin to the flaking cork. He was the only person she knew who didn't use his phone as a diary. Scrolling her finger along the columns to the right date, she saw that he was on a back shift. He wouldn't be home until after 10 p.m.

The hospital switchboard was painfully slow to navigate, and her impatience was unconcealed by the time someone answered.

"I need someone to contact Lochie Shields urgently – he's the charge nurse on ward forty-four, HDU."

"I'm sorry, but who am I speaking to?"

"It's his sister, Maggie Shields. And I'm sitting in his house. It's just been broken into. Can someone please get him to look at his phone and call me ASAP?"

Maggie hung up abruptly and made her next call to 999. She imagined someone loose on the streets of

Kirkcaldy, livid as hell that they failed to find what they were looking for.

*

Lochie never went near his phone during a busy hospital shift. He'd leave it in the staff locker and often not have time to check it during his breaks. But she hoped someone had passed the message to him by now. She was considering calling back and asking the hospital to confirm he was there when the doorbell rang.

Two uniformed officers came to take a statement, followed soon after by the crime scene folk, who got busy looking for fingerprints, asking questions about locks and alarms. She explained it was her brother's house and that he would be home from his hospital shift soon.

"I'm technically still a co-owner, but I've not lived here – in this house, I mean – in a long time."

"Have you noticed what they've taken?"

"Nothing. They've taken nothing. But I still wanted to report it, obviously. They've ripped through the place. It's… it's just grim."

She realised that sounded odd. But Maggie knew what she was saying.

"Do you think you interrupted them before they took something?"

This was getting too close for comfort.

"No. I don't think so."

"OK, did you see anyone suspicious outside the property when you arrived?"

The questions kept coming like rapid fire.

Has the property been broken into before? What is your brother's job? Does he keep any medical equipment/needles or medication here?

She wanted to tell them she had a pretty good idea what they were looking for. And that it wasn't some expensive telly, or needles, or any other run-of-the-mill stuff. But she didn't. Something was holding her back from divulging all she knew about the photos in Lochie's house. Instead, she answered their tick-box enquiries, let them do their work and listened whilst they told her they needed to speak to Lochie ASAP.

Pulling the door shut behind them, Maggie looked at her watch. It was now almost 9 p.m. Why was he not home? She called him again, twice, and left another message on his voicemail.

"Lochie – what's going on? Tell me you're OK, right?"

She knew she couldn't leave the house like this. Maggie had to put her brother's home back together. Maybe because she knew her mum would like it that way. As she worked, she imagined him fixing patients and making them as comfortable as possible before handing over to the night shift. Because that is exactly what he would be doing right now. He didn't deserve to come home to this.

*

There was something pure about the silence of cleaning alone. She felt it made space for the sounds of memories. It allowed her to imagine noises which brought her mum back to the home. The gentle humming of her singing as she cleaned up after everyone or stood ironing clothes without complaint.

But she also liked silence because you didn't miss when it was broken – by someone or something. The unmistakable sound of Lochie's front door opening was followed by footsteps that she knew with certainty were not his. They had a slowness of movement. They sounded intrusive – foreign to this home. Laying down her dust cloth silently on the coffee table, Maggie was back on high alert. She couldn't remember closing the front or back door when the cops left.

Don't let that bully take over now. You've always closed the doors, Maggie.

That's what Lochie would say. But did she actually *do it* this time?

You've always closed the door, and switched off the lights, the oven, the fan heater.

That's what he'd tell me, and every time, he was right. But tonight – no, tonight was different. It wasn't the bully speaking to her, trying to mess with her day. To take hold again where therapy and artificial therapy had been pushed out. It was real.

Searching the room for something that would injure a person on contact, she found the old steel coal shovel that Lochie kept as an ornament. Maggie crept towards the hallway, watching for any shadowy movements coming from the back of the house. Her breathing was shallow, but something hit the furthest reaches of her throat. It was a strong taste or scent. Musky. Not unpleasant, but not off until I bottomed it out a bit, but this thing could affect thousands of NHS patients. This is big. And I'm all over it well before the authorities catch up. Why aren't you letting me do my job?"

Nothing pushed Maggie into top gear like the whiff of censorship and, for a moment, it numbed the pain of her brother's lies.

Lexi thrust her right hand in front of her body as if to physically restrain Maggie from continuing.

"Enough!"

The tone and volume of Lexi's voice stung the air.

"In my office, now."

Lexi rose sharply to her feet and moved without looking back, knowing she'd be followed. She switched on her computer and motioned to Maggie to sit down opposite her.

"I need you to listen for once, Shields. And I mean, really use those lugs of yours."

Relief flooded through Maggie at the thought she was going to tell her about the email from COPFS.

About bloody time.

"Remember when Clarkson and Symington paid us a friendly wee visit recently?"

She was hardly going to forget that in a hurry, and the reminder twisted in her gut.

"Oh, aye. All in the name of collaborative working – only to be instantly followed by a complete police communication blackout."

Lexi nodded quietly.

"Aye, well, when I walked them out of the building,

carried through the house by her brother. She tightened her grip on the coal shovel, but her hands were wet with sweat, and it felt like it might slip from her fingers any second.

A silhouette of a figure she knew stood square on, in front of her.

26

MONDAY P.M.

Maggie dropped the shovel, causing an almighty clang of metal against wood.

"Stay away from me!" She heard the tremble in her own voice as she warned him to back off. Pete McGill did as he was told. He lifted his hands, showing his empty palms.

"What the hell are you doing here?"

"Sorry. Please… I won't hurt you. I rang the bell, but it didn't work, and then I saw the side gate swinging open and the window smashed to shit."

Maggie kept her distance, the pounding in her chest as strong as ever.

"Still doesn't explain how you knew I'd be *here*?"

Maggie searched Pete's face for any signs of lying. It was expressionless.

"I didn't. I wasn't looking for you. I was looking for Lochie."

She noticed he hadn't moved from the spot. He was slowly lowering his hands back down to his sides. Maggie straightened her body in front of him.

"You OK?"

It felt genuine enough for Maggie to relax a bit. She nodded, silently. Mistrust still filling every pore.

"Yep. Except for dealing with a feckin' mess."

He looked around but there wasn't much left to see. She'd completely tidied away any hint of a robbery from the ground floor of the house, except the broken windows.

"Mess? What's happened?"

Maggie shook her head, feeling a rage building inside that she had to channel somewhere.

"The house still smells of them. You know that unclean smell that criminals leave in your life?"

"Was someone here?"

Maggie noticed Pete looking at her in a way that made her feel like a victim.

"What do you want with my brother?"

Pete was walking slowly towards her now. She reacted with a step back.

"It's OK, Maggie. Whatever you think is going on, I'm no threat to you, I promise. Breathe."

"I'm breathing just fine. I just didn't enjoy mopping up a crime scene for the last three hours. I asked you a question."

Maggie caught her reflection in the hall mirror and shrank away from Pete, embarrassed by her weakness. Sweat drenched the skin of her face, and her eyes looked bloodshot.

"I want him to tell you the truth."

The words repulsed her. Who? What truth?

Then it hit her like a brick that Pete was talking about Lochie.

"What do you mean? Lochie tells me everything. Why would I listen to you?"

"Listen, for just a second. Please. He's been visiting my mum with medication."

She wanted to tell him to leave, not to mess with her mind. But she couldn't. She remembered the prescription that fell out of Lochie's pocket. The one she'd not plucked up the courage to ask him about it. At least Pete wasn't lying to her.

"What did you say?"

"My mum. Lochie has been visiting her for weeks, bringing her medication to help with her… with everything, really."

They'd moved into the kitchen, and she collapsed backwards onto a wooden chair. She'd not mentioned the prescription to anyone. He must be telling the truth.

"Why are you telling me this?"

"Mum was cagey at first. Tried to pretend she'd never heard the name Lochie Shields. But she is a shite liar, my ma."

"Why? Why would he be doing that? Lochie is a hospital nurse, not a chemist's delivery service. You're telling me he just rocked up to her house like some door-to-door salesman? And she let him in with open arms?"

"There's a way of tackling my mum, and it sounds like he knew what he was doing. That lad's got more charm than you give him credit for."

There he goes again, she thought. Talking about Lochie like he really knew him. Liked him even. Maggie dropped her head into the seclusion of her own hands, but Pete kept talking into the silence of her thoughts.

"My mum despises doctors. Always has. And medicine. And pretty much anyone who has tried to help her manage her grief. Claims it's all a waste of time. Apparently, she's got some messed up fear of being around medics in uniform – white coat syndrome, they call it. That's why she drinks. Self-medicating, so she tells me."

Maggie thought of her own fears. The day she ran away from a therapy session and how that NHS invitation to an AI therapy trial made her feel. Trust between patient and carer must be the hardest to win.

"I'd noticed a bit of a change in Mum. Can't describe it. Like some of her fog had lifted. She seemed less dragged down, I guess. I thought she was just having a good run of it. It's happened before but doesn't last long."

"But... why Lochie? Why *him*? There's something else you're not telling me."

"Honestly, Maggie, I don't know much more. That's what I was coming to ask him. He just turned up on her doorstep one day. Apparently, there was something 'in his magic blue eyes' that made her feel safe."

Maggie understood. She knew those eyes well. The dots were joining up in her head.

"Did she say why? Had someone sent him from the hospital?"

Pete edged a little away.

"No, I got little more sense out of her – she seemed extra sleepy. The pay-off from those pills, I guess. She just moaned a bit about not getting them this week. Something about him losing that wee note for the chemist. Said he'd get a new one and come back another time."

Maggie's thoughts were spiralling out of control again. Her adrenaline rising. And with the adrenaline came its master and commander – mistrust.

"Lochie's a nurse – he can't write prescriptions. She'd need to be seen by a doctor."

Pete said nothing. He just shrugged his shoulders, as if he knew that was no insurmountable problem.

"Please don't lie to me, Pete. I've had enough of shit liars for one week."

Maggie heard the desperate tone in her voice, and she despised herself for it. She'd just worked out who killed Pete's brother, but she was the one angry that he was keeping her in the dark.

"I'm trying to help you here. Why won't you trust me like you trust *him*?" Pete said, a genuine look of hurt written on his face.

His words felt sharp. Bitter. Loaded. She couldn't bring herself to tell him the truth that her trust in Lochie was crumbling away with every new twist and turn of this sorry tale.

She needed her mind to catch up. Pete was watching her closely, though. Still watching her every move. Then he looked to the scene around them. The mess and damage.

"Maggie, can I help you here? Just until Lochie gets home?"

It felt like he was trying to get inside her head. Just like that bloody robot therapist, ANT, had. And look where that got her. How could she be so naïve?

"Can you just leave, please?"

He ignored her, so she headed upstairs to Lochie's

bedroom and closed the door behind her. It was an instinct that took her back to childhood. Whenever she got into trouble from their parents, she'd run and hide in Lochie's room. It didn't matter if he was there or not.

This room still looked so like how Maggie remembered it from when she lived there. His bed was still in the same position, up against the wall. There were no Baywatch posters, though, or football boots infesting hidden corners. He'd changed the carpet once and painted the walls a couple of times, but that was it. Someone had forcefully evicted the contents of the sliding cupboards – shirts, jeans, jackets strewn across the floor and on the bed.

She hung everything back up as best she could, taking a moment to breathe in the smell of her brother. His jackets smelt like his hugs and the faint whiff of cheap Lynx body spray hung around his T-shirts.

Exhaustion was taking control of her body in waves, pleading with her to rest. To go home. Slumping into a corner, she gave way to the uncompromising need to stop. Just stop.

Letting her eyelids gently close as she leant against the edge of the wardrobe door, she saw the briefest glint of red shooting out from one shelf. She almost missed it completely. Her eyes opened wider, and she stared intently at something that should be of no significance at all. Just another item tucked in the back of a shelf. Like an ant's nest left undisturbed for years. Nestled among a sea of other untouched items, she found single socks, a football scarf, some gloves, and a red cap.

27

MONDAY P.M.

For the next five seconds, she considered walking away.

If I hadn't seen this, I would never have to think about it again. I could walk away and erase it from my memory.

But it was too late. The damage was done. She moved like lightning, grabbing the red cap with one shaking hand, desperate to find the thing that reassured her. The thing that told her it was not *that* red cap. Not the red cap that was worn by the third person in the photo – looking on when Archie's life was stolen. It would be there. She'd find the thing that meant it wasn't Lochie in the shadows of that photo. Standing, watching, and doing nothing to stop it unfolding. When she found it, she could relax, let her heart rate return to normal and breathe comfortably, again. Just as she'd done so often before when her obsessive worries turned out to be unfounded. That warm, sedating feeling that spread through her veins when she got the reassurance needed.

She turned over the red canvas in her shaking palm.

The cap was distorted out of shape from being wedged between other items in his wardrobe for so long. The next thing she saw was the Adidas logo.

She wanted to throw it against the wall like a ticking bomb and run as far away as possible. The room spun around her. Reaching for something to hold onto as an anchor, she found the corner of Lochie's bed.

Maggie pulled the hat from her brother's bedroom floor, tore past Pete and carried on downstairs, stopping to grab the USB stick from its hiding place under the floorboard. Then she ran out of the door without looking back.

"Maggie?"

Someone was following her. Then a hand on her shoulder.

"No, Lochie!"

"Maggie?"

"Go away, Lochie!"

"Maggie… it's Pete. What the hell?"

"Leave me alone – don't come near me!"

She was shaking her head. Everyone was lying to her. She would not listen to any more lies. Pete reached out and tried to unclench her fists.

"The red cap. It's the red cap."

"What? What cap? What are you talking about?"

How could she tell him this? How could she tell him her own brother was there when Archie was brutally murdered?

"I thought he was protecting me by telling me to keep quiet. But he was just protecting himself."

Her words trailed off into silence. She thought of Archie, Pete's brother, lying in the woods – the life ebbing out of him. Just as she'd seen it leave her mother's eyes.

"Maggie! Talk to me!"

But she ran. As long as she was running, she didn't have to speak to anyone else.

28

MONDAY P.M.

Maggie ran from an ugly and terrifying new truth. For so long the questions had haunted her, but now the answers – the truth – were so much worse. The acid in her legs forced her to stop. She counted her paces in threes between each lamppost, avoiding cracks in the pavement, and trying to piece everything together. But each time it looked like the jigsaw was solved, she found bits that must have been thrown in the wrong box. Like the image of her own brother, standing watching in the shadows as someone's life was stolen from them. Wearing that red cap. A deep red, like the blood on her mother's dying face, and the blood seeping through Archie's clothes as he lay in the soggy woodland path. Lochie didn't belong in this picture. She tried to push him out, but the facts worked against her.

Maggie was close to the safety of home now. There she could shut the door on it all. Her heart rate stabilised as her pace slowed. But the bully reminded her to fear what might wait around every corner. Even in the eyes of the people she trusted the most.

Until now, evil had found its home around people that meant nothing to her. People whose families were faceless, nameless additions to their lives. But evil had entered the closest parts of her world and stopped her from doing the job she lived for.

There was no way she could tell this story and protect her brother now. Not after what she had just found. The belief she had in his innocence was shattering into pieces like glass in front of her.

Crouching down on the cold stone of her doorstep, her body began to shake with panic. Maggie cradled her arms around herself and searched for peace, but all she could feel was resistance. She couldn't bring herself to go inside. Even her own home felt hostile, unfamiliar. Poisoned by the fear engulfing her mind. All she could do was sit with it. Feel it and not try to fight it.

She promised herself she would move again on the count of three. One, two…

No, I can't.

Try again. When three cars have passed on the street, it will be safe to move again. One… two… was that a car? No, I think I counted that one twice. No… I have to start again. One… two… three.

Oh God, Lochie's right. What is wrong with me? I can't even count to three.

Defeated and exhausted, her thoughts fell away from the present and into the past. She let herself go too far back. Back to the day a couple of lost, motherless kids watched their dad – broken by his own grief – walk out the door forever.

It was Lochie who'd picked them both up and put them back together. That was the good that made her brother. She couldn't forget that – no matter where life had dragged him to since. The same component parts still made him who he was. The same vital organs. The same mind. She needed to find him again. But first, she needed to find somewhere to feel safe. There was only one other place she could go.

*

It was almost midnight when Maggie made it through the back doors at the *Standard*. The night shift security man, Tony, looked like he'd fallen asleep reading his paper. She coughed lightly to wake him up. He jumped, snorted and hid the folded tabloid under his seat.

"You again, doll. D' ye jus' no sleep or what, luv?"

Maggie smiled awkwardly as she ran her ID card through the scanner on the wall, waking the elevator up too.

"Aye, somethin' like that Tony. Don't suppose Lexi's in?"

"Are you having a laugh, ye donut – you seen the time? This is the witching hour for that one."

"Fair enough."

"You OK there, lass?"

She kept walking towards the lift and away from Tony's face. It was full of questions she didn't want to be asked.

As the lift doors closed in front of her, she caught Tony's eyes. His look of concern irritated her. Her hair felt greasy, so she pulled it back in a low ponytail, leaving some strands stuck to her skin with sweat. Her top lip was cracked and dry from exposure to the cold, salty air. Maggie hadn't changed her clothes since she'd gotten up at 6 a.m., so she'd have to improvise.

Standing alone in the lift, the panic began to rise. She forced it down again, somewhere deep. At least for now. The doors opened, and she headed to the loos. Memories of the day Lexi found her there, slumped in a corner, scratching at her own hands, rushed back. She scrubbed her hands and her face, and her hands again until the skin came up red raw and burnt when she held them under the dryer. But today, at least, she would get out of this room herself.

As she moved through the deserted office, the odd light sprang on as she triggered a sensor. There was a secret stash of individually wrapped T-shirts, leggings, and underwear in the bottom drawer of her desk. Nothing warm enough to protect her from the cold of the office at night but at least she could shed off the days' clothes. Things might feel better then. She might clean some of the horror of what she'd found and what she was told in Lochie's house.

The effort served her well and a greater calm took over. It would only be a moment's respite, but she was determined to use it. Switching on her computer, Maggie tried to focus. There must be a way through this that made sense.

A faint noise broke the stillness of the air. Like a door shutting in the corridor outside. An open window allowed an isolated draft to blow through the office. After getting up to close it, the second noise followed – it was unmistakable. The lift shaft was in motion. Someone else was in the building. Then the sharp ping of the doors opening on her floor. Maggie swallowed down what little moisture was in her throat.

"Tony?"

But the movements were too subtle to be his. The footsteps sounded more hurried – and a familiar raspy breathing sound was audible with each step. They were getting closer now, turning onto the main reporters' floor.

Why are people following me everywhere? It must be those hackers. Have they got into my phone somehow, too?

As she grabbed her mobile phone from her pocket, she saw the ANT app firing notifications out. It seemed to pick up her pulse rate. *How the hell?* She tried to disable it on the screen, but the phone wouldn't unlock. There was nowhere Maggie could hide. She leant back against the window she'd closed. This time, there was no tree to hide behind, no forest darkness to camouflage herself inside. No choice but to wait and listen.

"Lochie? Pete?"

No, it can't be them. Neither of them would get access to the building without a fob. And Tony would have stopped them from coming any further.

Then came the voice that could break glass from a hundred feet.

"What the chuffing hell are you doing here, Maggie Shields?"

Lexi was standing with her hands jabbing into her hips and a look that bridged disgust and pride.

"Jeez, boss. You scared the living shi…"

"Are you mad? What are you doing here in the middle of the night?"

There's that word again. Mad. Just like 'paranoid'. They keep coming up. Maybe they are all right?

What did Lochie always say to her when all the evidence pointed in the same direction?

If it looks like shit and smells like shit, it's no a bunch of roses, is it?

She dropped her gaze, stared at the carpet and tried to come up with a decent response.

"I've got stuff to write. Like you said, this paper's not going to save itself, eh?"

Maggie retreated to her own desk, where it occurred to ask why the boss was here too. It was the obvious comeback, but the moment had passed. But Lexi must have read her mind.

"Old Tony down there was worried. Said your face was tripping you – white as a sheet, he reckoned, like you'd been in some trouble. At least that was his excuse for waking me up at one in the friggin' morning – and he's not known for his oversensitivity is Tony. Interrupted a perfectly good sleep, so he did."

Maggie wondered if an apology would help. Or at least lowering the pace and pitch of her voice.

"Sorry, but I'm fine, and I've got a key. There's no need for you to stay."

"Save it for my cat. The grumpy old hag was sprawled across me like a fat, lazy lump. Bloody thing hissed at me like a cobra when the phone went."

Lexi was striding with a purpose now, towards Maggie's desk, making a fuss of pulling her coat off dramatically, before pushing a seat next to her desk. An overwhelming odour of sickly perfume orbiting her. It struck Maggie as odd, considering she'd just peeled herself off the sofa. Her make-up had also been applied, albeit badly. Maybe it was just last night's make-up that wasn't washed off yet? The thought made her stomach turn.

"So, are you going to tell me what the hell you *needed* to write at this time in the ni—day... whatever the hell it is?"

The weight of expectation hung in the air. She imagined Lexi's purple glasses-framed eyes were directed right on her. There was nothing about Lexi's body language that suggested a change of heart from the last time she was told to back off from Anderson, or the many times before that.

"I read that latest piece you wrote, lass. All that pulling on the heartstrings stuff about a family lost for answers and let down by the cops. Pretty heavy stuff, eh?"

Maggie looked up, bewildered but relieved to have more time to think.

"Eh?"

"Is that your idea of working in collaboration with our friends down the police station?"

Lexi's smile made the lines in her face deepen, giving her a more vulnerable quality that relaxed Maggie a little.

"Well... I'm not sure I expected to see it in print after you made your feelings clear on that one. It was just a download. Needed to get it off my chest after you killed the story. Just ignore it. I need to speak to you about something else, though, seeing as you're here."

"Ah, you do? I thought you were just in here to write?"

Maggie was tying herself in knots, but Lexi just sat there, leaning back and looking uncomfortable in a reporter's overused chair.

"Do you remember that murder in the woods ten years ago?"

Lexi tensed slightly in her seat, unfolding her arms and gently clenching her fists by her sides.

"Aye, I do. Went cold years ago, Shields. It's dead in the water – so to speak."

"Yeh, well, there's a connection between Mark Anderson's disappearance and what went down that day. I know that for certain now."

Maggie looked straight at her boss, but Lexi dropped her gaze and started picking at something on her blouse before releasing a low mumble.

"Is that a fact?"

"It's as close to fact as I've got for now. I've got a potent source – like – as strong as they get, boss. There's a whole bucketload of shit behind this one. Trust me."

"Trust you? I thought I told you to back off from the Andersons – more times than I should've had to."

"I know. I know you did. But the thing is, the man – Ranald, not Mark – just keeps popping up everywhere, like a bad penny. It makes no sense to just let it go."

"Try harder."

Maggie was feeling her rage rise to the surface now.

"Christ, boss. You'll want to hear this. I've just found out the old man Anderson has been involved in some shady medical data breach cover-up, too. Was holding this

they told me there was a perfectly good, sorry, a 'valid operational' reason Anderson's disappearance was being handled the way it was, and if we 'stir things up', it could have dire consequences – their words."

Lexi's cheeks flushed as she was talking, her eyes searching for something on the screen in front of her.

"This case goes higher than the local force. I got an email from the Fiscal's office echoing the advice to back off, and those guys don't mess around. I'm too close to cashing in what's left of my pension to risk some shower of shit raining down on me from that lot."

"The Procurator Fiscal? But boss… I don't get how…"

"Look at this."

She motioned for Maggie to come and look at it next to her.

"Remember that arrest of the pair who were allegedly stalking Anderson's girls?"

"Yup"

"Those lads never had their day in court."

"Eh?"

"It was a textbook weekend arrest," said Lexi. "That pair would've been in the cells over the weekend and should've been first up in the Sheriff Court on Monday morning. But it never happened."

"I don't follow."

Lexi had the upper hand again.

"I've checked all the court records myself. It was like their arrest was just written off the books."

The cogs in Maggie's brain whirred again. Her forehead warmed with the effort.

"There's something weird there, Maggie. And I don't like it."

Maggie thought back to what Tetchy had told her about the car following the girls.

"It was a copper's car following those girls. Of course, they weren't going to be in court to answer questions about why they were monitoring Olivia and Rebecca – if it was all legit. You know, an unmarked car operating in the line of duty. But why fake an arrest? Feels like an elaborate show for the benefit of onlookers to me. If you won't let me touch the miss per investigation, why won't you let me chase this new line about Anderson senior's rotten software leaking highly sensitive medical data?"

Lexi's face stiffened, and she reached down to her desk cupboard and pulled out a bottle of gin. This was the first time she'd ever done this in Maggie's company.

"Want one?"

"Nah, you're OK, thanks."

She poured liberally into a glass, adding no mixer, and her first mouthful drained half the contents.

"I just want you out of that man's orbit. Something in my cynical old bones wants to keep you safe."

"Don't…"

"Don't what?"

"Don't say it. Don't say it's for your own good. My protection or something like that."

Those words had haunted Maggie long enough. Lexi shook her head, letting an exasperated sigh escape.

"Look – I get it, Shields. I'm only going to say this quickly when no one else is around to witness it. You're a bloody excellent investigator. Hard as nails and better than half the lads in here. But you don't need to chase this one down to prove that to me. Ranald Anderson mixes in some miserable company. You need to keep your distance."

"Aye, easy for you to say when—"

"Stop. I'm not finished."

She took another large swig of her gin.

"This goes no further, right?"

Maggie nodded furtively, knowing she'd entered unfamiliar territory with Lexi.

"I have a history with Ranald Anderson that'll haunt me for the rest of my days. I DON'T want you being caught out like I was."

Lexi stopped speaking abruptly, running her tongue over her top lip as if savouring the remaining alcohol sitting on her mouth.

Incredulity was crawling over Maggie's skin. There was only one thing worse than being on the receiving end of Lexi's uncontained wrath. Seeing her weakness and vulnerability was so much worse. Someone, somehow, had got the better of this woman.

"Oh?"

Was this the moment that someone else she saw as a tower of strength crumbled a bit?

"You mentioned Ranald's data breach? Let me guess, you've been speaking to Mitchell Stevens?"

Maggie nodded.

"I found that story myself when it happened. I was hungry then – aiming for promotion from deputy editor. Anderson and Stevens thought they'd swept it all under the carpet, but I have contacts everywhere, lass. One of the lads in the IT consultancy that shut down the leak for Sapphire overnight fancied making a quick buck himself and set me up with some great evidence on the QT."

"I don't understand. The story never ran anywhere. I checked."

"No, it didn't. It was as good as sitting on the printing press, but Mitchell Stevens came knocking at my door and started throwing cash my way to keep it under wraps."

A bit of something inside Maggie died at the sound of her words. Lexi was fierce, unforgiving, tactless and unafraid. But as far as Maggie could ever tell, she always put the truth first. But Mitchell? She didn't expect that.

"You took a bribe from Stevens, boss?"

Lexi refilled her glass with another considerable measure of gin.

"My dad was being destroyed by Parkinson's disease and needed constant care at home just to hold onto his dignity. That doesn't come cheap, you know? Stevens told me he was just following through on Anderson's orders. It was his hush money, apparently. But I wasn't convinced. There was something even more sinister about him than Ranald – and that's saying something."

Maggie wanted to tell Lexi just what an excellent judge of character she was – even back then – but she couldn't. She considered telling her what she knew about Mitchell – the man whose face she'd held in her head for ten years but could never put a name to, until now. Every fibre of her being urged her to tell Lexi who he really was. But then she'd lose control of a dark truth that had led her back to her brother's door. At least if she thought a bit longer, she might figure out a way to write about some of this and keep her brother's name clean. The secrets she was carrying about Lochie and Mitchell Stevens were too much to share with someone who'd just ruined her trust. Why was everyone around her disappointing her?

"Shit, sorry. That's rough, boss."

"Aye, but don't feel sorry for me. I still fell into the age-old trap. I got greedy. May have been for my dad's benefit, but it's greed and laziness all the same. Once their type get you on their payroll, they'll never let you go. Anyhow, that's why I can't let you run that story, Maggie."

Lexi's honesty hit Maggie hard. Instinctively, she wanted to return it with some of her own.

"It's not just the historic stuff with Stevens and Sapphire though."

"What are you on about?" Lexi asked.

"Ranald Anderson has not learnt his lesson. Apparently, he promised Stevens that any medical software he touched again would be tested properly before he launched it anywhere near the public."

"Hang on just a minute, lass. Did you mention an NHS data breach earlier? You must be well off the mark there. Anderson only ever dealt with the private sector. That's why he first crossed paths with Mitchell Stevens. The private operators were the only ones with the budgets to spare for fancy new IT toys."

Maggie thought back to what Lexi had told her about her dad's struggle with Parkinson's disease.

"You must've seen how stretched the NHS are – even

back then, when your dad was sick? Well, look at the state they're in now. Chronically underfunded, post-Covid hangover and the rest."

"Aye, why do you think I had to get into Ranald's payroll to get additional private care for my dad?"

"Right, well, imagine you were running an NHS waiting list and someone came along and offered to give you a free trial of a groundbreaking system that has already transformed lives in the USA and around the world. Imagine if this trial would halve your waiting list for initial treatment of mild to moderate anxiety and depression overnight. Would you not bite their hand off for it?"

Maggie continued, telling Lexi everything she had learnt from Tetchy about how hackers, stalkers, and others might have gained access to the most private data from thousands of ANT's users. When Lexi asked if she had sourced a first-hand victim account, she didn't hesitate. She didn't pretend it was someone else. She told Lexi the truth – that it was her own experience. That she couldn't face going back to the woman in the clinic with her stares and judgement.

Lexi was motionless. Maggie had the floor. Until Lexi's desk phone rang out. Maggie got up to leave, but Lexi stopped her by gesticulating with one finger whilst listening to what she was being told at the other end of the call. She wrapped it up quickly and hung up.

"Well, Maggie, I'm not sure I could sleep well at night if I didn't let you pursue that money-grabbing shoddy shitbag Anderson for all he's worth. But it'll have to wait. Looks like your self-imposed night shift has put you in prime position to attend an unfolding story."

"Oh?"

"I've just had a heads up from my guys in the first responders team. There's been an incident down at the Rankin estate – potential murder attempt – off the record. Go and have a fish around, will you?"

Maggie felt the blood rush to her head as she caught up with Lexi's words.

Attempted murder.

She knew the Rankin estate well. It was next to where she grew up.

29

TUESDAY A.M.

Lexi insisted Maggie took a car to the scene.

"You're not turning up to an attempted murder scene on a bike, luv. Don't care how much of a ball breaker you think you are."

Maggie was sick of the shared reporters' cars. Apparently, they were cleaned inside and out every so often. But it didn't get rid of the dirt that no one saw. The invisible dirt. The prints left on steering wheels that contained the worst filth. She couldn't face sitting in one again. Not today.

"I'll be quicker cycling."

Lexi gave her a stare that meant she wasn't budging on this one.

"That excuse might work at five o'clock on a Friday when the whole town's rushing home from work. But not just after midnight, when you'll be lucky to meet a scabby fox out there."

Backed into a corner, she headed to the basement to get a car key off Tony. It was a creepy hole down there at the best of times. It smelt of car fumes and wee. But she wasn't missing out on this job. Digging deep, she made her way down the stone steps. Tony wasn't in his pokey wee office, so she called reception on his phone. He'd be trying to use coins to get a chocolate bar from the fancy new vending machine that only took card payments. It had been his nemesis since it arrived a few months ago. When he still didn't answer, she started raking around in drawers and cabinets for car keys. They were in an old, battered biscuit tin inside an unlocked cabinet drawer. Each had handwritten labels showing which car they belonged to. Grabbing the first one she could, she wandered out into the parking floor and scanned for the right car. It was hard to see all the vehicles, as some were hidden behind large concrete pillars. She spotted the one with a number plate that matched the keyring fob.

A noise like footsteps came from behind her. Just one or two steps together, and then nothing.

"Lexi?"

She walked on towards the rust-coloured Vauxhall in the corner, checking its number plate matched the keyring label clasped in her shaking hand.

The sound of heavy material rubbing against itself got louder, followed by a rhythmical swishing sound. Like the rough material of trouser legs rubbing against each other in a repetitive motion.

"That you, Tony?"

Again, there was no one to be seen across the car park.

She stood in the dark underground vault, nothing but questions about her own sanity for company. Paranoia had raised its ugly head again, trying to interfere with a job and it made her want to scream at someone. A lingering regret crept in that she'd ditched her pocket therapy app. But then she remembered what she'd told ANT just before finding out that weirdos sitting in dark rooms might be accessing her innermost thoughts.

Just get in the car – and – drive.

Everything fell quiet again as she walked around to the driver's side, but the silence bothered her more than the footsteps. She was more scared than ever to hear the thoughts in her own head.

She was going to a suspicious death at the Rankin estate. The estate had maybe twenty-odd streets. One of them was Denny Court. The McGill's family house. The first place she met Pete McGill a few days ago. There was no rational reason for that to be anything other than a coincidence. Lexi had told her to get on the road and she'd text her the full address when it was released by her source.

When she turned the key in the driver's door, an image appeared on the reflective surface of the car door's metal.

Her whole body spasmed uncontrollably. It took all of her basic instincts not to lash out with a fist or a foot. A man's face she knew well, but the angle of the glass distorted it.

"Mother of… Lochie! What the hell?"

He didn't speak at first. Just stood there, staring at her. Sweat formed in her right hand where she gripped the car key, but she held it more tightly, feeling the sharp edges of its cold metal dig into her palm. Memories of the photo, the red cap hidden in his wardrobe – it all came flooding back.

"Where the hell have you been?"

Her words sounded stronger from her lips than she expected. But, again, there was no reply.

He took a couple of tentative steps towards his sister, and she scrambled to open the car door, but her hands wouldn't work at the speed she needed.

"I need to speak to you…"

His voice sounded desperate. There was a darkness to his words that she couldn't remember hearing for a very long time. But at least he had spoken. There was cold comfort in that, somehow. But she wasn't ready to see him – not here, not now.

"No. Lochie. Ten years ago, maybe. Or the year after that, when I made you promise we were doing the right thing. Before I knew who that lad that I saw killed was. And I mean who he *really* was. But not now. Right now, you need to get out of my way and let me do my job."

"Please listen to me, Mags. You think you know what's going on but… I need to… are you OK?"

"Don't do that, Loch. Get away from me."

She tried again to open the car door, this time with success, but then paused and forced herself to look at his eyes, searching for something familiar.

"The house… have you seen what someone has done? What is going on? Who did that?"

Lochie nodded silently.

"Yeh? I thought as much. Well, I know what they were looking for. I *know*… about the photos, Loch. You told me they were gone. Gone. Deleted. Why did you lie about that? Did you have something to hide too, then?"

"Mags, please. You don't understand..."

He was close enough to reach for his sister's arm, but she felt his touch and shuddered at the sensation.

"Don't you dare touch me. Not now. You were there, weren't you? When Archie was killed. How could you? You were involved, weren't you?"

He stared at her but gave no response.

Maggie unlocked the car and threw herself down in the driver's seat, then she slammed the door shut in his face. Getting the key into the ignition took another few crucial seconds. Long enough for him to appear at the passenger door and force himself into the car beside her.

"Jesus, get out, now. Or I swear I'll call the police. I promise, Lochie. I will have you arrested. Get the hell out of this car."

"Maggie, look at me."

She couldn't force herself to make eye contact with him. Not today. Not now.

"Whatever you think you know, I need to tell you more, OK?"

"What?"

"Trust me. Please. If I tell you everything you will understand. I know you will."

"Trust? What the hell do you know about trust? Don't you dare do that again."

"What?"

"Don't convince me that my mind is messing with me, either. That I'm not fit and well enough to make proper judgements. Whatever is going on in here, let's not confuse it with my issues. I have fixations, habits, ways of keeping safe. That's all. I am not mad!"

Maggie was pointing at her own head and felt her eyes sting.

"I never said you were mad. I don't think that, Mags. I don't. But – please – calm down and listen."

Maggie's breathing thundered through her head so loudly it felt like a pounding drum.

One, two, three… Start again. One, two, three… Breathe in, breathe out. Just that. Nothing else. Nothing else for now.

She tried to transport herself to a different place. Somewhere magnolia, somewhere empty, where there was no stimulus. No danger. Just nothing. But then he touched her again. His hand was resting over hers on the steering wheel. Or was it trapping hers? Stopping her moving. It threw her back into a dangerous reality.

"Why were you there, Lochie? That day in the woods? Because I know you were now. So don't try to deny it."

"Maggie…"

"It's a simple question. Do me the decency to answer it. Why? Why were you there – watching over a fucking murder? That lad may have killed our mum by accident and been too scared to face up to it. But please tell me you didn't have him killed. Please…"

The tears were forming now, and she heard her own voice falter. For a moment, Maggie allowed herself to look up at his face. She had to see his reaction to this question in real time but instantly regretted it.

"It's not that simple. Trust me."

Hearing that word – trust – again was too much. The rage took over her like an explosion. She felt a primal force inside her.

"I found the photos, Lochie. The photos that show someone else was there – standing in the background, watching the life being taken from Archie McGill. Someone who was wearing a red cap. Do you own a red cap, Lochie? Guess what… I know the answer to that too. I found the red cap in your wardrobe. The red cap you were wearing in the bloody photo that day. Don't even think about lying to me."

His voice remained deathly calm in response.

"I'm not going to lie to you. I'm not denying I was there. But please let me speak."

Maggie said nothing but turned her head away from him and stared out of the car towards the dark grey of the car park walls. She was spent, exhausted. There was nothing he could say that would take any of these facts away.

"I was there. Yes. But I had no idea it would end the way it did for him. You *have to* believe me."

He was begging now, but she still couldn't bear to look at him as he spoke and kept her eyes fixed firmly in the distance.

"You need to give me more than that. And fast."

Remembering she was on her way to a suspicious death, a sickening feeling played with her nerves. Maybe she wasn't made for this job. She didn't have the stomach for it. Not when it involved so much death and pain. Pain that was no longer anonymous. Distant from her own life.

Lochie talked and she had no option but to listen.

"We were destroyed by debt back then, Mags. After Mum died and Dad… well, wherever the hell he went. I tried to keep it from you. To help you heal, but I needed to find a solution, or we would lose our home. I had to keep the roof over our head. To keep you safe."

"So, you hooked up with murderers?"

"No, no. That's not what I signed up for. It was supposed to be just a straight exchange. Pure and simple. And I'd just get a cut – enough to pay off the credit card hounds and get our heads back above water."

Maggie's breathing settled a bit. Something in her brother's voice was pulling her back from a cliff edge. She let her head fall slowly back into the car rest, closing her eyes as he spoke. Praying for the full truth – whatever it might be.

"I'd been hearing stuff at the hospital. About Mark and Ranald Anderson from a gobby shite in A & E. These guys see everything. Even the rich folk have to use the same A & E as the rest of us."

"So, what, you wanted to target someone who had money and buried secrets?"

"Just give me a chance, Mags, please. That A & E lad told me Mark Anderson was slowly destroying his heart with all the steroids he'd pumped into his veins over the years. And Ranald – the old man who was making his fortune selling IT software to the medical industry – was afraid the truth about his son's drug use would hurt his business."

"So you sent Archie out to pick up your blackmail

money and Ranald had him murdered? Why did he have to die?"

"I don't know. I honestly don't know why he was killed, and that is the truth – I swear. Ranald didn't even turn up himself – had someone else do the dirty work for him. But… I guess you'll know that too."

She wondered if her brother even knew who Mitchell Stevens was. Or that he was hiding in plain sight right now with Mark Anderson's ex-wife.

Lochie had more to say.

"I found an excuse to work at Anderson's ward myself. They were desperate for any extra night shift workers and before I knew it, I had access to Mark's files. It was all there – in black and white. Chapter and verse of his various admissions: acute heart problems, mood swings, detox, you name it."

Maggie opened her eyes again and saw her brother's face, ghostly white with shame.

"Lochie, what did you do?"

He broke off eye contact now. She saw the pain in his whole body.

"I just took photos, Mags – like you always say, a picture tells a thousand words."

"Photos of what? Jeez! How could you risk your job like that?"

"Did you hear what I said? We were one more debt collector away from homelessness. We would've been out on the streets. I had to do something."

"So, you took a photo of Mark getting his stomach pumped and threatened to send them to the press?"

"Jeez, no. Maggie. Not of him. Of his medical records. All the recent entries. It made for compelling evidence."

They were looking directly at each other now. She, of all people, knew how these things worked. Desperate people wanting to make a buck out of selling a story. Those medical records would've given the media plenty to run with. *Go to print today – worry about the repercussions tomorrow.* That was Lexi's motto in the bad old days, so she'd told her once.

"I sent a copy of the medical notes to the Andersons' home address and told Ranald that they'd fallen into the wrong hands and if he wanted to keep his son's drug use out of the press, he would need to find fifty K fast."

"But why was Archie Ross involved?"

"I knew I couldn't pitch up to the handover myself. I had zero street smarts for that kind of shit. I needed a middleman – and I'd heard a lot of chatter about this local kid. He had a reputation for settling scores and getting shit done on the quiet. Drug deals. Debt collection – all that kind of stuff. If you wanted something seedy taken care of, he was your man."

Maggie remembered the fleeting image of a face through a car windscreen the day she saw him race away from the horror of what he'd done to their mum.

"How could you even speak to the man when you knew what had happened with Mum, never mind strike some dirty blackmail deal with him?"

"I didn't know I was dealing with Archie McGill, or Ryan Ross as he was known by then. I promise. I didn't even meet him in person. I was given a phone number and told he didn't like to share his name. Easier that way, apparently. Untraceable."

"Christ, Loch. What were you thinking?"

"I was desperate. Desperate people don't think enough, Mags. You must see that in your work. I just got his number and had a conversation. Told him where to be and when. He warned me to stay well away myself. Like, he *really* meant that."

A sickening thought occurred to her as her brother was talking.

"Ross would have known who you were though, wouldn't he? No wonder he didn't want you pitching up and seeing his face."

"Listen, Maggie. I know this sounds messed up, but I like to think that when he realised who he was dealing with, he committed himself to doing something for us – some sort of tiny way to make amends for what he took from our family."

Maggie wanted to scream at her brother.

"Why did you go, then? Why were you there that day?"

"I was afraid he'd pocket the cash and scarper. So, I went down there to make sure I got my cut. Then I saw… God, Maggie. Then I saw what happened. That's when I saw it was Archie."

"You should have gone to the police right there and then. You know that, don't you?"

"Of course I do, Mags. But I was mad and scared and stupid. Murder was so far from my mind, but none of it would have happened if it wasn't for me. If I'd gone to jail, who would have kept you safe then? And the McGills – I knew that family. Pete and I were pals. You discovered that for yourself."

The sorry tale was flowing out of him now. Lochie told her that, after he witnessed Archie's murder and fled, he confronted Ranald Anderson himself. It was Ranald who told him Archie was driving the car that hit their mum. Ranald was driving past that day. He saw them with his own eyes. He saw the driver flee the scene.

Maggie was lost in her brother's words. She wanted to feel relief. To be glad that he'd told her everything and, in doing so, had restored her faith in him. But there was too much to process.

She noticed the time on her dashboard, and haunting images of what was awaiting her at the Rankin estate job kept stabbing her heart. Her phone pinged. It was a message from Lexi:

Full address of near fatal just in – get yourself to 5 Denny Court.

Maggie's heart sank to a new low. She knew exactly whose house that was.

30

EARLY HOURS OF TUESDAY A.M.

The crime scene tape was billowing in the wind, illuminated by the flashing blue lights from emergency vehicles parked outside Anne McGill's home. Maggie looked for somewhere to abandon her car. She could feel the grim expression on Lochie's face without seeing it. He was swallowing hard, maybe trying not to vomit. Maggie stopped the car to think.

"Why were you visiting her, Lochie? Anne McGill? What were you doing at this house?"

She needed to hear it from him.

He was biting his nails as he began to speak.

"He was her second child – the baby of the family… Archie. That lad was so far from perfect, but she'd never see it. All he'd signed up for that day when I spoke to him was to hand over the medical notes I'd printed out and take the cash. He'd get a cut. I'd get the rest – and we'd all walk away into the sunset."

"How could you be so stupid to think someone like Ranald Anderson would be happy with a printout that could be replicated a thousand times more?"

"Let's just say I'm no blackmail expert, Maggie. I'm still from a world where your word is good enough – no matter who you're messing with. Anyway, Archie was just the messenger that day. No matter what else that lad had done before to our lives. It made no sense that Anderson had him killed. All I could think was that Anderson and Mitchell wanted to send a message to whoever sent Archie to the handover that he wasn't messing around. Let them know this was the end of the gravy train."

"Who told you about Anne's condition?"

"No one really. She was admitted one night after a neighbour saw her through the window, collapsed on her kitchen floor. And when she was here, she told me herself she had turned to the booze ever since her troubled child Archie abandoned her to live in London."

At last, everything was fitting together, piece by piece.

"Pete McGill said his half-brother Archie had returned to Fife after lying low in London for a year or so, but he'd kept his distance. He stayed a good distance away in Dunfermline. Nearer to Edinburgh, where there were rich pickings for a criminal go-fer on the make. At least he was wise enough to give himself a new name. There was little chance of being discovered by any Kirkcaldy folk – unless they got really close, you know?"

"But you got wind of his grotty underworld services, anyway? That's some reputation he'd managed to build up pretty quickly."

"It's amazing the doors that you find to open when

you're desperate, Mags. I only thank Christ you didn't know about any of this."

An overwhelming exhaustion began to seep into Maggie's core, taking the place of some anger.

"You protected me from it."

"I tried."

Maggie was softening again to the brother that she knew deep down.

"So you reckon Ranald wanted to silence his blackmailer completely and arranged for the cash handover to end in murder all along?"

"Guess so. Ranald no doubt had his own dirty jobs man on the books full time."

Maggie thought of Mitchell Stevens – the owner of a private medical group – being described in this way. The grimmest of evil hiding behind the veneer of respectability. But it felt a bit of a leap to imagine he'd commit murder just to keep his one-time business associate squeaky clean. Did he really shack up with Val Anderson and Ranald's grandchildren just to protect himself from being turned in by Ranald? People never fail to disgust you more than you can imagine.

"Did Anne McGill ever find out what happened to Archie?"

"Yes, the police told her before they released the name to the press. They agreed to formally ID him as Ryan Ross, keeping Archie's name a secret in return for her turning over all his belongings – diaries, burner phones, the lot. It gave them inroads on a truckload of criminals he was mixed up with across the central belt of Scotland. Anne

McGill could live the rest of her life in the shadow of a lie. No wonder her health problems got worse. Perhaps she was braver than anyone gave her credit for."

Maggie needed to get out of the car, but something made her feet feel like lead. She turned to her brother again. He had so much more to answer for.

"So, what… you just pitched up one day and convinced her you were going to nurse that woman back to health and she welcomed you in?"

"I had to do something. Grief had destroyed her. We know what that looks like, Mags, don't we? It's relentless. Takes you by the neck and won't let go."

Maggie watched as Lochie clenched his fists. She turned to the scene unfolding in front of her in Denny Court, struggling to find the strength to get out of the car and do her job.

"Why has Anne been attacked, Lochie?"

Maggie saw tears form in her brother's eyes.

"I have absolutely no idea. *Please* believe me. Maggie?"

The desperation in his voice was comforting. She pulled up the zip on her jacket, opened the door of her car and walked towards Anne McGill's house. A police officer was guarding the taped-off cordon and there was no way she was getting any closer. Through a sea of high vis vests, she saw Pete being guided to a police car. Maggie pushed her way through the melting pot of voyeurs and found her voice.

"Pete!"

He either ignored her or didn't hear her.

"Pete! Pete!"

This time, the paramedic that was guiding him to the car looked round first and Pete followed his lead.

His face was every inch the mask of a broken man.

"Pete… wait…"

Maggie wasn't sure what she was planning to say to him. He'd just watched his mother being wheeled out of her home on a stretcher to the waiting ambulance, but he stopped and was looking at Maggie now. Waiting. She had to say something.

"What happened, Pete?"

He managed a shake of his head in response.

"I'm going with her."

Looking at the sadness in his eyes, Maggie took a few paces towards Pete. His body was shaking so much that she felt the tremors ripple out through her own. She was being watched closely by the cop who was waiting by the open door of his panda car.

"Was it you who found her?"

He nodded gently, and she reached up to his ear.

He followed the direction of the officer, who was guiding him into the back seat of the car. His head bowed towards his lap. Maggie had turned to walk away when she heard her name.

"Maggie?"

It sounded like a question. He was holding the car door open with one hand.

"Uh-huh?"

Pete used his eyes to encourage her to lean forwards towards the passenger side of the car. His voice was barely a whisper.

"She was holding this when I found her."

Pete passed the note just low enough to hide it by the car door. Some words crackling through the police radio attached to the front of his jacket distracted the uniformed officer.

Her hand met Pete's, and she felt folded paper in her palm.

His expression told her to wait before opening it, so she stuffed it in her pocket and held his gaze as the car door closed on him. Remembering she'd been sent to cover the unfolding events, she needed something useable from someone in charge – a quote or something. But this was a major crime scene. Not one official was going to talk to her tonight. A young woman was standing with her hands on her hips and holding court with the gathering masses.

Her name was Judy, and she had an elaborate tale of coming home from the local pub to find 'that bloke they've just carted off down the cells' sitting on the pavement outside, shaking back and forward.

"The lad just kept saying, 'Someone's tried to kill my mum'. And I was, like, is she deid? And he just ignored ma question and kept, like, rocking back and for'd. And I asked him if he'd called an amb-lunce and he just nodded, and that's all he said until the blue lights all arrived, and it started kicking off like merry hell."

"Great. thanks. Can I take your full name and age to use with your quote, please?"

It was good enough. Maggie would rewrite it in her head on the drive back to the office.

Where did I leave the car? Shit… Lochie.

She saw her brother's ashen face staring out at the scene unfolding. He looked haunted by something. Stopping short of the car, Maggie prized open the crumpled note she'd been handed by Pete, read the words quickly once, and then again, her brain sticking on the name at the bottom of the note. An affectionate sign off, as if talking to an old friend.

Thinking of you,

Mark Anderson.

Her heart quickened at the thought of the last parts of the jigsaw finally falling into place.

31

TUESDAY A.M.

Maggie drove out of Denny Court in total silence. Lochie's stare was on her again, but he said nothing. He looked spent. She resented him for unburdening his secrets onto her shoulders. But she needed to take the lead. To be strong enough to see this thing through.

"I think they tried to kill Anne because she was the one person left who knew too much. Apart from you, of course. It was the same person that turned over your house for the photos. He needed to see what was in them and destroy them, and silence Anne."

Lochie looked pale as a ghost.

"I told her about the photos. I wanted her to know the evidence was mounting against Archie's killers and it was just a matter of time. To give her hope."

"That's what I feared. And I'm willing to bet that Anne mentioned it to the wrong person in a town full of loose talk and gossips. When Anne found out her son had been murdered, she never stopped hounding the police to find his killer, but the leads just dried up. Mitchell must have found out that there were photos that identified him as Archie's killer and knew he had to destroy all the remaining links between him, Ranald and the murder they were responsible for ten years ago."

Lochie looked at her so intently, she wondered if he might cry. She couldn't remember the last time he did that in front of her.

"I'm so sorry. I was desperate and stupid and full of guilt. You deserved better. You should've had at least one parent, but you got me, and I fucked up. The good news is that it's not too late to make good of what's left."

"Don't, Loch. Just leave me alone to think. There's a way through this. But I just need to figure out how to keep you out of it. I'm not bringing my brother down with those greedy, self-serving scumbags."

Lochie was shaking his head as she spoke.

"No, there isn't. You have to take everything you know – the photos, that sodding red cap, *all of it* – to the police. The story isn't complete without all of it. My testimony too. Do this properly, like you should have ten years ago."

She considered his words, and what it would mean for the brother who protected her for so long. He was only ever trying to look after her. She couldn't turn on him like this.

"I'll speak to the police. Tell them what I know about Ranald's links to Archie McGill's murder. But there's someone else that would complete the story. They need the man whose hands were on the knife that killed Archie that day – before he runs."

"Do you know who that is?"

"I can go one better than that. I even know where he is. He's using someone else as a human shield to protect himself. Just like the coward he is."

Lochie looked lost.

"You heard of Mitchell Stevens?"

"The name rings a bell, but that's about it."

"That man is every inch the respectable businessman on the outside. Just like his pal, Ranald. But theirs was an alliance cemented in corruption and the cover-up of faulty medical services to vulnerable people who were none the wiser."

Maggie looked at Lochie. Their mutual respect was slowly resurfacing.

"What I don't know is why he killed Archie. I don't buy the fact that it was on Ranald's orders, and that's the bit I've still got to work out."

Maggie thought back to the note in Archie's diary. That extra entry below Ranald's name was niggling at her again.

(+extra25 – off the books)

"I think there was a separate blackmail going on that day."

"What, you mean a deal that Archie struck himself with Ranald, to squeeze more out of him?"

Maggie searched upwards, looking for something. Inspiration, perhaps.

"I don't think it was a separate blackmail against Ranald. I think it was Mitchell he had on the hook for something else. And when I find out what that is, I'll know why he killed Archie."

Maggie looked at her brother again. The colour had not yet returned to his face.

"These animals don't care who they destroy to protect themselves. Please keep out of their way, Mags. I couldn't bear it if anything happened to you."

"I'll be careful, Lochie. But if I don't see this through, then what's the point in any of it?"

His expression changed again. This time nothing but defeat – raw and real.

"I think there's a way around this. I can lose that red cap – and destroy the photos for real. It's the only barely useable evidence that you were even there."

"NO, you can't. Because you can't erase this conversation. And you think those cowards won't land me in it to get their own sentence reduced? You tell them everything or I'll do it myself. You have to."

Maggie looked straight into her brother's eyes and saw a calm that felt out of context.

"It's OK, Mags. Really. It is."

"Why? Why is it OK *now*? You've been holding me off from doing this for ten years. The stuff you've had to tell me to stop me from coming forward as a witness. Oh, God, please don't tell me that was a lie? That Archie killed our mum?"

Lochie's face took on a pallor of disgust.

"No, of course not. Ranald told me that himself. He described the driver he saw in detail. Archie McGill had this weird tattoo across the back of his neck. It was exactly how I remembered it from the day he got it done just after leaving school – his mum went mental, but that was Archie. No one told him what to do – even back then."

"When did Ranald tell you this?"

"Not long after Archie was killed. Like I said, I was only there to make sure Archie didn't run off with the cash before he gave me my cut. But when I saw… I had to confront Ranald about it. At first, he looked mad as hell. I'm not sure that was part of the plan. But then he told me to save my tears. And why. And sure enough, that was the last that Anne McGill ever saw of her son in Kirkcaldy – until the day the police came knocking on her door."

Maggie felt fresh waves of nausea wash over her as he spoke. This wasn't just some tragic local crime that she had to condense into a few hundred words for the next day's paper. This was her brother's life. *Her* life too.

"I can't do this to you. I can't send you to prison."

Lochie was almost smiling now. There was an odd calm about him.

"It's different now, Mags. It's like you keep telling me. You're not that daft wee lassie in the woods all those years ago. I don't need to protect you anymore. You can do that fine yourself. Now, piss off and write your story. Talk to the police – but make sure you get back as much as you give them. Finish the job you started."

Watching him get out of her car and walk through the gates of his home, Maggie ached for a time when life had none of this. When there was no deceit. When she didn't even know what blackmail meant or why people go missing or die suddenly. She remembered two young children standing at their front door, dressed in school uniform and smiling for their dad's new school term photo – hair brushed properly for the first time in weeks.

Hurry up, Dad. We'll be late for our first day back!

Back then, it wasn't anxiety she felt. Just impatience. Normal, healthy impatience to get on with life. She wanted her brother to be the perfect one. Needed him to be her rock. But now she knew his secrets. She had to find a new way to understand him. Switching her engine back on, the alien sensation of tears filled her eyes. Real, uncontrolled, tears. Tears for the loss of a perfect brother who was only ever a figment of her imagination.

*

She didn't sleep that night but lay in bed, staring at the words on the note taken by Pete McGill from his mother's hands. Pete gave it to Maggie for a reason. Was it just for safekeeping, or for some other reason? Whatever it was, she had to honour that.

She read it again for anything she might have missed.

> Dear Mrs McGill,
>
> This is Mark Anderson. I'm writing to you from a place of hiding. I'm risking everything that has been put in place to tell you this, but it's the least I owe you. I know my own behaviour and my father's obsession with protecting his reputation and money contributed at least in part to your son's death, and nothing I say or do will bring Archie back. But at least I can try to play my part in ensuring all those responsible will serve time for their crimes. There are other people involved

and I cannot tell you where I am or this will all fall apart and I will not be able to give the evidence needed to bring them down, but please know that I will do everything possible to bring justice to your family.

Thinking of you,

Mark Anderson.

*

Internet searches consumed the dark night hours. Clinging to the words Mark used – *a place of hiding, everything they've put in place* and *give the evidence needed to bring them down* – she followed where her research took her.

Maggie had heard about the country's witness protection programme from chatting to other crime reporters from the nationals. But facts were not easy to find. Eventually, Maggie stumbled upon a scattering of stories about men and women who'd chosen to do the right thing. They put justice for victims over protecting their own skin. There were hidden stories of family members who'd turned on their brothers, parents, uncles and even their own children because their conscience had nipped at their head for too long. Some spoke of the haunting nightmare of living in the shadow of others' crimes. Shrouded in fear. She thought of Anne McGill and the different life she'd chosen to lead – hiding behind the lie that her son had just gone to London and never came home. Unlike Anne McGill, those who agree to witness protection take their chance to step out of the darkness – as terrifying as that may be.

Bringing down your own father – when he's cut in the mould of Ranald Anderson – was not going to come without risks. Maggie considered how well Ranald constructed this empire. She thought about how he had used his family as assets – steps on the ladder he wanted to climb. And his alliance with Mitchell Stevens. There must be a reason that their friendship continued after the data breach was silenced. Maggie still refused to accept Stevens was the moral arbiter to offset Ranald's utter lack of decency. It bothered her that Mitchell Stevens didn't fit neatly in either the 'good' or 'evil' box yet.

Mark Anderson's sporting talent was a strong enough foundation to build a media profile and generate adoring headlines for the whole Anderson family. Ranald's choice of Valerie Rollo as a wife for Mark was the perfect addition to his plan. By marrying his son into old money and generations of consultants, Ranald was introduced to the world he craved to be part of. Even the brightest, sharpest, life-saving doctors around needed more efficient IT systems to make them slicker and quicker at handling greater demand.

They knew how to fix someone's vital organs, but they would put complete trust in others to provide a solution to their data management or IT challenges.

And then there was the chronically under-funded, cash-strapped, overstretched NHS, desperate for any help it could find to tackle crippling waiting times. Maggie thought of her own need for mental health support from an NHS system that was being stretched to breaking point.

What better opportunity for a groundbreaking

artificial intelligence psychological therapy program to cut its teeth? To be the bright savour and the answer to their nightmares.

It was all going so well for Ranald until the ugly reality of human imperfection emerged. The glittering sports celebrity couldn't be a drug user. Ranald's medical software products couldn't be leaking data like a sieve. None of that had a place in his master plan.

There were too many cracks in Ranald's world. The first signs of Mark's steroid use leading to the hospital admissions. It was all in the medical report that Lochie had photocopied.

Then there was the corner cutting with Ranald's software testing, confirmed by Stevens. Followed by the media threats to expose him, which took up more of his time and money. He'd preyed on the weaknesses of otherwise fiercely strong people like Lexi Brodick to make the headlines disappear.

Maggie understood family loyalty. She knew what it felt like to protect those we love at all costs. But was he protecting himself more than his son?

Then there was everything she had learnt about Mark himself. When Pete McGill found evidence of Archie's connections to Ranald and confronted Mark in the Harbour Tavern, that was when the deceased Ryan Ross went from meaningless local waster to Anne McGill's absent son. It was then that Pete McGill made Mark Anderson stand back from his father and saw him for who he was. And finally, the diary entry that meant little at the time, but now so much more.

(+extra25 – off the books)

What would Mitchell Stevens's obvious move be, if Mark found the courage to testify against his father and bring him down for these crimes? He'd claim to be acting on the orders of a threatening and manipulative man.

But what if that's not the truth? Everyone was so quick to condemn Ranald Anderson for the villain he undoubtedly was. But could it be that Mitchell Stevens had his own reasons to silence Archie Ross permanently?

Whatever the truth was, without Mark's testimony, it was a gamble whether this would hold together in court. The police would have known that too. That, as Maggie could now see, was why Mark Anderson had to be taken into a witness protection programme whilst they planned their move to arrest Ranald and Mitchell.

But surely time was not on their side? Maggie knew that Ranald and Mitchell would have figured out the real reason for Mark's disappearance. They would already have a plan underway for getting to him, wherever he was hiding, first. She just had to figure out what it was. There was one person who might be able to point her in the right direction. But speaking to Val Anderson again took on a whole new meaning, now she was painfully aware of the company she kept at home. She'd have to get her out of there first.

32

TUESDAY P.M.

Maggie clocked Val Anderson as soon as she arrived at the restaurant. A long coat with an exaggerated hood shrouded most of her body and hid her from prying eyes. Maggie raised a hand in her direction and watched as Val kept walking to the back of the room. The venue was Val's suggestion. Maggie was never one for fancy eateries. They made her feel uncomfortable – on show and out of her depth. But putting Val at ease was more important today. This woman was the key to the minds of two men Maggie had only just begun to understand. The thought that this woman was knowingly living with a man who killed Archie Ross ten years ago turned her stomach.

"God, I hate this town sometimes."

It was a bitter greeting from Val. She was in no mood to hide the burden she carried.

But it was a complaint Maggie could relate to. Small towns can be suffocating when you become the centre of attention. Stares crawled over Maggie's young skin from all directions for weeks and months after her mum was killed. The weight of pity bore down on her shoulders everywhere she went. Until they moved on to the next tragedy in town. Yet here she was, in a job that fuelled the rumour mill. Cultivated it. Profited from it. She told herself that's why she had to keep it real. She had to cut through the crappy town gossip and stream of inconsequential nothingness that filled up column inches. Maggie Shields would become the journalist who'd get to the heart of the stuff that mattered. Tell the truth, no matter how ugly.

"I can imagine it's not easy – being out and about and all that."

"Can you? … Really?"

She wanted to scream at Val. To say, *Yes, actually, I know what it feels like to have the eyes of the town on you in every shop. Pity and sorrow seeping out of every face because you're from* that *family where* that *terrible thing happened.* But she didn't.

Val took a seat with her back to the room and attempted to remove her coat quickly and without drawing attention. The dark shadows beneath her eyes showed through the mask of make-up she'd applied. Her hands shook as she adjusted the strands of hair around her face, misplaced when she lifted her hood up.

"I need a coffee, or a gin. I'm not sure which."

Maggie caught the attention of the passing waitress and did as she was told.

"How are your daughters, Val?"

"Their dad is still missing. But at least there aren't any curb crawlers tailing them outside school now."

The coffee arrived quickly, and she began to sip on it in

the same hungry way she inhaled a cigarette the first day they met. The caffeine injected some life into Val's drawn face.

There was so little Maggie had in common with this woman, but something between them seemed to click. It was a tough pill she was expecting Val to swallow, but she was committed now. Maggie saw a bravery in her, behind the foundation and the labels. She just had to convince her to use it.

"How's the big investigation going, Maggie? Are you any nearer to finding my husband?"

Maggie opened her mouth to form a sentence without really knowing what would come out first.

"How much do you know about Mitchell Stevens, Val?"

It was a bolder start than she expected from herself, but Val's response would be vital. If she pretended not to know the man, it would confirm she was up to her neck in at least a fair chunk of shady shit. Maggie paused, clinging to the uncomfortable silence.

"For someone that I live with and at times share a bed with, surprisingly little. And I enjoy it that way."

"Oh? How long have you been…"

Maggie had no idea how to finish the sentence.

"Shacked up together? I don't even know what you'd call it, to be honest. The man breezed into my life shortly after Mark left home. I guess it was just good timing. And, before I knew it, he was there most nights. During the week at least. I think he preferred to be at home at the weekend. It was nearer Ranald's home. That's where they went hunting together. Hideous sport in my opinion, so he knew I didn't want to hear about it."

Maggie knew she'd have to cut through the chatter soon. Cut to the chase. The bit where she told her that her father-in-law and the friend she'd been living with for years were responsible for the murder of a young lad ten years ago. She knew the risk was high that Val would turn on her and move to protect the men in her life. That would be the easier option. But Maggie wanted her to take another path. To help put them away for their crimes. To make the case against them irrefutable in the eyes of the law.

What if she simply refuses to believe everything I tell her?

Maggie knew the evidence she had gathered – from Pete, from Lochie and from her own painful discoveries – was compelling. But she also knew that the loyalty one woman is capable of to protect others knew no bounds. And Val Anderson was surrounded by men that didn't deserve her loyalty. Maggie thought of her own willingness to play down or hide Lochie's part in the sorry tale of Archie's death. Until he reminded her why she could never choose that route.

"Val, I've found out something about Ranald and Mitchell and I don't know how to..."

"OH for God's sake, girl. Get on with it. What could you possibly have to tell me about Ranald Anderson that would shock me now?"

Maggie took one deep breath and locked her eyes on Val's face. She needed to read her reaction in the very instant it appeared.

"Do you remember the murder of that lad in the woods ten years ago? Ryan Ross, as he was identified at the time."

Val looked at her, the embers of horror beginning to spark across every line on her face. She managed a silent nod.

"I have very good reason to believe that his murder was ordered by Ranald and carried out by Mitchell Stevens."

Maggie took a breath. She left the words hanging out there between them, hoping they would land as well as possible. There was no turning back now. She had shown her hand, and it was decision time for the woman who sat before her. Not only did she need Val to believe her, but she needed her to trust Maggie enough to help bring these men to justice.

But in that moment, she knew it was every bit as likely that Val Anderson would run out of the door and never see Maggie Shields again. She could tip off Ranald and Mitchell before the police had a chance to follow up on Maggie's evidence, and Maggie would spend the rest of her career regretting this day.

Val looked up at her through a dark ridge of fake eyelashes. Her lips were pursed but the rest of her expression was flat. Giving nothing away. Perhaps none of what Maggie had just said was news to her. Perhaps she had been harbouring a murderer and protecting his paymaster all along. It was a sobering thought. Then she spoke again, and it sent Maggie's thoughts in a direction she didn't expect.

She laughed.

It was the kind of laugh that was more suited to a

horror film, or the darkest of moments in someone's life, when life had turned so foul that it disrupted everything, including your ability to make appropriate responses.

"And here's me thinking I knew his darkest secret."

Maggie wondered which man she was talking about. The more she learnt about Ranald Anderson, the more she realised there was always one more secret around the corner. But, she could never escape the fact that it wasn't him that plunged the knife into Archie's young flesh that day.

"Mitchell, I mean."

She must have read Maggie's mind.

"I thought that supplying drugs to his best friend's son whilst slowly making his own fortune in so-called gold star healthcare was as low as he had fallen. But no, here is young Maggie Shields telling me that he went much, much lower. Christ, what a gullible old fool I am, huh?"

There was no rage in Val's voice. No defiance and certainly no hint of the will to protect either of these men. Maggie contemplated her words.

"Mitchell was supplying drugs to Mark Anderson?"

"Aha! There are still pieces of the Anderson tragedy that evaded you, then? But it looks like that little nugget has been somewhat overshadowed."

33

TUESDAY P.M.

As soon as Maggie stepped inside Kirkcaldy Police Station, the old fears returned. In the air she breathed as soon as she walked through the doors. On the door handles, the countertop and the seats. Each of those things and hundreds more were carriers of life-threatening viruses. It was almost unbearable, but today she had no choice. She'd promised too many people she'd see this through. Even *if* the police had the time to listen to a reporter who wouldn't get out of their way, it would be on their terms, in their house.

Maggie sat awkwardly on a blue plastic chair, waiting for someone to appear behind the glass screen that divided them. After five minutes of patient toe tapping and leg rubbing, she approached the desk and rang the bell. She'd promised herself she would press the goddamn thing if no one appeared after three minutes – which became five minutes. Five minutes of staring at it from a distance. That time passed, and she had to uphold her own promise.

Pulling the sleeve of her shirt down over her fingers,

she created a shield between her skin and the round, black buzzer.

She was rewarded quickly, as a middle-aged female in uniform appeared from the inner sanctum. Maggie clocked the stripes on the desk sergeant's arm.

"How can I help you?"

Maggie cleared her throat and pushed the collar of her jacket down from her mouth to respond.

"Hi. I need to speak with Julie Clarkson."

The woman's brow raised slightly, but the tone of her voice remained flat.

"Is that a fact? Well, I'm afraid DI Clarkson isn't based at this station."

"What about DS Symington, then?"

The woman lowered the glasses down the bridge of her nose to get a proper look at Maggie.

"Sorry, what did you say your name was?"

"You didn't ask me my name."

She regretted her own comment. It wasn't meant to be insulting, but sometimes things like that just came out without warning when she was this on edge. No filter. A bit too matter of fact. But it was too late.

"Okay, luv. Well, I am now. Name, please."

The last word was followed by a forced smile.

"It's Maggie Shields."

"Right, Miss Shields. If you tell me what this relates to, I'll see if someone who *is* actually based at this station can help."

"I'd like to speak to someone working on the Mark Anderson case."

The sergeant's face took on a more animated look, and Maggie guessed what was coming next.

"Hang on a second. Did you say *Shield*? You're at the paper – the *Standard*, aren't you?"

"Shields, with an s. Yes, but…"

"You've been doing that job a while now, haven't you?"

"Almost six years. Why?"

"Well, surely you'll know by now that any media enquiries have to go through our press office – or media relations team, as I believe they're known in this modern age?"

"I do, yes."

She saw the irritation growing in the woman's face.

"Well, in that case, is there anything else I can help you with?"

"It's not a press enquiry."

Again, it wasn't meant to be rude.

"Is that a fact?"

Maggie realised she had encountered a police officer who was pretty keen on establishing facts.

"Yes, it is another fact. I'm here as just a regular citizen of Fife."

The sergeant shook her head and exhaled through her teeth.

"OK, then. And this is still about Mark Anderson?"

She'd softened slightly and glanced behind Maggie, presumably to check if anyone else was on the blue plastic chairs. But they weren't.

"I know where Mark Anderson is, and I want to help the police build a case against those responsible for Ryan Ross's murder ten years ago."

The look on the Seargent's face was harder to read this time. Maggie had expected cynicism, but what she got was very different.

"I think you should follow me, Miss Shields – with an s."

*

Maggie was taken into a meeting room, furnished with four more plastic chairs and a wooden table, which smelt faintly of heavy-duty bleach. It reminded her of the local swimming pool. There was nothing on the walls except cameras, one oddly high window (with rusting black bars) and a sad-looking ceiling lamp hanging above them, illuminating the room in an offensive white hue reminiscent of a pathologist's lab. But it was the hidden stuff in this barren space that rattled her the most. The thought of the underside of the interview table with its multiple buds of abandoned gum, clinging on like pustulant warts, ready to drop off at any minute and land on her lap. And that window – sealed tight and stubbornly blocking out any hope of fresh air penetrating the stale mass of airborne viruses within. She wanted to run, there and then. Just like she had from that *human* therapist, into the clutches of an online robot. She bottled it that day and look where it took her. Into the hands of a corrupted jumble of algorithms – being manipulated by a sick weirdo.

Stick with it. You can do this.

The detective constable offered her something to drink, which she turned down. He started fiddling with the recording equipment on the desk and had just pulled out his notepad when his superiors arrived.

"We will be recording this interview, Miss Shields. Just to make you aware."

A brief rush of self-satisfaction energised Maggie. They must be taking her seriously if she was worthy of an audience with the big guns.

"Maggie Shields, we meet again."

Detective Inspector Julie Clarkson and Detective Seargent Lorne Symington were clearly a tight outfit, Maggie thought. She nodded quietly at them both and waited, sensing she had the upper hand for now.

"My colleagues tell me you know where Mark Anderson is?"

Maggie was leaning back in her chair, trying to keep her distance from everyone else in the room. She folded her arms and tried hard to block out the counting in her own head.

"In a manner of speaking, aye, but I reckon what I've got on Ryan's – or should that be Archie McGill's – killer will be of more interest to you. All in the name of closer collaboration, like you said."

Maggie couldn't resist shooting Symington and Clarkson a loaded wink. They shared a brief glance between them which leaked an unease in each other's company that felt new.

"Oh? And why would that be?" said Clarkson.

Maggie relished the question. This was why she did her job. Nothing would ever beat the feeling of being one step ahead of everyone else. The briefest laugh escaped from the corner of her mouth.

"Because you've known where Mark Anderson is for a long time, haven't you?"

Clarkson's jaw dropped first, a look of mild paralysis on her face. Symington's reaction was more animated. He sat up straight in his chair and leant forwards across the desk. He opened his mouth to speak but Clarkson beat him to it.

"What makes you think that, Maggie?"

Having the upper hand felt good, and she briefly remembered Lochie's last words to her.

You have to take everything you know – the photos, the cap, all of it – to the police. Do this properly, like you should have ten years ago.

Maggie still had the letter from Mark that Pete had handed to her outside Anne's house in her pocket, but she couldn't betray him by showing them that. She was pretty sure that would constitute a violation of rules on his part, and she couldn't be responsible for them pulling him out of protection.

"How is Anne McGill bearing up, by the way?"

It was a stretch to think they'd tell her anything, but she genuinely wanted to know.

"Let me assure you that Anne's next of kin will be made aware of any developments. Now, you were about to tell us your theory about Mark Anderson' s whereabouts."

"I've been handed evidence that Mark is hiding somewhere for his own safety and been told by a very strong source that he's preparing to testify against his father, Ranald."

Clarkson's cheeks flushed with what Maggie had to

assume was rage. No one spoke for what felt like minutes, but was probably about five seconds. It was Symington's turn to chip in.

"Can I ask how it is you think you can assist us, Maggie?"

Maggie felt the vindication that she'd be searching for. It was as close to a confirmation as she was going to get.

"You want to bring Ranald in but you're waiting to make sure your case is strong enough, yes?"

"Let me guess, you're going to give us the final evidence we need?"

Clarkson was back in the game.

"Well, I think I might go one better than that."

This time an eyebrow was raised in response, but no words.

"I can tell you who carried out the murder, and why. Oh – and where to find him, too."

Clarkson and Symington were both silent now. She had their undivided attention.

"Everyone has been making a mistake, you see. All along, you have been working on the assumption that Ranald was pulling the strings. He'd been blackmailed and needed to silence his blackmailer before the truth behind his son's drug use came out and threatened their perfect family image. But that never felt like a strong enough motive for murder to me. Don't you think?"

It was a question which both cops in front of her declined to answer.

"That's because it wasn't ever his idea to murder Archie – or Ryan Ross, as you knew him to be."

Clarkson's face was motionless – giving nothing away from her side.

"Go on."

"His friendship with Mitchell Stevens. They both wanted to be Billy Big Balls in the world of private healthcare services. One ran a group of private hospitals and the other provided high-tech software to the medical industry. It was a friendship that was built around the potential glory and riches that would bring. Oh, and hunting animals – but that's another matter."

"Maggie, where are you going with…"

"Oh, hang on, just bear with me. But then there was Mark. The prodigal son on whom Ranald held so much hope and expectation. The poor lad desperately wanted to please his father but was just never quite good enough, strong enough, fast enough… whatever. So, can you guess where Mitchell came in?"

Neither of them responded, once again, so she continued.

"I've just been with Val Anderson, who told me that Mitchell Stevens admitted to supplying Mark with an eclectic cocktail of performance-enhancing drugs behind his Dad's back, as he knew that keeping Mark in the top flight of international sport would keep Ranald happy and off his back. What a warm-hearted fellow Uncle Mitch was, huh?"

Clarkson struggled with Maggie's dominance of the airtime and broke her flow.

"Can you get to the punchline please, Miss Shields."

"I'm sure Mark's told you about the blackmail attempt

on his dad to hush up his son's drug use? Well, guess who was on the receiving end of a side hustle?"

"Are you saying Ross blackmailed Mitchell, too?"

Maggie nodded, secretly delighted it was Symington who beat his poker-faced superior to the chase.

"Exactly. Ryan decided to get greedy and, when he found out that Mitchell had been supplying Mark with his drugs, there was no way that Mitchell could take any chances. His whole healthcare empire would crumble before his very eyes."

Clarkson had heard enough.

"Maggie, are you seriously telling me that a man who was making a fortune from the private healthcare industry would feel the need to risk it all to supply Mark Anderson with some steroids – or whatever else he was using?"

She was ready for this one. It occurred to Maggie herself when Val told her about Mitchell's sideline in steroid supply.

"Ah, well. It all comes down to image, doesn't it? Mark's profile as a successful sportsman with an adoring fanbase had to be protected. But, if Ranald found out that his close business associate was the one who supplied his son with steroids and other nasties on which he became dependant, there's a damn good chance that they'd have an ugly fallout, yes?"

They said nothing in response. Maggie took a breath and revelled in the attention.

"And what would that lead to? My guess is that the tidy little hush-up they had agreed to at the time of the data breach would be used as a pawn against each other. And my money would be on Ranald coming out top on that. Wouldn't you say?"

"Why?"

"Think about it. Mitchell Stevens is a grafter. An ambitious man with hard work driving him through life. But the medical industry is cutthroat – especially in the private sector. And Mitchell Stevens does not have the profile and connections that the Anderson family do. He's just a bit of an outsider, really. And deep down he knows it. Which is why he could never afford to fall out with Ranald. And that, I believe, is why Ryan Ross had to die. It kept everything neat, tidy and permanently sorted."

"OK, and how did Ryan Ross find out about Stevens' drug supply to Mark Anderson then?"

"I'm not sure we will ever know. But he was a man who operated in an underworld. Remember that. He spent a lot of time working for drug dealers. Maybe Mitchell Stevens had a reputation for back-door steroid supply from his hospitals? I'm guessing there is more to this story yet to be uncovered. Aren't you?"

Maggie wanted to be finished. She wanted that to be enough. But she knew there were questions that had still to come.

"We have another problem with all this talk of blackmail, or extortion as we call it around here, Maggie. Do you know what that is?"

Maggie nodded. "You need proof?"

"Correct."

This was it. The moment of no turning back.

"I can give you that too. Because it was my brother,

Lochie, who arranged the blackmail against Ranald Anderson, and he's willing to come forward and tell you everything."

34

THREE DAYS LATER...
(FRIDAY A.M.)

Maggie sat in silence in the back of her own car, a safe distance from the house, as they pulled up at Val Anderson's gate. Val was there, in the front window of her home as she promised, watching the world go by. She'd said the view from that window was one reason she'd never sell the house. Even with its bittersweet memories of happier times. Before her marriage of convenience fell apart.

It was the same window they set up their Christmas tree in every year, she'd said. They'd take turns to let Olivia and Rebecca place the fairy at the top. The memory had sparked something in Maggie's own mind. She'd always got the job in her house, and Lochie would lift her up to reach the top branch each time. He held her tight – pretending he might drop her at any minute. But he never did.

Straining through the car window glass, she wondered what Val was thinking right now. Was it fear of what was to come? Or pride? Was she imagining Mitchell's arrogance being deflated for the first time in his life? Maggie had to fight past years of Val's lingering loyalty to these men to get her onside with the plan. But it was the only way.

A message came through on the earpiece Maggie was wearing.

"Awaiting confirmation of Stevens on site. Stand by, Shields."

She was chancing her arm to ask for a ringside seat when they brought him in, but in the end she compromised. Maggie would convince Val to help them bring Stevens in, and they'd let her watch from a safe distance. It wasn't long until the man of the moment appeared behind the window glass, next to Val.

Maggie leant into her microphone.

"Confirmation of Mitchell Stevens in view now. Front room, standing behind Val."

"Right, we're on. And remember, Shields, you stay exactly where you are until we're done here. Right?"

His imposing outline appeared behind Val. She imagined the sound of his brogues tapping on the varnished wooden floors and the heavy scent of him lingering in the room. Very little had changed in his appearance in the ten years since Maggie saw him in the woods, knife in hand. Still the same gait, the same bald head, and the same rotund belly. The sight of his body triggered the memories.

"You're sure that's the man you saw at Val Anderson's property last week? You can testify to this in court?"

"It's him. That's the man I saw sticking a knife into Archie Ross, too. As sure as night follows day."

Val was staring straight out of her window towards the unmarked car. Maggie told her she would be there, watching, looking out for her. But there was a fear in her eyes she'd hoped not to see. Even from a distance, Maggie sensed it. Fear was an expression she knew well. She sensed it in those who thought they could hide it.

You'll be safe. I promise. We're right here.

She willed the words to reach Val somehow. The grim weather helped to hide the unmarked car from Mitchell's line of sight. He was standing next to Val, staring out onto the front garden. Tall, pompous, and alert. A man guarding over another's property and family.

"Watch your backs, team. Be advised Mitchell may be armed."

A warning from Val that he kept guns in the house had been relayed via Maggie. He kept them in a locked box at the back of the building. Under the same roof as her children. Claimed it was just for his recreational hunting with Ranald. Just like those knives. Maggie imagined him in that shed with Ranald, mentally selecting the best knife for the job. And grabbing one when Ranald wasn't looking. Because he already knew it had to end that way. But using one of Ranald's knives was a bit of an insurance policy.

Her stomach turned like a washing machine drum, and she tried to refocus.

The cops had reached the front door. The younger one took a cue from the other and disappeared around the back of the house. Val's face reacted to the sound of the doorbell ring. Too quickly. Her whole body jumped, and Mitchell noticed. She moved to answer the door, but he put his arm out to stop her. Maggie strained to see more clearly, adjusting her position in the car. By the time she looked up again, Val was out of view.

Shit.

Maggie couldn't help herself. She was out of the car before anyone could stop her – looking for a tree to hide behind – to get a closer view of the scene unfolding. Seventeen again. Sheltering from the same man behind a different tree. But this time, others were in control. No one was visible through the window now. Resting her head against the bark of the tree, she shut her eyes and searched for some belief.

She thought of all the ways Lochie had protected her. The decisions he'd made so that she didn't have to. Then she thought of the McGill family. Torn apart from the beginning by sheer lack of opportunity. The lottery of birth. Archie – a child born into struggles. A teenager who made one terrible choice in a blind panic and ran from the repercussions. He'd still been running, surviving on a wing and a prayer, when someone more evil than he could imagine caught up with him.

She thought of Pete McGill. The man who was there from the start of everything. Ready and eager to help her find answers. Always there, encouraging her to uncover the truth behind the Anderson charade. Always listening to her. Helping her. Being there… even when she didn't understand why he knew where to be.

Maggie's own thoughts rebounded back into her consciousness.

Oh God, he was always… always… just… there. How did he do that? How did he know where to be?

She was never a fan of coincidence. But then she thought of her paranoia. Was that what was going on here? Her mind was playing tricks again – spinning out of control just when she needed to stay focused. She was almost at the finishing line of this investigation.

Please don't mess with me now, please. Let me get through this first. Just think about the facts.

Maggie thought back to the last time she saw Pete. At his home – in his own house. She remembered the glare of screens behind a closed door. It was the same unmistakable glare that filled the offices where Tetchy worked – an oppressive sickly hue created by artificial light from banks of screens. *What was on those screens, Pete?*

Could Pete really have been manipulating her AI therapy just to keep an eye on her – or to send her off course?

But why?

Something coming from Val's house pulled her back into the present. Remembering where she was and what she was doing there, Maggie tried to quiet the noise in her mind. She heard loud voices, swearing, and then the muffled sound of physical resistance. The briefest pause in the chaos was followed by the sight of Mitchell Stevens being led to the police car in handcuffs. They had their passenger for the return journey to the cells, but there was one more person they needed to bring in. Maggie had not been invited to the stop but that wasn't going to prevent her catching the action. This time she had to think a little bit ahead of the game.

35

SATURDAY A.M.

Mark Anderson arrived at the gates of his father's home at dawn. The woods around his house were alive with early birdsong and a fine mist had drifted in from the coast. His car wheels crunching over the gravel drive shook Maggie out of her half slumber.

The back of a reporter's car was not the best place to get a decent kip, but she was here, and that was all that mattered. This time, Symington and Clarkson had given her a hard no on watching from the sidelines. But when she told them she'd tell them exactly where to find a murder weapon, they agreed to turn a blind eye if a certain reporter's car was noticed parked nearby.

There was no guarantee that Mitchell had returned the actual murder weapon to the collection, but that was less important. Using Maggie's witness statement to identify the very distinct style she saw in Mitchell's hand ten years ago would be enough. Photos of the rest of Ranald's collection would do the job. So, here she was. Maggie Shields, the investigative reporter who put the pieces of this jigsaw together, waking up to witness the day Ranald Anderson's alliance with Mitchell Stevens came back to haunt them.

She watched as Mark Anderson began the walk from his car to the front door. He was a different man to the one Maggie saw online in photos from his sporting glory days. His face had lost its sense of pride in a hard day's work on the rugby field. This man looked like he'd been drawn with a limited palette of colours. Any muscular definition left was well hidden under a plain checked shirt and faded jeans.

Maggie watched the unmarked surveillance van parked out of sight of Ranald's security cameras. She imagined the assembled police unit readying for action inside. Mark touched his chest lightly, no doubt indicating where the recording mic was located. He was clearly not a natural at this. Mark's mother opened the door as he approached, no doubt alerted to his arrival by some internal camera system. It looked like she was still in her dressing gown, the bleariness in her eyes giving way to a raw disbelief.

Maggie imagined what private family moment the police were listening to via Mark's microphone. Would they hear the tearful sobs of an overwhelmed mother, desperately hugging the son she feared had come to harm? The son she knew was imperfect, but still had so much more to offer the world. Would the police airwaves be filled with extremes of human emotion? The sound of two girls being reunited with their father, and a father with his son. Would Ranald be able to hide his suspicions about Mark's intentions? Or would he take the bait? Would he seize this opportunity presented to him to come down on his son's plans like a tonne of bricks, threatening, manipulating, and convincing him to change tack?

Willing him to show his true colours, Maggie's need to hear the moment of proof for herself got the better of her. She opened her car door quietly and moved closer to the police van parked a few metres in front of her. Everyone was distracted now – no one would notice her approach.

How the hell will I hear what's coming through the radio from outside?

She checked around the vehicle for any windows that had been left open – even a little. But there weren't any.

Shit.

Reluctantly resigning herself to defeat, she began to retrace the five or six footsteps back to her car. Then heard a click.

Turning back, she noticed the sliding door of the van had been opened a couple of inches. Straining to look through the gap, she made out the face of DS Symington sitting closest to the door. It was hard to tell if he'd seen her and opened the door on purpose. Thrown her a bone that she felt had been earned. Whatever the case, she wasn't going to waste the opportunity. She leant her body tightly back against the rear of the van and rested her head against the side, straining to hear what she could. The crackling of an audio feed made the hairs on the back of her head stand on end.

Here we go!

Mark Anderson was the first to speak again, his voice crumbling with each word.

"I'm so sorry, girls. I just had to take some time out. I

didn't mean to hurt anyone. There were things I needed to deal with. Work out, you know?"

"No, we don't know. What the hell, Dad? You didn't even text or write to us. You could've been dead in a ditch for all we knew."

"I always would have come back to you. I just didn't want you to... I mean..."

"How could you not call us, or anything? Or if not us, then Mum? She was a state too – even though she pretended not to be."

"I couldn't. I just couldn't. You have to trust me. That doesn't mean I didn't want to."

"And then what, you just decided to walk back into our lives when you were ready? Are you even back to stay?"

"I don't know yet, Olivia. But I do know I was missing you both so much that I couldn't bear it anymore. I had to know you were both OK. Your mum told me I'd find you here today. And it was safer than going to the house..."

"Safer? What the hell? Who are you running from, Dad?"

Maggie strained to hear more as Mark continued, choosing his words carefully. There was a nervousness growing amongst the surveillance team. Mark had to find his chance to make it count. He needed Ranald alone – to set the scene for his own downfall. Maggie knew people like him eventually tripped over their own ego and landed right where they needed him. Maggie's neck was beginning to stiffen at being twisted in the same direction for so long. But she could tell emotions at the other end of Mark's recording device had calmed.

"Girls, who wants to make your dad a strong coffee from the silly machine your grandmother bought? You know I could never work that thing, could I, Mum?"

Bingo.

Maggie leant her ears in closer to the cold metal of the van, sensing Ranald's hunger to be in charge again was growing by the second. He'd be desperate to tell his son what he really thought of his devious little plan to turn against him and persuade him to see the error of his ways. To tell him that it wasn't his intention to have Archie killed, but that Stevens had gone rogue on him and lost control for some reason he could never explain properly.

Some muffled swearing dominated the audio feed from one of the girls.

"Becca, go with your grandmother and help her cut some of that cake she made. You might need a strong arm."

Maggie imagined Ranald overflowing with arrogance, thinking his control of the situation was as iron tight as ever.

"You're clearly going to talk about us behind our back, aren't you? We're not eight years old anymore, you know? We're old enough to hear what's been going on in our dad's head. Who or what he's running from. In fact, we deserve it."

The sound of a door closing was followed by Ranald's voice again. This time it was different. It was the Ranald Anderson Maggie met in his hunting shed.

There wasn't a sound from the police van. She imagined them all in there, sensing the final act about to unfold.

"Well, now I have my prodigal son on his own for as

long as it takes three women to boil a kettle and cut a cake, I'm very pleased to see you have come to your senses and agreed family are more important than anything."

"Dad, please be quiet. Before you say anything else, I need to tell you…"

Maggie heard DI Clarkson's voice.

"Oh Christ, he's going to bottle it. Tip him off that we're listening before he gives us what we need. Back up on standby?"

"Confirm, back up on standby."

But she'd misjudged the moment.

"Don't insult my intelligence, Mark. I know exactly what's going on. Even before Anne McGill opened her drunken mouth and spilt the beans about your nice wee letters to her. That was a stupid move, even for you. Trying to ease your conscience by writing to her, eh? Telling her about your cosy wee arrangement with the coppers to throw me under a bus? After everything I've done for you. You've got her blood on your hands too now, son."

"How did you get to her?"

Mark's question echoed Maggie's. How did Ranald manage to get close enough to Anne McGill for her to tell him this? Mark's voice sounded stronger now – his breathing sped up – and Maggie knew things were back on track.

Stay calm, Mark. You're nearly there.

"It's amazing what a visit from the head of a private healthcare operator and an offer of help to sober up at one of our five-star residential facilities can do to loosen tongues. As usual, Mitchell was only too happy to accommodate a special resident – or offer to, at least. Not much that man can say no to, what with me hiding his murderous secret and all that. You know I won't let you get away with this? I will see to it that your girls suffer if you go through with this."

"I just had to do the right thing, Dad. For once. That family were destroyed when they lost Archie. And it didn't need to… to happen. Did it?"

Ranald made a noise that sounded like an eruption of anger, making the surveillance team edgy. They ran a quick check down the radio to ensure the team on the ground were still awake and ready to move if things got lively.

"Don't give me your soft shit again, son. That lad's reckless driving left two kids without a mother. And all I was doing was saving your skin. Your reputation as a former pro athlete trying to make it as a personal trainer to the rich and stupid."

"No, Dad, I really don't think I buy that anymore. Tell me, were you really saving *my* reputation, or was it your own? How the hell didn't you know that Stevens was getting blackmailed too? You're not as bright as you think, are you?"

"You know nothing, you spoilt little shit. Stevens just lost it. I hate people who lose control like that. It's so… so weak."

Maggie looked at her watch. This was electrifying stuff, but they'd been alone for seven minutes. Time would run out when the women returned to the room. But Ranald was increasingly stirred by the exchange.

"So, you didn't know your best friend was being blackmailed too because Archie found out he'd supplied me with steroids for years?"

Silence cut through the exchange for a few seconds.

"Stand by, Mark, we're losing audio I think."

But Maggie knew better. They weren't losing audio. Ranald Anderson had just been silenced. But not for long.

"Bullshit. Why would he do that?"

"You were so desperate to have a son that was good enough on the sports field that you didn't even notice how scared I was to disappoint you. But Mitchell did. He saw a way that I could stay competitive, bulk up, and be the competitor you desperately needed me to be. And, by helping me achieve that, it kept your anger at bay and your focus on business. Christ, the man felt sorry for me, Dad."

"Bullshit. I don't believe you. He killed Archie because he lost control – simple. And that's what I'll tell the cops if you go through with this. And I tell you what, son. If you do go through with this. If you sit there in the dock and get your old man sent to jail just because his stupid pal couldn't keep control of his anger, this is only going to end badly for you."

"Well, it might, Dad. But at least I'll be doing something right at last. You don't get that, I know. But I'm finally starting to understand what it means."

"Have you thought how this will go for your girls, Mark? Do you want them to have a grandfather *and* a father in jail?"

Mark didn't respond, but the mood in the police van was jubilant. They'd got their moment of proof. High fives and fist pumps were flying. Then a soft female voice crackled through the speaker.

"Who's going to jail, Dad? Grandpa?"

Rebecca was back in the room.

Maggie heard movement from inside the surveillance van.

"Control to all units. Time to move in for arrest."

All that came next was the noise. The muffled sound of chaos whistled through the police van. What sounded like female tears. More banging. A scream. And then nothing. The audio signal went dead.

Time stood still and no one in the van moved.

Until the misty morning air outside was filled again with the sights and sounds of a battle at an end.

They led Ranald Anderson out of his own home into the waiting arms of a second unmarked police car. A sense of calm returned to Maggie that she'd not felt for a long time. She drank it in and let it wash over her. The win was not hers alone, but she let herself feel pride in the outcome.

36

SATURDAY P.M.

With Mitchell in police custody and Ranald soon to join him in the cells, Maggie had to turn attentions elsewhere. She couldn't shake her fears about Pete McGill, and even though she knew he'd be at the hospital with his mum, he'd have to come home at some point to sleep, or change, or something. She had to confront him at home.

She watched him arrive home just before 11 p.m. He cast a sad figure in the darkest hours of the night. Maggie hovered outside his house for a few minutes after he went inside until finding the strength to get out of her car and approach his front door. Inflated from her role in the day's earlier events, she felt bold and ready to challenge anyone.

As soon as he responded to her door knocking, Maggie pushed forward, unflinching.

"Let me in, now, Pete."

"Maggie? What the hell?"

"I know what you're up to."

Pete dropped his resistance surprisingly quickly

– standing back in the hallway and inviting her to take the lead. Once inside, she remembered exactly where the room was located – the second door on the left of the hallway. It was still closed, and the light was there. The same artificial glare as before seeping under the door onto the floorboards outside.

"How is your mum?"

She had to hold her anger back and show some basic courtesy for the man whose mother's life hung in the balance.

"The doctors have stabilised her. She's breathing well, and they're working as hard as they can to help her fight whatever she was drugged with, before they…"

His words were grim. Maggie did not have a heart of stone. She couldn't ignore this man's pain, but it was her only chance to confront him. She had to be selfish and protect herself too. She pushed past him, making straight for the door handle, but it was locked.

"Open this now."

"What? Maggie, what's going…"

"Open the bloody door right now, Pete – or I'll bash it down myself, I swear."

"Maggie, I…"

"Now."

"Did you read that letter I handed you? The one my mum got from Mark?"

Pete was stalling her, and Maggie was in no mood to hear it. He may have lost his mum, but there would be time for sympathy later. She wasn't ready to tell him what had gone down at the police station yet. Not until she had her answers.

She grabbed a heavy wooden vase stand next to his hall table, lined herself up in front of the door and took two steps backwards.

"Jesus Christ. Stop!!!"

Pete was holding his arms out to block the door.

"OK, I'll open it. The key is in the kitchen. Give me a chance to find it at least."

Maggie stood still, placed the vase stand back down on the floor and waited for him to return. It annoyed her that she didn't notice the Yale lock on an internal door last time.

Details, Maggie, details.

As the door swung open, the scene that met her stopped her momentum. A bank of four flat computer screens on a wide table. The room was colder than the rest of his house. Just like the IT power and back up room at the *Standard* and most of Tetchy's office. Optimum conditions for protecting electrical equipment that was working twenty-four seven.

"Pretty impressive set up for an estate agent, isn't it?"

Pete didn't say a word. He stood next to her, silently watching.

"Were you ever going to tell me?"

She watched his face for signs of something that felt like truth.

"Tell you? Why would I tell you?"

Christ he's got balls, this man.

Maggie walked towards the bank of screens and equipment in front of her, moving a mouse to see what would appear. But a wall of password prompts stopped her progress.

Thinking back to how quickly she'd been lured into the AI trial, it all felt too much. A lump of something heavy swirled in the pit of her stomach.

"How did you send me the invitation from an NHS email?"

"Maggie, what are you talking about?"

"You will answer all my questions, or I'll take you to the police station myself. I swear it."

She looked at him again – piercing his eyes with her own gaze. How could she have been so naïve to trust this man?

"Um, OK."

It sickened Maggie to think of his next answer, but she had to ask the question.

"Why not just hack my work email? Trust me, that's got to be easier. How did you know you could get to me like this? Through *this* route?"

Pete's face turned from apparent confusion to anger. He stepped forward, leant over his keyboard, typed something in, and brought the screens to life.

And there it was in front of her face.

One of the most elaborate gaming set-ups she had seen in her life.

Fuck.

"I… I… thought you had been…"

"What, Maggie? Carrying out some elaborate hacking of your NHS records? Really?"

Maggie's bluster crumbled in a moment. Embarrassment seeping in through each crevice in her brain.

"I just thought when you seemed to, you know, turn up when I was at my brother's house and these weird messages I had been getting. I thought you were maybe trying to..."

"Why the hell would I want to interfere with the one person finding answers for my family?"

For a moment, Maggie was silent. No words came to her that didn't sound ridiculous.

Damn that bully.

The paranoia was back with a vengeance, and it had taken a victory.

Then something lighter cut through her thoughts. She remembered her brother as a teenager. How he would spend time at friends' houses playing computer games for hours – especially when the weather was rubbish. Maybe Pete McGill was one of those faceless friends that he hung out with. She was too young to be aware of where he spent his time. Then she remembered Lochie's description of him a few days ago.

He always seemed to hide in his room or play around with computers at school.

Maybe Pete McGill never really grew out of computer games?

Say something. Try to be normal. Make amends, Maggie.

"It's quite a system you have here for a bit of on-screen shooting action, eh?"

It earned her a half smile from Pete.

"Ever since Archie died, I was angry and needed a distraction. Something mindless. A place to vent the anger. I guess I just started playing around in my spare time. Thought it could break me out of the darkness of my own thoughts sometimes. Take my mind off the hurt of losing Archie and seeing my mum drink herself to death. Guess it just snowballed a bit!"

Maggie's head was starting to pound from the glare of the screens, but she joined his lead with a wry giggle.

"I just called you out on hacking but you're really just a gaming geek, eh?"

"How long will I get for that inside, do you reckon?"

She stayed with Pete a while longer. They chatted about Mitchell Stevens. Pete was as surprised as the rest of them at the fact that it was Stevens who chose to kill Archie. He said that his mum was full of drugs that must have been supplied by someone with access to restricted medication. There wouldn't be a huge leap to tie Anne's attempted silencing to him too, she suspected.

"There are some folk that should just never come together in life – Ranald Anderson and Mitchell Stevens being two of them."

Pete's words felt genuine, and it made Maggie think about alliances. People whose coming together can do nothing but harm. Something was brewing in her investigator's brain. It wasn't quite a fully formed thought yet.

"Do you think Mark knew all the stuff about his dad's corrupt business practices too?"

It was a question Maggie couldn't wait to ask him herself. She told Pete how she got caught up in the effluent of Ranald's product vulnerability to hackers.

"I don't know, but it looked like old Ran targeted the cash-strapped, overstretched NHS to use as a guinea pig. Predicted they'd be only too glad to jump on the bandwagon of an online psychotherapy option to chip away at a waiting list. Then Ranald used it as an unofficial testing process to iron out any more teething problems after his previous disaster with Sapphire Healthcare – a win, win all round, eh?"

Maggie realised there was an elephant in the room they were avoiding. She'd told the police everything she found out about Archie and Lochie – just like he asked her to. And now she had to tell Pete. He deserved to hear it from her, before it all came out in court.

"We should talk about our brothers, Pete."

"The bond between you and Lochie was… I get it. I had a brother too."

"He was no angel, Pete. You must know that. How much do you know about Archie's past?"

"I know enough."

"*Your* brother was responsible for killing my mum. Did you even know that?"

It was too abrupt. She realised that too late, but the words had left her mouth, and she couldn't take them back. His face gave her the answer. No.

She told him everything she had found out about Archie. What happened the day her mum was killed. But then she told him about Lochie's role in setting up the blackmail plot that led to Archie's death.

They stood in silence for a moment, with nothing but the whir of unrelenting technology to drown out the toxic air between them. Maggie didn't want it to be wasted. For the sake of either of their brothers. Perhaps it was up to them to make good on their mistakes – to turn the tables. Pull something worthwhile out of the pain and misery.

But she couldn't do this alone. For the first time in a long while, Maggie accepted she had her own mental health issues to tackle. But whatever was going on in her mind, no one was going to stop her doing her job.

Perhaps there was a way to use her own battles to tell a more honest story than she would ever have dared to before? But first, she had a double arrest to report on.

37

The Fife Standard. Date: July 25th 2023

Stevens and Anderson Snr Convictions As Decade Old Ryan Ross Murder Solved

By Maggie Shields

Fife software business owner and father of Scottish rugby star Mark Anderson has been convicted in relation to the fatal stabbing of local boy Ryan (formerly Archie) Ross. Anderson's business associate Mitchell Stevens was convicted of murdering Ross in retaliation to an extortion attempt on both Anderson senior and Mitchell Stevens.

Ranald Anderson (72, from West Anstruther), along with Mitchell Stevens (56), await sentencing from the High Court in Edinburgh this week. Stevens (originally from Leven) executed the fatal attack on Ross and was also charged with attempted murder of Mrs Anne McGill – Ross's mother – earlier this year. Stevens and Anderson were also found guilty of attempt to defeat the ends of justice after trying to destroy evidence linking him to the murders.

The conviction ended one of Fife's most high-profile recent trials which saw previously unseen photographic evidence of the fatal stabbing that emerged years after the initial investigation went cold.

When delivering his verdict, Lord Justice Crighton said:

"Whilst it has been proven that the co-defendant – Mr Ranald Anderson – was not present at the murder of Mr Ross, it is evident beyond doubt that his role was critical in the initiation of events which led to Ross's untimely death. It has been proven that the subsequent attempt on Ross's mother, Mrs Anne McGill's life was a heartless attempt to cover up knowledge of their historic crimes. Whilst there are several other parties who bear elements of responsibility for the ultimate outcome of these events, I am confident that the manipulation and direction provided by Mr Anderson senior and the self-serving violent tendencies of Mitchell Stevens were the primary leading cause in these heinous events."

Speaking outside the court on behalf of Anderson, Solicitor Advocate Alan Rutherford gave the following statement:

"My client, Mr Ranald Anderson, does not accept the unjust verdict given today. He maintains he had no part in the murder of Mr Ross which, as has been proven today, was carried out by his former associate Mr Stevens. We will proceed with an appeal in due course and continue to fight to prove his innocence."

It is understood that the successful conviction hinged on testimony from Ranald's son, Mark, whose recent disappearance is understood to have been related to being in protective police custody prior to testifying against his father. The court also heard evidence from both Mr Lochie Shields and Miss Margaret Shields, who were witnesses to the ten-year-old crime. Lochie Shields, a senior nurse at Kirkcaldy Hospital, had charges of attempted extortion dropped as part of a plea bargain to provide evidence. NHS Fife have declined to comment on his ongoing employment within the hospital.

38

SIX MONTHS LATER

Maggie Shields had never been inside a prison. A police station was one thing, but a prison was a step too far. A leap into the fires of hell, more like. But it was also a melting pot of her greatest fears and rewards together, so she had to fight the bully when he told her to stay away. Filth and contamination mingled with opportunity and answers – the very richest of stories that needed to be told by those whose path in life has taken them places others couldn't begin to understand. Maggie wanted to understand. The very worst and most beguiling aspects of the human condition all wrapped up together under one roof.

But today would be the day. The dust had settled after the trial, media restrictions had been eased, and she'd promised herself she would see this through. Lexi offered to assign someone else to the interview, given Lochie's involvement in the story, but Maggie would rather have pulled her own fingernails out with tweezers than let that happen.

The prison guard checked her over and watched carefully as she placed her mobile phone and watch in a small plastic tray. She'd been given special approval to take a recording device into the meeting area and they checked the Bluetooth and Wi-Fi were disconnected before giving it back to her. Then she checked it herself, three times of course, to make sure it wasn't going to let her down.

A prison warden with way too much humour on his face for the job he did led her towards a bright blue bench with a row of orange stools attached on either side. She thought about her school lunch hall. Is it meant to remind them of being school children? she wondered. Maggie was ushered to the far corner of the meeting area – well away from others. Feeling her pulse quicken as she prepared to sit down, she kept her gaze off any surfaces.

Come on, where is he?

For so long, Maggie battled to push the nerves out of her system. They had no place in her life. Nothing good would be achieved with them standing in her way. But today – perhaps it was time to surrender to them just a little.

The oversized grey joggers and T-shirt that Ranald Anderson wore when he walked towards Maggie did a fine job as the leveller it was intended to be. It revealed the true extent of his distended abdomen in a way that expensive, tailored suits could no longer hide. Prison food had not yet reduced his waistline. He was trying to carry off the outfit and his predicament with his customary arrogance, but she wasn't fooled. He placed his hands on the table between them before locking his eyes squarely on hers.

"And here she is, then. Fife's answer to Kate Adie herself."

"Kate Adie was a war correspondent."

Maggie's response was quicker than lightning.

Sod you, Ranald Anderson.

"Maggie Shields. *Fife Standard*."

"I'd say it's a pleasure to meet you but that would be a lie. Journalists are, in my opinion, among the lowest dregs of society."

"Good to know, Mr Anderson. All the same, you have agreed to answer some questions for the purposes of my report. This is by your own free will, I might add. Are you happy to proceed on this basis?"

Of all the people Maggie had interviewed following the murder trial, she was struck by Ranald Anderson's unshaken arrogance. In the face of two life sentences, even the most robust egos could be expected to crumble a little. But not Ranald. Holding his eyes on Maggie, he sat in front of her with the same pride and composure he'd shown on the witness stand.

"I'm all yours, as they say."

Maggie reached for her tape recorder, placing it between them and clicking it on. The quiet purr of the machine relaxed her.

All the facts had now been laid bare. Even the nationals had reported on each detail of Ranald and Stevens's conviction as soon as the judge passed his verdict. That wasn't what Maggie wanted. She didn't need more gruesome facts about how long Archie Ross had been dead by the time his body was found by a dog walker.

She wasn't interested in Steven's mitigating circumstances.

No, Maggie was here – fighting every terror inside – simply to understand why. Why he would do this to the McGill family. Was it just some inherent evil? Or greed? Or both, maybe? Something about this case had changed the way she looked at good and evil. It had shifted her thoughts and allowed her to consider something else.

She thought of Lochie's actions. As a brother. As a nurse. As a blackmailer. As an accessory to murder.

What if we all had the potential to dip a finger into that evil place? What if it had the potential to give us all something warm and comforting when we needed it – brief shelter, financial security, or just a meal on the table for the ones we love? That's OK, isn't it? As long as we don't stay in that place long enough to get comfortable.

Maggie knew that Ranald and Lochie met each other there once, a long time ago. But Lochie took what he needed and ran from it as soon as he could – hiding the memory of his time there somewhere deep inside. Ranald, on the other hand, built his empire there. And that's what Maggie needed to understand. What was it about his past, his childhood, and his life that made him feel at home in that world? But there were other gaps that she needed to fill first.

"Did it never bother you that the AI software you were peddling to a public health service on its knees could leave vulnerable people open to trolls and criminals?"

"Ah, Maggie. Yes, I heard you got a bit tied up in that mess yourself. Had a bit of skin in the game, as they say? Would your time not be better served chasing down the hackers instead?"

“Let me worry about that, Mr Anderson. I’m here for you and you alone today.”

Tetchy helped her make sense of the vulnerability of the AI software and she’d used it to start a campaign for better mental healthcare provision for those who struggle with face-to-face therapy. She knew it was the start of a long journey, but that didn’t faze her.

“Problem with your way of life, Ranald, is that you found yourself all out of friends when you needed them, wouldn’t you say?”

“They’re all cowards – quick to save their own skin. We can only ever look out for ourselves in this world, Maggie. Have you not learnt that yet?”

Maggie considered Anderson’s reduced sentence against Mitchell’s life term. It was yet another layer to the story that she could use in her exclusive. Lexi told her that they were going to run it over a number of issues, so she needed plenty of content. She was almost home and dry and the prison warden was beginning to hover around their table. But there was still somewhere deeper she wanted to go.

“Did you really do all of this to protect your reputation?”

He looked at her with the closest thing to vulnerability she’d seen in him yet.

“You’re not the only investigator here, Maggie Shields.”

“Oh, is that right?”

There was a devilment in his eyes that she tried to ignore.

“I know a thing about you, too. You and I – I guess we have a lot in common, really.”

She began to feel the overwhelming urge to escape to the comfort of somewhere clean. To her safety rituals. Her cacti, and the fresh Kirkcaldy breeze pouring through her lungs.

"Oh, and how's that?"

"It's simple really. We both know what it feels like to struggle. To be the family with not enough money to pay the bills. To watch from the wrong side of town as others wear better clothes, live in bigger houses and drive expensive cars."

His words were left drifting in the air as the warden moved in to tell them time was up. Maggie watched Ranald Anderson being led away from her, keeping his gaze on her face and enjoying the impact of his words. But Maggie Shields was never one to let others have the final word. Rising to her feet and clicking off her voice recorder, she looked deep into his eyes with strength that she'd not felt in a very long time.

"Trust me, Ranald. We couldn't be more different."

ACKNOWLEDGEMENTS:

I would like to thank all those who have supported me every step of the way as I wrote, re-wrote and edited *Keep Me Safe*. Without their encouragement, belief and patience, I would have given up on my dream to become a published author a long time ago. I would especially like to thank my Developmental Editor and writing mentor, the very talented Anna Britton whose guiding hand has kept me on track and helped to bring out the best in this story. I would also like to thank the team at The Book Guild for believing in my story and working their magic right through to publication.

Then there's my long-suffering closest family. My husband Bill and two boys, William and James, who let me disappear for hours on end to cafés, hidden rooms and countless weird and wonderful locations with my laptop to write because they understand how much it means to me to be an author.

To the people of Kirkcaldy, St Andrews and Fife at large, please forgive the liberties I have taken with the finer details of your beautiful kingdom in order to bring Maggie's world to life in a corner of Scotland that shows our wee country off to its wide and varied best.

To each and every person who may have been affected by OCD in their life or family. Keep your head up high and find the support you need. You are not alone.

And finally, to my readers. As a newbie in Scotland's crime thriller writing tradition – one with a daunting reputation to follow – I would like to thank each person who picks up this book and reads my words. I am more grateful than you could ever know.

If Maggie Shields gets under your skin or you'd like to follow news of my next publication – already well underway – please sign up for updates here: https://allisonmeldrumauthor.com/#subscribe.

With hugs the size of your favourite book reading armchair,

Allison. x

ABOUT THE AUTHOR

Previously a newspaper and magazine journalist, Allison Meldrum has had multiple short stories published and selected as Editor's Picks by *Toasted Cheese* and *East of the Web*. She has also contributed works to two short story anthologies through her involvement in Transcendent Authors, an international authors' group. Allison has previously published *The Life I Owe Her*, a novel about parenthood and friendship.

Stay up to date with Allison's work on:

Facebook: @allisonmeldrumwrites
X: @MeldrumAllison
Instagram: @allison.meldrum.1
TikTok: @allisonmeldrum